# RUST UPON MY SOUL

LUCY BRANCH

ABL PRESS

# ABOUT THE AUTHOR

Lucy Branch lives in North London with her husband and three children. She is a restorer of public sculpture and historic features and has worked on some of the UK's most well-known monuments including Eros, Cleopatra's Needle and Nelson's Column. The passion she has for her work inspires her writing.

Other novels by Lucy Branch
A Rarer Gift Than Gold
Girl In A Golden Cage

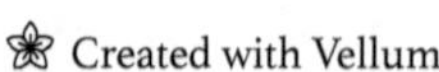 Created with Vellum

# DEDICATION

For Mum and Dad

**WANT TO KNOW MORE ABOUT…?**

THE GOLDEN ILLUMINATI
ALCHEMY
PATINATION
AND
THE ART THAT INSPIRES THE NOVELS

JOIN MY READERS' GROUP AND RECEIVE EMAILS
FROM LUCY BRANCH WITH CONTENT THAT DELVES
DEEPER INTO THE THEMES OF THE SERIES.

AT

www.lucybranch.com

1
——————

## ROBERT

I leaned against the display case and my eyes locked on its familiar contents. The diamonds in the salamander brooch caught the light and sparkled like the smile of a beautiful girl. The thought of how close I was to reclaiming them made every muscle in my body buzz with triumph.

'If I do it, I'd want these,' I said, catching a glance of my reflection in the glass case and shifting to avoid facing myself.

'Jewellery?' Philip's reedy voice echoed along the seemingly unending rows of display cases. He stepped forward out of the darkness. With his insipid blue eyes, thin red hair and transparent old man's skin, he glowed like a spectre in the low light. 'There are some very special items in the rest of our collection, but of course, my dear boy, the choice is yours.'

My anxiety eased. The jewels meant nothing to them, but their theft had cast a shadow over three generations of my family. I let my eyes cavort between the sapphire droplet earrings and the clasp made with emeralds cut to suggest delicate leaves around diamonds plump as buds. It was a shame about the ruby bracelet: it was made up of solid gold rods which had been hand twisted to give the impression of a flowing form. But the segments had been disassembled and now lay awkwardly in a disjointed row.

A barbed ball of grief materialised in my throat. It wasn't fair that the closest my da' ever got to them was when he lay dying in London Bridge Hospital. It should have been him here, not me. Though I couldn't imagine how a lowly gem-cutter, who worked his whole life at a polishing wheel in Hatton Garden, would ever have been offered membership of The Golden Illuminati – that seemed to be my path. It was cruel that he'd fallen before ever knowing that his meticulously researched theory of what had happened to these special jewels – and their maker, my grandfather – was correct. It would have been some reward for a life in which all else had been pushed aside.

'I could build you a world-class headquarters in London instead. From an investment point of view, that would be a damn sight better deal for the Society. You should give it some real consideration.'

I pretended to peer at the information card in the case. 'It says here that the collection is incomplete, and I think that bracelet might be missin' sections.'

'Choose something else then!' His temper got away from him for a moment.

Considering everything, he was tolerating me well. I was a hard pill for him to swallow, having no family money, no boarding school to reminisce about and being a ruffian Scot.

He exhaled and spoke in a measured tone. 'We are not in a souk, Robert. Abigail is the only deal we are interested in making.'

Disgusting as the deal was, I would have paid it ten-fold for a fifth of this collection, let alone a half.

'So, I am to befriend this girl, and observe her to see if there is anything truly unusual about her, and whatever the outcome, I am to hand her over to you?'

Philip nodded.

I didn't have any concerns about carrying out the plan. My strong friendship with the artist, Terry Gerrard, made me the ideal candidate. Terry was one of the few people on the planet whom Abigail trusted and a recommendation from him would go a long way. Given what she'd gone through last year, it might take more than that to make her trust me, but I had another advantage that I was sure would tip the balance.

'From what I heard last year, there was no evidence that the girl had any gift at all. She did pull off a perfect imitation of what we all wanted her to be capable of, but it was all a hoax: a trick to escape us. We could find a hundred foundry apprentices able to do what she did. Is it revenge you want her for?'

Disappointment in my question seemed to weigh down Philip's eyebrows. 'Abigail Argent planned and executed a cold-blooded murder of one of our own members.' He was using his courtroom voice. 'No-one knows better than I the kind of response a jury would give this type of case, but revenge could not be further from our minds. If it were, why would we be troubling you to set up her reassessment in a manner so informal that it cannot be in the least way traumatising to her? If we did not accept some responsibility for the mishandling of her case last year, we would not need you. We could just hand her over to the police. It would only be what our country's justice system would do.'

His expression was so pained, regretful, and at the same

time, firm, that I wondered if this eloquence in facial expressions, as much as anything else, had opened doors for him within the law. Philip was one of three of the country's most senior judges – that was the calibre of The Golden Illuminati's membership.

Did I care what their motivations were? 'If ye like the nut, crack it,' had been one of my da's favourite sayings. If I wanted to reclaim these jewels, I had to accept whatever effort was involved to bring it about.

'To my mind, the honour of serving The Golden Illuminati should be enough for a member to step up and do their part. I can't see the need for a bonus,' he nodded at the jewels. 'We have the chance to be part of the continuation of the Society's great history of discovering alchemists. It has been over eighty years since our last one.'

'Discovering and profiting from.' I couldn't help myself.

'Sorry?'

'Discovering and profiting from alchemists is our great history.'

Philip gave me a surprised look. 'Well, yes, of course, dear boy, that goes without saying. We are the overseers and protectors of the true history of alchemy.'

'I don't see these baubles as a bonus,' I inclined my head towards the case, 'more a gesture of appreciation.'

Philip cleared his throat. The noise bounded between the exhibits and the marble-clad room. 'Oh, quite, yes. It is a shame that this jewellery collection is no longer entire. At least half of it was lost, several valuable items, when the Society bought this building in the 1970s and moved from its old location. We suspect the moving company was involved in the thefts, but even incomplete, the value of these stones, stripped down and sold individually, is very high indeed.'

I closed my eyes to blot out the visual of such a heinous act of vandalism.

'Where did you buy them?' I asked, just to hear him lie.

'You know us, Robert. We are in the business of acquiring rare things.' Then the man's tone shifted back to our negotiation. 'There's also something we would require you to agree to first, of course. If by any chance you misinformed us, or it came to light that you kept relevant information to yourself, then we would have to invoke a penalty clause. We would require compensation.'

'A penalty clause, when it is you asking me for the favour? I never sign penalty clauses.'

Philip shifted from foot to foot, making the floorboards groan. 'Not a favour, Robert. After all, you will be more than compensated for your trouble with this exquisite collection, which we will be sorry to lose.'

This remark took some control to stomach.

'You must see it from our point of view. We need to know that you have an incentive to be completely transparent with us. Consider what occurred only last year – a member went rogue for his own ends. We must ensure that your commitment to us is genuine. I'm sure this is just an unnecessary precaution: a clause that will never be needed.' He opened his hands wide, the picture of reasonableness.

'My interest in this collection already makes me invested.'

'You wouldn't be the first man to feel the prick of conscience at a critical moment. We must act in good faith that you will fulfil your promise and we will honour our contract. But, if later we were to discover you'd deceived us for your own purposes, it would only be fair that we have recompense.'

I dredged my mind for examples of the foul depths I had

sunk to so far in my life. I had recently tapped the bicycle of a sandwich-seller as he squeezed between the cars in traffic and I'd damaged his wheel. I hadn't stopped to help. The truth was, there hadn't been much need for me to practise being savage to gain rank or recognition in my career as an architect. I was just a man whose path led to these jewels, and every time I tried to step off it, life provided a course-correction. Philip wouldn't understand, but the reason I was sure I could go through with betraying a woman I'd never met was because I could do nothing else.

'What is the penalty?'

'I believe you have a very nice residence in Scotland ...'

My anger flared at this outrageous request. My house wasn't just a residence, it was my finest piece of work! It took a moment to steady my indignation, but even as I struggled, I knew that it was the final buck of an unbroken horse about to be saddled.

'I'd like time to consider.'

'Of course.' Philip's voice was light as if it wasn't of the least importance either way. I knew to the contrary, though. Members of my rank didn't get personal requests from Domenico Milliardo, Supreme Head of The Golden Illumi-nati, as I had done, unless he wanted something very much indeed. 'Call me tomorrow. If you decide to proceed, it won't take long to get the paperwork drawn up.'

Business behind us, he switched to being host. 'Let's take a glass of something, shall we? I'll show you the latest item we've acquired.'

'Another time. After my decision is made, perhaps.'

Philip looked at me with a cold but patient expression. He was at least double my age and his family had been in the Society for six generations. That made him a king in this world and me a serf. His eyes lingered on my hair and he pursed his lips; its style was too long for men like Philip.

'I'll see you out,' said the gaoler of my jewels. Visitation was over.

We walked through the grand ceremonial hall with its large portrait paintings and marble columns, gilded top and bottom. I had been in this main hall several times since I'd been accepted into the Society. As we reached the entrance, I noted my own name, infilled with gold leaf, on one of the newest of six wooden panels listing the members. How my da' would have gaped if he'd seen that.

A doorman pulled open the bronze door and I stepped out into the damp night air.

'Always good to see you, Robert.' Philip offered his hand and we shook: a gesture of unity that left me feeling grubby.

2

## ABIGAIL

Sitting like a small child on the shoulders of a gargantuan bronze sculpture of John Lennon, I had a fine view over the many slanting roofs which made up the foundry buildings. My parents had built them over the years, one by one, with whatever materials were to hand, so they looked like a patchwork quilt from up here.

The statue was almost twenty-five feet high. It had been too tall for us to braze the huge segments together inside the main foundry and so we'd moved it out into the courtyard, built a scaffold, and assembled the casting. Mine was the final stage of the process: the colouring of the bronze.

The light was fading. I'd hoped to get finished by the end of the day, but that wasn't looking likely now – good light was essential to get the shade right. A mishmash of art and science, it was hard enough to create the right hue even when the light was good.

Lennon's head, which was wider than my whole body, was almost finished now. Aside from the scale of the sculpture, this was one of my less challenging projects. The colour required was a straightforward mid-brown-bronze shade: quite traditional. It had been commissioned by a wealthy super-fan who wanted the statue located on his land near the coast in Dorset.

My phone rang. I pulled it out of my back pocket. It was Anne-Marie on the reception desk calling. She was so excited she was having trouble getting her words out.

'I've just sent THE sexiest guy ever out to you. He's got this dreamy Scottish accent and is tall as a tree. Soulful eyes, too, and he teased me about reading romance novels, and then—'

'Anne-Marie, who is he?'

'Oh, yes,' her laughter filled my ear, 'friend of Terry's, Robert Kirkpatrick. Says you're expecting him.'

My throat dried. Bloody Terry! My exact words to him during our last conversation when we'd discussed this man had been, 'No, no, no, no and no!' I don't think I could have been clearer.

Caution reined in Anne-Marie's vivaciousness. 'Were you not expecting him?'

'It's not your fault, Anne-Marie. Thanks, it's fine.'

Damn Terry! But then I checked myself – I had already damned him. I'd destroyed the heavenly life that my father's closest friend had shaped for himself in Venice. He was now without Thérèse, his muse, his love, his best friend – The Golden Illuminati may have killed her, but it was because of me. If Thérèse hadn't opened their home and welcomed me into their lives last year, she would still be alive. What kind of dross was I to object to any request he made? I would never write off the debts I owed him, and now he was my only ally against The Golden Illuminati.

My eyes swept the almost empty scaffold, and then I tugged off my nitrile gloves and gauze pads. The disfigured skin mauled by psoriasis and a partially healed slit across one palm didn't make them a pretty picture, but ignoring that, I pressed my hands tightly against the sculpture's metal head. I felt a faint tingle at the surface of the skin, but nothing else.

Fear dried my throat and its prickliness began to work its way into my torso, but even it couldn't dislodge the main resident that lurked there: the yearning for the profound connection with metal which I'd achieved just once last year when I'd transformed a tiny piece of spelter into gold. Since then, it had dodged me continuously, only allowing me tiny glimpses of that power from time to time. My body ached night and day with the loss of it.

I moved my hands to Lennon's shoulders and tried again. I strained to hear any titbit the metal might have for me, even asking a question in my head –'Is it safe?' – but again, nothing. Since last year, sometimes metals sent me messages through my hands. It was a random occurrence, and I'd reached the conclusion that not all metals had something to say. But the ones that did often said something useful.

I swung my leg over Lennon's shoulder and dismounted – I'd been trying to finish the highest points of the sculpture, and these were most easily reached by sitting astride his neck. I pulled the gloves back on. There was nothing approaching a weapon up here apart from a five litre tin of wax. I suppose if the need arose, it could do some damage if I hit this Robert Kirkpatrick square with it.

I needed to calm down. Terry had said he was a good guy, on our side.

'Hello!' A voice came from the level below. I picked up my tin of wax and took a deep breath.

As the figure came into view, I couldn't do anything but agree with Anne-Marie's assessment: he was handsome. He wore a close-cut beard, but she hadn't mentioned his unusual colouring. To me, it was always the most distinctive feature in a person. His beard and longish hair were a blend of browns and russet shades with slight hints of silver. Colour was a tactile language for me and I felt my fingers tingle at the challenge of how I would coax and blend those precise shades on to the surface of a bronze.

He swallowed and then swayed slightly, grabbing on to the scaffold rail. Our eyes met again, and a flush came over his skin. He put his hand to his head and squeezed his temples.

'Must have run up too quickly. Need to get back on the old treadmill.' He spoke with a Scottish accent that was refined, but hadn't lost its Celtic warmth.

After a moment, he looked up at me, face ashen. 'Do you have any water?'

I stared at his eyes a beat longer than was proper: nice eyes, a blue-based hazel, but where Anne-Marie had seen soulfulness, I recognised wariness. Since the events of last year, it was a look familiar to me, and it didn't reassure me that Terry knew what he was thinking about, bringing us together.

I nodded and walked over to my site box on the corner of the scaffold. I had a half-dozen small bottles of water in there. Opening one up for myself, I brought the water to my mouth, my hand shaking. Since Thérèse's murder, Terry had turned away from his successful art career and focused entirely on finding a way to bring down The Golden Illuminati. He was sure that this man was the chink in their armour – someone on the inside, a fully paid-up member of the Society, but on the same page as us. To me, it was just too convenient.

As I passed a bottle to him, he leaned against the

guardrail to drink. As he did, I noticed his eyes run along the length of my neck, slip down my shoulders, and continue down. I was only wearing a vest top and jeans. The work I did was too physical to wear jumpers, apart from in the very cold months. The path of his eyes made me feel underdressed.

He held out his hand. 'I'm Robert Kirkpatrick.'

I didn't reciprocate.

'I know who you are, but not why you're here. I thought I was quite clear with Terry that, despite his faith in you, I'm not interested in your help.'

My voice sounded better than I'd hoped for, like I wasn't scared, but even though I knew it was stupid, I couldn't stop myself from taking a surreptitious glance over the side of the scaffold, just to check some Golden Illuminati SWAT team wasn't swarming the foundry courtyard.

'But why?' he said, shaking his head slightly as if he really had no idea.

'I should think that would be obvious, but if it isn't then let me steal a few words from the mighty man himself.' I put one hand on the statue's shoulder. 'The more I see, the less I know for sure.'

He turned towards the statue. 'Unusual piece of work. I'm a fan of large-scale sculpture, but I can't say that this would be my taste.'

He circled the boards that surrounded Lennon. I followed him, keeping an even distance between us. Then he leaned over the sculpture's shoulder so their heads were side by side. It looked comical: something which under other circumstances, I might have offered to take a photograph of.

'It's interesting to meet you, finally. You're almost a

legend within the Society, with all the trouble you've caused them.'

'Don't you mean, all the trouble I've caused you? You are one of them.'

He nodded. 'Aye, in a way, I am. They're going to come for you again.'

I shrugged. 'Well, I'm not that hard to find – right back where they found me the first time, working in my family's foundry.' This time my voice wobbled.

'You shouldn't joke. They will take you.'

'You think it's a sense of invincibility that keeps me here?' Anger and astonishment mingled in my voice. 'I don't know where else to go that's any safer. If they want me, they'll take me wherever I am. I don't know why they haven't moved sooner.'

'The Golden Illuminati is much like any large organisation. It's an unwieldy beast and many people need to approve any new step. Not everyone is sure that you are worth the trouble.'

'I'm not. And you can tell them I've lodged a statement with a solicitor about what happened to me last summer. It will be handed to the police if I disappear again. Currently, the police have said they'll look into my claims, and if I go missing again they'll be able to guess who has taken me.'

'There would be no evidence to connect you to them. They are experts at covering things up – they've done a pretty good job of hiding the real history of alchemy, wouldn't you say?'

'I'm not interested in your help. There's nothing you can say that will convince me.'

'Don't you owe it to Terry to at least listen?'

Bullseye.

I picked up a foam pad and cotton cloth from the scaffold boards. 'I need to crack on – talk if you want.'

I knelt on the pad and pulled the tin of wax close to my side – just in case. My cloth flew over the bronze's surface, making the shades stand out in higher definition.

He took another sip of water. 'You know I'm a patron of Terry's? I've admired and bought his art, promoted and helped him through his career, partly because I think he is amazing, but also because I owe his family a debt.

'Terry's dad, Billy Gerrard ran parts of the East End of London back in the 1950s. He had thumbs in a lot of pies – one of which was smuggling diamonds. At the time in the UK, it was illegal to import diamonds. My da' worked for Billy as a gem-cutter in Hatton Garden, but his extra-curricular role was as a diamond courier. He went all over the world for Billy, bringing back diamonds from places that, in those days, other people feared to go to.

'Eventually, diamond smuggling became unnecessary as the laws changed and Billy sold up to go live a quiet life in Essex. About ten years ago, my da' got cancer and he wrote to Billy to say goodbye. Billy swooped in and paid for the best private treatment that money could buy. He really did everything humanly possible to try and save him – experimental drugs, flying top specialists in from every end of the earth, but it was all a bit late. Unfortunately, the cancer had the jump on them.

'I couldn't be more grateful for what he did, though, because the most important thing was how he distracted him and cheered my da' up at the end. There was lots of talk of the old times, the scrapes they'd been in, the things they'd done, the people they'd known. That did him more good than all the extra drugs and chemo. I've always wanted a chance to pay that back.

'When I found out that Thérèse was dead and how, I got in touch with Terry because I knew that this was my opportunity to help him in a meaningful way, like Billy did for us. I've been a member of The Golden Illuminati for four years, and like Terry, I have a personal vendetta against them. My deepest desire is to see them exposed, but I'm playing a long game.'

'Seems to me you could just be spinning him a story about this convenient vendetta.'

'Actually, I didn't even have to tell him anything about it. Terry already knew because one of my da's eccentric tendencies was to talk to anyone and everyone about the scar our family bore because of them. The position I'm in means that I can help Terry, and you.'

I looked up at him, searching for the lie, but his expression told me nothing, and his eyes were just ... distracting. I turned back to my buffing cloth.

'I am offering to protect you, at least for a while, in my home in Scotland while we plan what to do next. It's not easy to bring down an institution that has been as successful in hiding itself as The Golden Illuminati, but we all want the same thing.'

'And they will never know I'm there, with you, right? I imagine I'd be rounded up as soon as I arrived.' I gave a slight but insincere laugh.

'No. There's another reason you can trust me. One that Terry doesn't know about. Something we have in common.'

'I doubt that,' I said, standing up to move around the statue to another spot.

'I can help you to develop your skills,' he said.

I tried not to react. He couldn't know quite how desperate I was to find someone who would help me with that. The last several months had been a frustrating spiral.

I'd tried so many times to repeat the miracle I'd achieved in that cell in Italy, but with not even the slightest glimmer of progress. The acute state of my psoriasis right now was another sign of how distant I was from any progress. Last year, the bonus outcome of creating the gold had been my skin condition clearing up entirely.

'What skills? As I proved last year, I have no gift, only craft skills,' I said, facing him. 'I doubt there's much you could help me with there.'

'They wouldn't come after you again, Abigail, if they didn't strongly suspect you have some unusual capability. I heard about your eyes. How they'd glowed last year. What-ever they've seen in you, it may not be a fully developed gift yet, but it's enough for them to consider you interesting.'

'They made things up to consolidate their case. My eyes didn't glow. Don't you think, if I could have, I'd have done anything to get out of there?'

'And you did.'

Something passed between us: a flicker of understand-ing. He knew I'd murdered Pierro. It was followed close behind by a flare of attraction.

'Aren't you curious at all what you might be capable of?'

Curious didn't come close.

'Give me one good reason why I should trust you besides the history you have with Terry. As for having some vendetta against the Illuminati, you've told me nothing convincing so far.' I tried to look as unimpressed as possible.

He smiled. 'I've a suspicion that whatever I tell you, you won't believe me, so there doesn't seem much point in giving you more details that could compromise me.'

It was getting darker by the minute. He came around the statue and stood close to my side. The wax tin was on the floor – damn!

'How about I show ye rather than tell ye?'

Reaching forward, he put out his hand towards me, upturned. I looked at it, unsure.

'Please,' he said.

I laid my gloved hand in his, and damn it if I didn't feel a blush reach my cheeks. But as I watched, he smiled, very slightly. Then he closed his eyes and I saw his expression calm, before I felt the strange sensation. It was as though I was holding a ball of static rather than his hand, and it was cloaking my hand. The hairs on my arms and the back of my neck rose up and quivered.

He opened his eyes and my mouth dropped open. There were bright dots of light buzzing around his irises like little hot coals in flight. The darkness closing in on us made them stand out even more brightly.

He gave me time to take it in. 'This is the reason. We have more in common than you think, and I can help you gain control of what's inside you. Very few people know about my own gift. If The Golden Illuminati did, then like you, I'd be locked up in a trice. Now I've trusted you with something that makes me vulnerable, I'd like you to reconsider my offer.'

I nodded mutely. It was the only carrot that could have made this ass move.

## 3

## ROBERT

Sipping my third coffee, I watched the train from London pull into the station in Edinburgh. Within seconds, people were filing off the train and marching up the platform. I sought her face in the crowd: today would be different. I was prepared. I didn't want to think about the last time we'd met. It had been a damned disaster.

I'd flown up those ladders, but when I met her eyes at the top, it felt like I was falling back down them twice as fast. Vertigo – I had fockin' vertigo. Me! Who builds skyscrapers for a living! The man who's been scrambling up and down scaffolds since he was fifteen years old and working on the fly in his holidays. I've been on scaffolds so high that they look down on clouds.

Angeline kept flashing into my head. She'd not been in my bed for at least eighteen months, but we'd seen each other for a long enough period for it to be categorised as a relationship, at least by her. It was her heart-shaped face that kept rising in my mind; I could even hear her Bronx voice.

'Her? With her hair tied back and skinny-ass boy's body? She bowls you over when you had an A-class woman like me?'

Angeline had been A-class in every way. The only thing missing between us had been attachment. In that first glimpse of Abigail, I'd felt the bond being forged. My experience of like-recognising-like was no warm, fuzzy feeling, but closer to being shot in the chest with a nail gun. Now, every time I moved, or even thought about her, I could feel the nail still in there, rusting.

She was nearly at the end of the platform and looking even more sexy today than she had at the foundry. I stared up at the ironwork in the station's ceiling and filled my chest with air. Sitting in the car after meeting her four days ago, I'd reassured myself that it had just been the foundry setting that had given her heightened appeal. She'd seemed so in control of the space and she'd been wearing tight jeans and a skimpy vest top. For all Angeline's perfections, one aspect I hadn't appreciated was her dressiness.

Today Abigail looked alert, even upbeat. It had to be some kind of mind-voodoo. I must be imagining her into being my ideal woman because she was the one female I couldn't have. But, as I looked at her shiny dark hair that swayed around her jawline, sunglasses complementing her ivory skin and long laced boots exaggerating her lengthy, lean legs, those details didn't feel like figments of my imagination.

'Hi.' She stopped a foot away from me and took off her glasses, bringing the end of them to her lips. I was unable to look anywhere other than those lips. Attraction howled in my stomach and began to spin down lower.

'Looks like you don't have a care in the world.' It escaped

my mouth before I'd engaged my brain and came out like an accusation.

Surprise lifted her eyebrows. 'Would you be happier if I were throwing stray glances over my shoulder and running into your arms to beg for protection?'

As that image swept across my mind, I thought how nice that would have been. Her lips became all curves as she guessed my thoughts, though she didn't quite smile. I pulled her bag from her hand, more roughly than I needed to, and turned, marching towards the exit.

It took a moment for her to catch me up. 'Actually, you wouldn't think I was quite so cool if you'd counted how many times I moved seats on the train. It's amazing how easy it is to become consumed by paranoia – normal behaviours like elderly ladies calling their daughters can morph into code for "She's sitting in the middle of carriage D".'

My thoughts ran to Philip. Maybe she should be warier of elderly men.

A void seemed to open up in my head and swallow all topics of polite conversation. As we made our way across the station, I couldn't think of a single thing to say to her. The silence became awkward in no time. Anxiety was like a tight band around my throat – how would we manage the next several hours in the car together? Last time I'd felt this way, I'd been fourteen and about to kiss my first girlfriend. If only the circumstances surrounding Abigail and I were as simple.

'Do you always walk this fast?' she said, running the odd step to keep up.

'No.'

'Is the car far?'

'No.'

More painful silence. I cast my eyes around, hoping for some inspiration from the shops in the station.

'Robert, is there something wrong?' She faltered and then came to a stop, looking at me with huge eyes. She quivered like a deer. People were moving around her in both directions; a bag hit her shoulder as someone passed too close and she jumped and swung around a half circle, about to bolt.

I put out my hand, meaning to reassure her, but as I took hold of her arm, she began to twist and yank herself from my grip. People were looking at us with frowns as they passed by.

'Abigail – I promise you there's nothing wrong – no-one here.' I was supposed to be putting her at her ease, getting her to trust me, and all I was doing was terrifying her. 'Ay'm sorry,' I said, putting as much feeling into it as a repressed Scotsman can. She stopped struggling. 'I was just thinking of getting on the road. Long journey ahead and all.'

She glanced up at me and I tried to smile, but it felt tight, and I'm sure it was anything but reassuring.

She stayed where she was a moment or two and I watched her chest rise and fall. She took a step towards me and looked up; her dark, long lashes were so appealing that they smashed through the void in my head and all I could think of was the possibility of dipping my head and kissing her deeply.

'You've nearly given me a heart attack because you're thinking of the drive ahead?'

I nodded. 'Aye.'

She rolled her eyes, and then struck out with her hand, hitting me on the arm. 'If I hadn't grown up in a foundry full of men, I might not have believed you.'

I rubbed my arm and a tentative smile was exchanged between us.

I had to concentrate very hard not to walk fast again. We made it into the car park and I could see my car.

'It's just this way.' I pulled my key fob from my pocket, ready to open the boot for her bags.

'Nice. Aston Martin DB11?'

I was surprised she knew.

'One of my brothers is car mad.' She shrugged, and as her eyes met mine, I felt myself respond. As I did, my chest tightened.

'I wanted to ask you about—,' she began as I opened the car's door, but a large, hairy nose followed by two mournful eyes forced themselves forward and interrupted her. Abigail squeaked in delight. His tail made a dull thudding against the back seats.

'You've got a dog! Is he a deerhound?'

I nodded. 'Remi.'

'Hi, Remi. Hello, Boy!' She bent her head towards him and the dog licked her face as she stroked and tugged his ears gently. He pushed further forward for more, until his front half occupied her entire seat.

'You need a different car for this dog, something with a large boot.'

'We manage fine. There's plenty of room. I tried to leave him behind, but I never win an argument with Remi.'

I climbed in and pushed Remi back far enough to allow Abigail to get into her seat. Putting the car into reverse, I manoeuvred out of the space with the dog's tail marking time as it banged against the seat, his head thrust between the two of us.

'Settle down, Rem,' I said as we wound around the traffic

flow towards the exit. 'I can't concentrate with ya making all that racket.'

Remi moved backward and let out a wounded sigh as he settled himself down along the back seat. But he laid his head on the armrest next to Abigail.

Just as I was about to make it on to the main road, a man appeared from nowhere, walking straight in front of the car. I slammed on the brakes and Remi was thrust forward. He gave a yelp as his nose hit the radio.

The man, in a dark leather trench coat, thick-set with beard, had one hand on the bonnet of the car while the other was lifted to steady a sculptural red woman's hat complete with netting that trailed coquettishly across one bristly eyebrow. I swore as Remi scrabbled backwards. Fenrear was the last person I wanted to run into: it couldn't be a coincidence.

We stared at one another. I revved my engine and Fenrear lifted his hands from the bonnet. I wound down the window.

'Get 'oot the way, man!' I yelled.

I glanced at Abigail, and she was wearing a puzzled expression: the one most people wore when they encountered the surprising cocktail that was Fenrear Leighton. I was determined not to give away that I knew him. The last thing I needed was Fenrear joining us on the journey.

He didn't shift, and I played with the clutch a little, making the car kangaroo, nudging him backward.

'Wait, Robert, you'll run him over!' Abigail exclaimed, grabbing hold of my arm.

That was exactly what I wanted to do.

Fenrear bent his knees and put his hand to his eyes to shade the sun's glare as he looked into the car. An exaggerated expression of surprise spread over his face.

'Robert!' He waved. 'Hello!'

This couldn't be good.

'Damn you, Fen,' I said under my breath as he walked over to Abigail's side of the car. He tapped on her window, then removed his hat as she wound it down and leaned in. His grin was wide and wolfish, his solid shoulders filling the width of the window.

Fen glanced into the back. 'Hello, my old friend,' he said to Remi, who thumped his tail on the seat.

'Don't be nice to my dog, you reprobate. Nice little charade you just put on.'

'You know him?' Abigail said this like she was putting two and two together, but in this, if nothing else, I was innocent.

He offered his hand to her. 'I'm Fenrear. Honoured to meet you, Abigail.'

She began to yank at the door handle.

'Wait! This isn't what you think,' I said to her back, putting a hand out to her shoulder, which she jerked away. Fen put his weight against the door, preventing her escape. Abigail turned to look at me with the dirtiest look of accusation in her eyes and she shook her head slightly.

What was Fenrear up to?

'Don't be mad with your handsome chauffeur – he didn't know I would be here, but I just couldn't miss out on meeting a real alchemist.'

My stomach turned over – the way it does when you realise you've missed a critical step. How had I not anticipated something like this happening? Of course, knowledge of Abigail's gift, or potential gift, had leaked out.

A loud horn blasted from a car directly behind us. Abigail and I both jumped at the unexpected sound, and Fen seized his opportunity. He had the back door open and had slid inside the car with his small bag in the time it took for me to put the car into first gear.

'Shove-up, puppy,' he said, giving Remi's long body a push as he squeezed in. He had a small, battered brown leather holdall with him which he wedged into the footwell. The fine red hat he laid on his knee carefully, giving it a small caress.

I pulled out of the car park and drove towards the A90. I looked into my rear-view mirror and Fen stared back at me.

'I'm watching you. Be on your best behaviour.' Uneasiness was all over me as I pieced together the possibilities of why Fenrear was there.

He pretended to look wounded. 'Of course, my dear boy. Wouldn't dream of doing otherwise.'

'Aye, right.'

Abigail was looking at Fen like there was a black mamba on the back seat.

'Pull over! Stop the car, now!' she yelled at me. 'I'm not going a yard further with this man – whoever he is.'

Fen leaned forward; he was a braver man than I was because her expression was rabid.

'Oh, darling—'

She spun so fast, I thought she might leap in the back and attack him.

'Don't you "darling" me! I want to know who you are and how you know my name!'

Remi started to bark; I swerved to the side of the road and stopped just in front of a bus stop. Fen had his hands up like Abigail had a gun and was making shushing noises to both Abigail and the dog.

'Be quiet, Remi,' I snapped. 'We don't need your opinion.'

Remi ceased his barking.

'Abigail, I can assure you that I didn't know Fenrear was going to ambush us like this, but it's okay. He's a chancer, but he's on the right side. Nothing to do with them.'

Abigail's chest was rising up and down, fast.

'There's no need to deny your talents to me. If anyone can keep your secrets, I can. We are kin,' said Fenrear in his most soothing voice.

Fenrear has many faults, but he also has the golden quality of knowing just what to do to make people like him, however badly he behaves. I saw Abigail's tight jaw soften, though I could tell her mind was still whirring with questions.

'Let me introduce myself properly. You know my name, and I'm definitely a friend, not foe. I'm an art dealer, of sorts, which is why Robert and I are so *simpatico*.'

I couldn't help huffing at this comment.

'I'm sorry if I startled you. I do so adore a bit of drama and I had a sneaking suspicion that my dear friend here wouldn't be keen to share you with me. There's no mystery – I know your name because I ran into Terry Gerrard recently. Him and I go way back – he wouldn't be the artist he is if he hadn't met me.'

'The artist he was.'

'Yes, yes, awful business that.' Fen looked down at his hands and paused a moment. 'Terry told me everything that happened last year, and the minute he mentioned The Golden Illuminati, I knew what you must be – I mean, it's rather like why McDonald's are interested in cows.' He gave me a little shrug. 'He's incredibly worried about you, you know. Told me all about finding you in Italy with your wrists slit?'

'My hands, it wasn't my wrists.'

'Says you've done it since then, too.'

Her expression gave nothing away.

'There's a few things Terry doesn't know about me, and one is that I know quite a bit about that secret society that is after you, and it sounded like you could do with a friend. Maybe one that's more like you than he is.'

Abigail glanced at me.

'Abigail, can I start driving again? That's the second bus I've been flashed by,' I asked her, and she nodded.

'Okay,' she whipped her head round to Fen, 'but I reserve the right to chuck you out of the car at any point.'

Fen nodded with a wry smile, and as I got the car moving again, he shuffled forward in his seat so he was cosily wedged between us.

'Whether you are or aren't an alchemist, I'm what's known as a spook and I always tell our kind that immediately as they tend to react badly if I'm not upfront about it.'

'Our kind?' Abigail studied him as she said the words. Her eyes ran over each of his features: the elegant female hat that he'd placed on his stocky legs; the iron-grey beard and longish Byronic hair with silver highlights; eyebrows that were shrub-like in their density, but rose to an apex and then fell towards the wedge of his hawkish nose. 'What do you mean, our kind?'

We paused at a set of lights. 'Well, I'm guessing you don't cross-dress, so I obviously don't mean that,' said Fen, who enjoyed his own joke so much, he followed it up with, 'Eh, Robert?', but I was looking at a helicopter that hovered and then took off across the city sky and away into the clouds.

'Actually, Fen, I hadn't gotten to the stage of telling Abigail about our kind yet.'

'Start with what a spook is,' she said.

'You're not gonna like this,' I said under my breath.

Abigail caught my words and concern made its way across her expression.

'A spook is a little bit of several things. I can leave my body, as your friend here can, but unlike Robert, I have some limitations.'

She swivelled her body towards me and brought her hand to her lips. 'But, you can do more than that, though. You're like me, right?'

Expectation is a tangible thing, but I'd never been aware of it until that moment. As I shook my head and saw her take on board the mistake, the car felt empty despite all its passengers. No wonder she'd been so upbeat getting off the train. Why hadn't I been more specific at the foundry? When I thought along those lines, the fact I'd persuaded her to come at all was a minor miracle.

I watched as she slipped one hand beneath the fingerless glove she was wearing on the other and scratched at the skin.

'I'm sorry ... if you misunderstood. We have things in common, but I'm not an alchemist.'

Fen gave a deep laugh. 'Of course he's not. Do you know how rare alchemists are? Let's see, they're probably in the same category as something like unicorns.'

'Well, I'm feeling much closer to being a donkey than a unicorn right now,' said Abigail, looking down at her hands.

As we drove further on, buildings fell away, and broad trees lined the road. The urge to comfort Abigail stole over me and I clenched the steering wheel tightly instead. My dog must have been thinking the same thing, though his conscience was clear. He stood up and pushed himself in front of Fen, licking her ear. She leaned into him appreciatively. Lucky dog.

I carried on my explanation. 'What I can do is move

outside of my body. My consciousness isn't tethered to it. As a child, the doctors thought I had all sorts of dire illnesses – rare forms of epilepsy – but really, I was just bored in lessons and would wander out. I didn't realise that my body had been left behind. In fact, I don't remember a time when I couldn't do it.'

Fen cleared his throat and took over. 'I'm a little different from Robert. Some people can see me when I leave my body. My form often seems opaque to those who are more sensitive. I imagine what people call ghosts are actually my kind, which is why they call me a spook.'

'Don't stop there, Fen – don't leave out the good parts,' I said, my voice as heavy with sarcasm as I could manage.

Fenrear swallowed, then sniffed. 'I also ... have a ... few other talents.' He spoke more quietly then. 'But, I think the one Robert is referring to is that I'm able to enter a person's body and access their thoughts.'

I almost laughed. Abigail looked like she'd swallowed salt. Fen hurried on.

'It doesn't last long. Seconds really – I can only sense what they're thinking in that tiny window of time. Then their brains seem to know there's an intruder and the curtains close.'

I gave Abigail a look that said, 'See why I didn't want to stop the car?'

'Can you control them?' she asked.

He shook his head. 'It's more like being a parasite than a puppet-master. I don't always go undetected, either – many people can sense me inside them. I can't communicate with them, though I've come across other spooks who can.' Fen clearly saw the look on Abigail's face. 'You've nothing to fear. I'll be on my best behaviour, I promise.' Fen put his hand to his head in a salute. 'Scout's honour.'

She turned away from him and stared out of the window, her expression sceptical, and then gave a start.

'What's that helicopter doing?'

I'd seen it, but didn't want to panic her again. Was The Illuminati checking up on me already? It was to our left, flying parallel to us over a wheat field, but not going a lot faster than us.

Abigail whipped her head towards me and grabbed my nearest arm off the steering wheel. 'This is you, isn't it?'

I looked at her anxious eyes and glanced at Fen, who was watching our exchange. 'No! Of course not!'

'Why else would there be a helicopter following us?'

I felt a flash of annoyance at her being so continuously suspicious of me. Not exactly fair, seeing as her instincts were on point. I hoped to God she wouldn't say more in front of Fen. I really didn't need him knowing all my business. He may be playing out his eccentric-Englishman act, but there was a lot more to him than that. His story about Terry only rang true to a degree, but I'd wager any kind of money that he hadn't turned up just to play nicely with Abigail. I couldn't think what his angle was, but I was certain he had one.

Fen patted her arm and looked at me thoughtfully.

'It isn't following us. Look, it's circled away now. Probably a private pilot. I understand that you have a nasty case of a secret society coveting you, so I can imagine why you are a bit jumpy, but you can't live assuming everything is about you. Believe me, it's the surest way to lunacy.'

Fen relaxed back against the seat and rubbed his shoulders into the leather. Remi laid his head across his lap.

'Among our kind, you'd only be unusual if you didn't have someone after you. It's the thing that's shaped our community and our culture more than any other. We are a persecuted race.'

'There's that phrase again: our kind, which means—?'

'I'm referring to Underworlders – our tribe. We aren't many in number, but we have abilities outside of the ordinary. We can't fly or become invisible or anything; we don't have superpowers, but much of what is considered folklore has roots in our kind – astral projection, for example, like our friend Robert here, or ghosts like me. I'm incredibly sought after by several groups as well, you know. Five years ago, I was taken by a group of researchers. They were worse than the South American arms dealer who got hold of me a decade before that.'

'Researchers of what?'

'Everlasting life.' He paused for effect. 'You see ... hasn't your journey been improved by my arrival? I'm much more interesting than Robert.'

I noticed in my rear-view mirror the helicopter in the distance again. Despite Fen's dismissal of it, uneasiness prickled my skin. Not that I was about to tell Abigail that. I'd lived in these parts for several years and never remembered seeing a private helicopter before. Maybe when I got back, I'd make a phone call to Philip – drop a few hints that I didn't appreciate micro-managing of the situation.

Fen's phone beeped. He pulled it out and looked at the screen.

'Oh, Robert, that's Richard at The Coach House. Meeting you and Abigail is grand, but really, I was en route to see him. Could you, perhaps, drop me there? It's not out of your way, and we should get there around dinner time, so you could take a little driving break, too.'

'I don't need a driving break.'

'I'm sure Abigail wouldn't object.'

I sighed. 'I'd be very happy to leave you at The Coach House, Fen.'

'Jolly good. It's all worked out splendidly. Oh, don't be so sulky, Robert. Mind you, perhaps Abigail appreciates a little Scottish scowl?' His eyes danced from me to her, seeking a reaction which neither of us yielded. 'Tzz!' He made a sizzling noise. 'I sense tension,' he said in a sing-song voice.

'Do you want to get out now? Because you're going the right way about it.'

'Oh, come on, misery, you'd have to stop somewhere.'

I concentrated on the road and kept a firm patrol in place around my thoughts. The last thing I could afford to do around Fenrear was drop my guard, no matter what he promised. His nature was to slip inside people's heads and feast on their thoughts. I did not need Abigail discovering my real plan on Day One.

4

———

## ABIGAIL

R obert pulled up at a traditional white farmhouse-turned-pub on the winding road between Pitlochry and Bridge of Gaur. The pub was the only one we'd come across for quite some time though we'd passed endless fields, forests and hedges interspersed with cotchels of houses.

As the three of us got out and stretched, Fen replaced his hat and Remi loped after a grouse. It was strolling past the car nonchalantly, but ended up scarpering as the dog gave chase. I walked stiffly across the wide shale driveway towards the silent road and admired the ripe light of the sun. It seemed to have stopped for a rest on its descent and was lolling on the peak of a particularly craggy mountain which flanked the road. Any moment, the sharp points would be sure to poke through the sun's membrane and liquid sunshine would pour down the mountain like egg yolk.

Fenrear's worrisome chatter rattled in my head: spooks, Underworlders, gifts, enemies and Robert - disturbingly attractive, *one-of-them*, Robert. To that, I also needed to tack on Fenrear himself, who may, or may not, have already rifled around in my brain. I wondered if I'd ever be able to trust them.

I had to get my desperation under control. I'd jumped to conclusions about what Robert could do because I'd heard what I wanted to hear. He'd only said he could help me develop my gift, but in my head, I'd seen him as a master able to teach me all the secrets of alchemy that I was longing for.

I rolled my shoulders and stretched my neck backwards. Ever since Robert had come to the foundry, only four days ago, it had felt as if I'd had a steel rod implanted into my neck. My shoulders and jaw ached with the strain. The muscles burned with tightness as my mind tossed and turned the likelihood of whether I was being a naïve fool to believe him. Physical work was nothing to the toll on my body of mental strain. I'd worked fifteen-hour shifts at times when we were busy in the foundry, but at least my sleep afterwards had not been infringed upon by fears.

It wasn't just fear, though. That I had risen above in the past, but my common sense was now having a bare-knuckle fight with my vanity. To protect myself, I'd taken every precaution to hide from The Golden Illuminati that I could transform metal. I'd shown them only that I had sound foundry skills, and yet I hankered for someone to believe in me; someone to acknowledge what I did. Last year, when I'd told Terry and my boyfriend David the truth, they'd strug-gled to believe it. A lot of looks and hushed discussions had passed between them in the days after my disclosure. Although David hadn't said it in so many words, I was certain he thought I'd made a suicide attempt while imprisoned by The Golden Illuminati. His expression had been incredulous when I'd explained that the cuts had been critical in the transformation process: it had been my blood that had made the final change.

Fenrear and Robert were different. They knew what it was like to be able to do things they shouldn't be able to do. They would believe me if I was brave enough to admit the truth.

I closed my eyes and lifted my face into the warm wind which was bounding down the valley.

'The air is marvellous here,' Robert said, just inches behind me. The surprise gave me a jolt. He was standing so close, I unbalanced as I turned to look up at him. As he put his hands out to steady me, his thumb settled across my wrist and I felt my pulse skitter under his touch.

I pulled my hand away, but couldn't help looking up into his inviting hazel-blue eyes. Remi raced past, following an imaginary rabbit, and I felt a bubble of happiness pop in my chest. It was unexpected – just an ordinary, nothing-much moment, but the novelty of the feeling couldn't be ignored: happiness had become something unusual in my life.

Fenrear put his head out of the pub. 'Come on, you two!'

Robert whistled for Remi to follow and I made my way towards the pub's entrance. Robert fell in behind me. It felt disconcerting to walk in single file, and I glanced over my shoulder and smiled.

'Am I holding you up? Feel free to overtake me, your legs are a lot longer than mine.'

'That would ruin the view,' he said so quietly, I wasn't sure if I'd heard right.

I was glad that the back of my head couldn't blush.

Inside the pub, warm lamplight introduced dark

wooden floors and whitewashed stone walls. There were photographs of the landscape of the area a hundred years ago, which looked just the same as today. The pub had a nice atmospheric feel, though any custom but us was absent.

Fenrear removed his hat, laid it on the bar and raked his fingers through his hair. I moved alongside him.

'What will you have, Abigail?' Fenrear asked.

I looked at him. Did I want a drink from this man?

'Okay, I get that you trust me about as far as you can throw me, but just for now, can we suspend hostilities and enjoy the rather spectacular comforts that this establishment has to offer?'

I gave him a slight nod. 'If we're friends for now, then I should tell you that you look younger without the hat, and I'm not sure red's your colour.'

His mouth dropped open. 'And I was sure I was going to like you! Just goes to show – first appearances are as valuable as muck. It's not a hat – it's a Jean Barthet, a genuine 1950s piece of art. I was about to tell you that my friends call me Fen, but now you can call me Mr Leighton.'

'It may be a piece of art on a supermodel, but what she is pointing out is that it's not on ye',' Robert said, indicating his choice of draught lager to the barman.

Fenrear made a tsk noise and turned his attention to the bar. 'This man is the man I aspire to be – one day. Richard, meet Abigail. She is with us,' he said, giving Richard a knowing look.

I passed my hand over the bar and we shook. Richard smiled self-consciously. He was stocky and had the ruddy complexion and large hands of a farmer.

'Richard is an artist who shuns capitalist norms and

creates for the sake of it, without any desire for financial validation.'

Richard cleared his throat. 'That's not quite true, Fenrear. You will be providing financial validation by paying your bill tonight.'

'What type of art do you create?' I asked, not able to see any obvious displays of his creativity on the walls, which would have been the ideal private gallery space.

He turned to the shelves of bottles behind him. There were rows and rows of different coloured glass bottles decorating the shelves and the length of the bar.

'They're all my own work. I micro-brew and distil here.'

As I gazed at the bottles, I saw that not even one was a labelled brand. Each concoction had a not very expertly designed sticker on the bottle with a small stamp saying The Coach House.

Richard picked one up from the eye-level shelf. 'This one is schnapps with rosehip and honey.' He poured each of us the tiniest dram, though Robert refused it. Fen chinked my glass when I picked it up. It was heavenly: the sweet thickness of schnapps with a tiny edge that made it pleasant rather than sickly. 'The honey's my own and the rosehips are foraged. My land here is self-sustaining.'

'Doesn't he sound smug?' Fen laughed.

'It's divine, Richard. Don't you sell this to other outlets?'

Richard shook his head. 'I like the quiet life. I'll make up things for people if they ask, but I usually give them it as a gift. Stops them asking for too much.'

Fen looked at me. 'I've tried many times to make him see sense. He could be the Heston Blumenthal of the alcohol world. I have the perfect people lined up to do business with him. You can't help some people.' Fen shrugged. 'Okay, away with the sweet stuff – give us a taste of something that will wake us up.'

Richard's eyes twinkled. 'You sure? I just finished a little project you can try, but haven't bottled it up yet.'

He left the bar for a small room on the right. From the angle I was at, it looked like a kitchen, but with its sides covered in glassware. He returned in seconds, carrying an earthenware jug – the kind that may have held water a century ago. The jug was a large beast and was full to the brim. Richard managed quite well to pour a couple of samples from it, only spilling a little.

Fen gave me a knowing look before taking up the glass. 'Hold on to the seat of your pants,' he said and knocked it back. I followed suit. It was like the hottest chilli I'd ever eaten combined with the kind of spirit that made every organ in my body clench.

'Achhhhhhh!' We both hung our tongues out of our mouths.

'I like the first one better,' I squeaked.

'I call it The Grim Reaper. It's chilli whisky made with the Carolina Reaper chilli.' Richard laughed. 'Go on through, you guys. I'll bring you some wine, Fenrear.' He lifted a hinged segment of the bar and gestured for us to move past and into another bar area beyond.

'Beer for me,' Robert said as he passed Richard.

I hung back and watched Robert go. I admired his height. He had a rangy body, long torso and arms. His shoulder span was wide, too, but not in a beefcake way.

'I'll just have a palate-cleansing tonic water for now, please,' I said to Richard, who moved about the bar for ice and glasses. 'Have you always lived around here?' I asked. 'It's very quiet.'

'True. Nothing much ever happens here. I grew up at the pub, then left and worked in banking for about a decade in Edinburgh, but when my mum got sick a few years ago, I decided to come back and take over the old place. It's always been a safe place for people like them,' he said, casting a glance in the direction that Robert and Fen had gone. 'My mum was one, you see. She was a gazer.'

I shook my head. 'I'm sorry, I've no idea what that is.'

'She could see memories in people by looking into their eyes, like watching an old-fashioned camera reel.'

Richard passed me a tall glass, pouring in the tonic water.

'From the way you talk, it sounds like you don't have abilities?' I asked.

He shook his head. 'No, but I'm one of them by association, perhaps the way you are.' His smile was kind, but he didn't pry as I had done – the perfect barman.

'So, tell me how it is that no-one knows they exist?'

Richard scrunched up his brow. 'I don't think there's any formal reason why, but being incognito has always been their way. They really are a very tiny group. There isn't a census or anything like that for Underworlders, but from what I've heard, there are probably below twenty thousand in the entire world. Blending in is safest, I guess – evolution's most primitive means of protection.'

'So where do they come from?'

He looked at me with a smile. 'Planet Zon.' He laughed. 'They aren't aliens. They just have natural abilities, like singers and artists, which they cultivate. The difference is, what they can do is rarer.'

'I don't understand how it's all kept so quiet. How do people not notice children doing something incredible? Do all the people around them take a vow of silence? Do they get visited by another Underworlder and told the rules?'

Richard sat on the stool behind the bar. He had a placid face which was unlined – a life with little worry.

'That's a lot of questions. You should ask your friends.'

I nodded. 'Sorry. Of course.'

'No problem,' he said, picking up his book. I began to make my way through to the other bar, then stopped and darted back towards him.

'Richard, do you know anything of Fen and Robert?'

'I know them both.'

'Can I trust them?'

He looked taken aback for a moment, and then he nodded. 'I would.'

'Good. Thank you.'

I knew I shouldn't consider the word of a man I'd only known for ten minutes valid, but I was desperate for even the slightest reassurance. I breathed a little more easily as I moved through to the other side of the pub, until I saw Robert and Fen, heads almost together, both jerk apart and stop speaking as I approached.

Remi stretched himself out on the floorboards, clearly revelling in the unlimited space after the cramped car. I had to wide-step over him.

'Don't let me interrupt your scheming,' I said, sitting down.

'Us, scheming? Never!' said Fen, with a big smile. Robert shook his head at him.

'You just can't tell when it's not an appropriate time to joke, can you?'

'Oh, she knows I'm joking. You've got all that money, Robert. Why don't you buy yourself a sense of humour? Lighten up.'

I looked around the private bar, which was similar to the one we'd entered through, but cosier. It had a corner fireplace with logs stacked up ready to be lit, and in the opposite corner, a staircase led upstairs with a piano in its alcove. The light was dim, the room having only two small windows.

Richard came in and lit a couple of small lamps which were positioned on side tables, and placed iron lanterns hosting candles on others.

'Richard! What have you got in the kitchen? I'm starved,' asked Fen.

'I'll sort something out for you.'

'Now, isn't this nice?' said Fen, looking very satisfied with the situation.

'So, you plan to stay here?' I asked him.

He rubbed a finger across his lips, 'Surely you can think of a better question for me than that. Go ahead, fire away.'

I had so many questions, but for now, I put the Underworlder ones to the back of the queue.

'Okay, you said that Terry told you about The Golden Illuminati and that was how you knew why they were after me – so what else do you know about them?'

My eyes slid to Robert to see how he'd react to my question, but he was checking emails on his phone. I'd been bursting to ask Robert all about this, but Fen joining us had got in the way – I suspected Robert wouldn't want Fen to know *that* secret, though it was possible Terry had already told him. I'd burst if I didn't find out more about this group who seemed to know so much about me. What I'd gleaned last year were the bare bones: they had wiped history clean of alchemy; removed every shred of physical evidence that it was possible and curated it all in their personal collections. They were occult slave lords, as far as I understood it:

snatching people for centuries and building massive fortunes from the very few who had the gift.

It was so difficult to plan how to outfox my enemy when I knew so little about them. I hadn't been idle over the last few months – I'd tried, but failed to find out anything. I'd searched online, hoping for a tiny morsel in conspiracy theory forums and alchemy history sites, but nothing had turned up. Not the tiniest shred of anything. I'd worried about venturing into physical libraries or archives as that had been where all my trouble had started last time.

Fen nodded, looking pensive suddenly. 'They're a Rolls Royce organisation. Not your grubby little upstart gangsters, who are often the bugs that irritate our kind these days. The Golden Illuminati are entitled extremists, but they should demand our respect, because they are one of the few secret organisations which have survived several hundred years, and you have to be wily to manage that.'

Just hearing Fen mention The Golden Illuminati in broad terms made my hands clammy and their rawness made the flesh sting. I turned one over and peeled off my glove. Fen looked at my skin, ravaged by psoriasis and scarred from the incisions I'd made during my experiments, and pushed his chair back in shock.

'Good heavens! Did they do that to you?' His face was horrified.

We both looked down at the scars that ran from beyond my wrist across my palm and along my fingers. There was the fresher cut across my palm, too: evidence of a recent failed attempt to engage with a gift that didn't seem to have any inclination to come out to play.

I laughed, but not in a happy way. 'No, I can't blame them for that. This is all my own work.'

Robert caught my eye. Did he flinch? Probably horrified

by the scars, but damn that kind of reaction. A year ago, I'd never have revealed the skin on my hands in public for fear of other people's disgust, but now I felt completely different. Proud at what those scars meant: evidence of self-discovery; a message that only I understood.

I left my gloves off so the air could get to my hands. Fen shuffled his chair back towards me.

'Well, I'd advise you to be more careful chopping salad in future, dear.'

'Yes, they are a bit of a mess. They got better for a while, but whatever improved them seems to have regressed. Go on, please.'

His eyes were drawn for a final look at my disfigured skin before he got back on track.

'Most people have heard of The Illuminati: the not-so-secret society with such lofty aims as to sever public life from religious influence and reveal the corruption of state power, bringing it to heel. What most people don't know is that they are only a splinter group, derived as a reaction to an existing group called *Et Illuminati Aureum* or The Golden Illuminati. The members are highly influential. They do abuse state and religious power, and endorse superstition with their fixation on the occult, particularly the study of alchemy.'

'How do you know about them?' I asked, fascinated.

Fen's eyes twinkled. 'I make it my business to know about anyone and anything that affects our community. If you remove the hideous human rights crimes that The Golden Illuminati have enacted, you have to admire them for their sophistication.'

'I don't have to admire them at all, actually.'

'Well, quite, I just mean in theoretical terms – there haven't been many secret societies that have had the life-span of The Golden Illuminati. It was after the Enlightenment that they did something very clever indeed, which made them grow rather than diminish. At that time, alchemy was being laughed at as old-thinking. Science-mania was sweeping the world, and their leader saw this as an opportunity. They would fan the flames of ridicule; they would undermine the alchemical premise; they would fund the emerging sciences and let the new thinking crush alchemy's credibility.'

'But why?'

'It made everything easier for them. It left the field wide open, in fact – rich pickings to exploit without competition. People discarded treasured objects and literature on alchemy which before had been coveted and prized. They scooped it all up. People disappearing? Well, it could be any number of reasons, but certainly nothing to do with alchemy – what a joke that was. Real alchemists? Ha!' His laughed filled the little room. 'Unlike the rest of the world, they knew it could be done, but only by certain people.'

I glanced across at Robert to see if he was listening to all this, but he was swiping at the screen of his phone and showed no sign of even hearing Fen.

Richard arrived with sandwiches: big doorstops of bread and clumsy slices of cheese and ham, with salad and pickle on the side. As he bent to lower the plate to the table, his attention was caught by something out of the window. Fen and I followed his gaze.

'Looks like a helicopter in that field over there,' he said, and we all looked out. It was far enough away to be hard to make out, but he was right.

Adrenaline splashed through my insides, making them burn. I got up and moved closer to the glass.

'Isn't that farm next to yours for sale, Richard?' Fen asked, his mouth partly full of sandwich.

'Yes, has been for nearly two years.'

'If the helicopter's anything to go by, you'll have a footballer and his wife as neighbours. You know what that means? Bulldozers, builders, cranes for at least two years, then that sweet little farmhouse will be a monster mansion. Some people have no taste.'

'You've got to be kidding, Fen? Robert!'

I looked at him – surely, he was concerned. Robert's face was grave, but he met my eye for only a second before dropping it and shrugging at my concern.

This was unbelievable! I was breathing like I'd been for a pacey jog.

'Abigail, please listen to my advice – I am a seasoned Underworlder,' said Fen, lifting up his sandwich again. 'You can't live your life scared. It will make you deeply unhappy, not to mention a basket case. All you can do is take every opportunity to equip yourself, so whatever arrives at your door, you can cope with it, and enjoy a good bottle of wine while it's on the table. Think about being a dragon, not a mouse.'

'What?' I felt like kicking him in the shin. Why was he talking to me about dragons? There was a damned helicopter out in the middle of nowhere. Platitudes were no use to me.

Echoes of last year's events ran through my head. My friends, my boyfriend, all saying the same thing: I was paranoid; it was all in my head. But weren't they wrong, and who'd had to deal with the mistake?

Robert walked over to Richard, who had gone back to the bar. They exchanged a few words, and then Robert passed him some cash.

'I'm going upstairs to use a landline in one of the rooms. My signal keeps dropping here and I have to make a call to Berlin.'

'There's a landline on the bar.' Fen pointed.

'I'd rather not have an audience.'

Our eyes met again for a moment, but Robert looked away mighty quickly for someone who only had a work call to make. Remi followed him upstairs. Who the hell was he really ringing? I didn't like the obvious answer – he was telling whoever was over in that field to come and get me. I chewed the side of one nail as I looked out the window to the helicopter again.

Then, for no obvious reason, the hairs on the back of my neck rose up and tingled. I looked around the room, which revealed no change, but to me, the air felt charged.

'Do you feel that?' I asked Fen, who was pouring himself some more wine. He shook his head, but continued to gaze at me.

I moved over to a different window, long and rectangular. Was there someone outside? The road, as far as I could see, was quiet and the driveway was still. I circled the room and approached the bar, asking Richard if anyone new had arrived.

'Not that I'm aware of,' he said, bending his eyebrows down in concern. The vibration had gone to my ears now; I could hear a buzzing noise.

'Something feels off,' I said to Fen. 'I'm going to speak to Robert.'

Fen raised his eyebrows, which I ignored – I was in no mood for teasing. Fen stood up and moved across to join Richard at the bar. As I made it up the stairs, I felt the sensation of the buzz increase. By the time I was on the first floor, every inch of my skin was humming like ten thousand tiny drum rolls.

There were only three doors along the corridor. I knocked at the first one – no answer, but the humming was turning into a frenzy, so I opened the door. Robert was passed out on the bed with Remi beside him. I stepped up to the bed and leaned over him in concern, and that was when I sensed something touch the back of my neck.

5

———

## ABIGAIL

Fear was my first reaction. I whipped around, but the room was completely empty. I put my hand to my neck, rubbing the skin there.

What was Robert up to? I gave his arm a gentle shake. Nothing. I shook him some more. Nothing.

My heart felt like it had stalled as I realised Fen must have slipped something into his drink. Damn my good feelings about people!

I was almost out the door when I felt it again – this time, a touch to my shoulder. A feeling so subtle, it almost wasn't there; a slight warmth of the skin. I stopped and stayed very still, and it began to move – a slow flowing motion, running up my neck and along my hairline.

The hairs on my skin stood, as intrigued as I was at this invisible stroke. The fear didn't vanish, but it was muted – overtaken, perhaps, by a longing for the touch not to stop. I tilted my head back and gave a delighted shiver. It was like a shower of warm water spilling across my scalp. It travelled down the crevice of my temple to the lobe of my ear, where it circled. I closed my eyes and indulged in the warm waves of pleasure that my body was being introduced to. It was so intimate – the caress of a lover.

I opened my eyes and turned, looking again at Robert's body on the bed. Was this him? Outside of his body? As the thought passed through my mind, I felt certain I was right.

Now that I understood the source, the sensation felt different: still as light as silk on skin, but the knowledge that it was him made it sexual. He continued along the line of my shoulder and travelled more slowly over my collarbone, down my inner arm and along to the bridge of my wrist. There was a pause, and then the ripples fanned out across the palm of my hand and along my fingers to their tips.

We must be facing each other; it was so odd staring into nothing, yet my imagination sketched him in. He was looking down at me, and then I felt a warm tingle build on my lips. I was no longer sure what was real and what was imagined.

As the sensation faded, I regained control of my brain, which had temporarily blissed-out. I was kissing Robert: the man who may already have betrayed me.

My phone rang in my back pocket. It jolted me away from any further speculation. I pulled the phone out and stared at it: David, my on-off boyfriend, of all people. The universe must have told him I was in a compromising position.

Swallowing down the gallons of guilt that threatened to block my throat, I opened the door and moved out into the corridor.

'Shouldn't you be asleep? What time is it in LA?' I tried to sound bright, but anxiety started gnawing at me again. It was nice to hear his voice: a voice that reminded me that there was a normal world out there where people weren't continuously on red alert every time they saw a helicopter. Suddenly, I had the urge to cry.

'You'll never guess where I am,' I blurted out. 'Scotland. It's a long story. I—'

Downstairs there was a loud bang, followed up by a crash. A split second later, Robert rushed out of the door with Remi at his heels. Someone shouted.

'What was that?' David asked.

'Not sure, let me call you back.'

I ended the call and ran after Robert. I stumbled down the stairs in my rush and met the last couple with my backside.

What I found as I re-entered the room was the complete opposite of what I'd left less than a quarter of an hour before. Remi was barking. There were three men in all, with crew-cut hair and black cargo-style trousers. One guy had a colourful tattoo that began at his jawline and ran down his stout neck. It disappeared beneath the parameters of his T-shirt, but was revealed again on his arms. He was about to grab Richard, who was swinging a chair at another man with an earring. This man had a gun aimed at Fenrear's chest.

Fen held the serrated knife that Richard had provided with the sandwich and there was blood pouring from the cheek of the man with the gun. All the jovial warmth had gone from Fen's expression and he looked every bit the bad bastard now. As the chair connected with the man's shoulder, Fen jumped out of his line of fire, grabbed a decorative brass feature off the wall behind him and swung it over his head. He roared as it connected with the man's skull and sent him crashing to his knees.

Who were these guys? They didn't look like Golden Illuminati henchmen, but I'd only known the Italian ones. Maybe this was the British branch.

In the next second, Richard was hit by one of the guys right in the temple and his bulk slammed into the floor. He tried to crawl towards the bar, but his attacker stamped on his fingers, triggering a scream of pain. Robert launched himself at the man. Then the guy with the gun, who was still on his knees, turned it towards me.

I was paralysed and stunned, watching the fight unfold, feeling powerless to help. All I seemed capable of doing was holding my breath.

Fen barged the man holding the gun, throwing his shoulder into him like you might if you wanted to flatten a locked door. The impact made him drop the gun and it spun across the floor towards the fireplace. As the man scrabbled for it on his knees, Fen's foot crunched into his jaw. The impact made him crumple, and Fen proceeded to direct further kicks at the man's head. I was impotent – why in the months I'd been at home hadn't I learned karate, hand-to-hand combat, or self-defence even? Anger pummelled my chest: I was utterly useless!

Robert was still grappling with the other guy, while the third was on his back, too. Fen glanced my way and a micro-expression darted across his face. Remi's barking made it hard to hear, but I caught Fen's words.

'We need a dragon, not a mouse!'

My brain activated and my body seemed to know what to do instantly. I wouldn't be a victim to the Illuminati again. I sprinted for the bar, dodging Richard, Robert and two of the attackers, and grabbed the jug of chilli whisky which stood where we'd left it. As the same time, someone seized my hair and yanked me backwards, making me slop the whisky down the bar and on to the floor. I twisted around, and he let go of my hair in the instant that he swung at me. I saw the fist coming and, whether by luck or judgment, rolled my head to the side. His jab swept so close that his knuckle ran right along my cheekbone.

Seeing the man off-balanced from missing his target, Fen aimed a kick which connected at the perfect moment and the man staggered, knocking one of the tables over. I scrambled through the chaos, still carrying the jug of whisky, and moved towards the lantern which flickered merrily on the only table which hadn't been upended. I fished out the lit candle, and standing up, threw half of the contents of the jug over the man with the tattoo, who was now booting Robert repeatedly. There was something familiar in the way I felt as I brought the candle down and the flame burst over the man's colourful shoulders, consuming his head. It was like being trapped in an over-heated airless room and then being let out into the sweet sunny freshness of the outdoors. This was precisely how it'd felt when I'd prepared the cyanide to kill Pierro last year.

The man's screams made everybody stop fighting and stare at the horror of the scene. There was a group intake of breath. Robert staggered to his feet and looked at me as if he didn't quite recognise who I was. The man fell and rolled, and some of the spilled whisky caught light. In an instant, flames were leaping up over the floor and the bar. I hurled the rest of the whisky at the next nearest man and tagged it with the candle. It fanned across the back of his body.

Flames were all around Richard, who was lying on the floor, and my spike of adrenaline began to recede to cold dread. Robert was the first to react. He got past me to where Richard lay and hoisted him on to his feet, shoving him towards the bar entrance. He caught my eye and his jaw stiffened. Fen was right behind him. The remaining attacker's attention was entirely focused on beating out the flames on his teammate's back, allowing me to grab my bag and Fen's hat from the floor and get out of the bar.

Once out of the door, Robert slammed and bolted it.

'What the fock, Abigail?'

Richard slumped against the door. I looked at his eye, which was already closing. Blood from his nose ran down his shirt, and the way he was holding his left hand, he probably had some fingers broken.

'We need to get him an ambulance!' I said to Robert.

Robert's expression was like thunder. 'And call the morgue.'

'Go!' Richard said, gesturing with his good hand. 'I can manage from here.'

'There might be two alive in there, but they'll all die if you leave them,' said Robert.

'Just get going and then I'll let them out. I can still swing a baseball bat if I must. I doubt they'll stick around. I know what to do.'

Richard's face was anything but placid now. Pain and stress were pressed into his features.

'I'll make some calls, send help to deal with the mess,' said Fen. Richard nodded.

Robert looked torn and then pushed me towards the car. We all raced across the gravel and dived into the Aston Martin. Fen was scrabbling with Remi to get into the back seat. Robert had the car in gear and was speeding down the quiet road within a few seconds. All of us were breathing heavily and trying to gather our thoughts.

'I can't believe you set those men on fire!' Robert squeezed his temple and ran his hands through his hair.

I stared straight ahead but the road in front of me skittered up and down forcing me to look down at my hands.

They too tremored with shock while pins and needles circled my palms like the path of Catherine wheels. I didn't want to think about what I'd just done. It was like my brain could only take so much stress and then it hurdled any sane middle-ground. This landed me directly in extreme and, I had to admit, occasionally murderous territory. The part of it I daren't admit was how good those clear-headed, action-orientated moments felt in comparison to the tame, fear-filled months I'd been living.

'Well, I for one appreciated your psychotic response,' said Fen. 'I wasn't liking our odds until you intervened. And, I owe you an apology. When you ran towards the bar, I thought you were going to desert us.'

'Don't make Fen your conscience!' Robert's voice rang with fury. 'He hasn't seen his own since before his voice broke.'

'And I've been all the better for that. There's no room for being kind to those sorts of people, whoever they were. They were pointing guns at us, for goodness sake.'

'It wasn't a proportionate response!' Robert's voice was loud. 'And look what we left Richard dealing with.'

My anger flared. 'I left proportionate back in Italy last summer. If you want a measured reaction, then you shouldn't be helping me. Who the hell were they anyway?' I asked, looking at Fenrear because I couldn't face Robert.

Fen shook his head and shrugged his shoulders. 'Probably just bounty-hunters, looking for Underworlders. The Coach House has never been targeted before, but plenty of other places have that are frequented by our kind.'

'Liar!' Robert's voice was so loud, it made me clap my hand over my ear. 'It has to have something to do with you. They knew that we were going to be there. We wouldn't have stopped if we hadn't met you.'

'It could have been Abigail's Illuminati guys – that heli-copter's been tracking us since Edinburgh.'

'It wasn't them,' Robert said in a quieter voice, to me rather than Fen. 'I'm sure of that.'

'Oh well, if you're ... sure,' said Fen, sitting back in his seat and pulling out his phone.

My stomach churned, and I opened the window slightly for some air, leaning my head against the cool glass as I listened to Fen making his call. Robert's words only added to the burden in my mind: who the hell was Fenrear? Not just a colourful character, clearly. The kind of man who knows people who can clear up messes like these. Still, maybe I shouldn't knock that – I certainly needed their services.

When he finished, I turned to him. 'I saved this for you.'

I passed him his red hat. He ran his fingers over all its angles, looked into my eyes and there were tears brimming in his own. In a heartbeat, that expression was gone, replaced by an accusatory expression.

'Well, I hope you didn't get any of that nasty chilli whisky on it. I mean, that stuff could really stain!'

## 6

## ROBERT

I was desperate to increase my speed, but the roads looped one way and then another, making it impossible to put my foot down. Being on the road home was some comfort, though. The serpentine motion seemed to make Abigail sleepy, as she closed her eyes and leaned her head against the window.

The adrenaline from the fight was dropping off and my body began to moan at its injuries. Whoever those men were, they'd fought dirtily. One had stamped on my foot with the heavy heel of his boot, while slamming me in the ribs with his elbow – I was pretty sure that I had a pair of broken ribs to match my broken toes.

I ground my teeth and strangled the wheel in my grip. I was a bloody fool. A moron beyond any I'd ever come across. I'd projected out of my body just as she'd entered the room. I'd been intending to investigate that helicopter. In my out-of-body form, I could slip across those fields in no time, but then, seeing her standing there, I'd been deserted by my common sense, and suddenly I was touching her. Astonishingly, she'd sensed me there. No-one has ever done that. When she'd responded to my touch, there'd been a moment of true connection between us; radiant happiness, even. In that instant, I'd have walked away from my jewels and my home for her, and prepared to be at war with The Golden Illuminati for the rest of my life.

I should be thankful for what followed. It tilted everything back in the right direction. I wasn't naïve. Those men weren't messing around. God only knows what they'd have done to us if they had managed to take us, but her response had exposed the part of her I'd found hard to believe: the murderous part.

After we'd met, I'd found myself rewriting her story. It had to be wrong. Maybe someone else in the Society had murdered Pierro and she'd been an ideal scapegoat – in the wrong place at the right time. But, witnessing her setting that man on fire tonight had given me the slap upside the ear that I needed. My mind ran forward to my beautiful home and back to the exquisite jewels waiting for me. How could I have thought about risking them for someone I didn't even know properly? I should be feeling relieved – without something this extreme happening, I might not have woken up. So why did I feel like ripping apart the steering wheel, winding down the windows and swearing like a docker into the evening air?

Fenrear broke into my thoughts. 'I'll have to stay at yours at least for the night. I'd like to go back and check on Richard tomorrow.'

I didn't like having guests, particularly not ones with Fen's capabilities. I glanced at Abigail, but she seemed to be asleep. I asked Fen the question that had been on my mind since he'd joined our journey.

'Why are you really here, Fen?'

He shuffled forward so he was on the edge of the seat

and turned his face inwards, so he was almost speaking into my ear.

'There's no denying that everyone in the community has a genuine interest. I mean, an alchemist, for crying out loud! That is pretty special, even in our strange circle.'

'She's only a potential alchemist. No-one knows for sure what she is,' I said in a hissed whisper. 'I'll bet it's politics. It's always focking politics with you.'

'It's a good job someone takes care of the politics. If it was left to the likes of you, who never sullies their eyes by looking to our kind, never mind trying to help or protect our community, then life would be pretty sour, even for you.

'You were born into a privileged era,' he poked my arm with a forefinger, 'with people to look out for you. It takes pesky fellows like me to bring that about.'

He poked me again and breathed out slowly.

'If you're asking whether I'm here on official Collective business, then yes, I am. Now I have a couple of questions for you: why has Terry cast you as protector of the wee lassie? And what makes you so interested in the affairs of this particular Underworlder when you've never been interested in any of us before?'

'We are good friends. Our families go way back, and I don't think Terry knows many people with my resources. You've seen her hands? He's worried she's suicidal.'

'I can tell you she's not.'

'What do you know?'

'I just watched her fight for her life. Suicide?' He shook his head. 'No way.'

Silence fell between us for a while before he sat back against his seat.

'No, that's not it. There's a piece I'm missing, I'm sure of it.'

FEN WOKE Abigail about an hour later as we reached my driveway. Remi stood up, recognising home.

'You won't want to miss this,' Fen said softly to Abigail as she rolled her neck and dug her fingers into her shoulder muscles.

The road began to rise slightly, and as it did, mature trees flanked both sides of the drive. I'd had delicate lights threaded through the branches so that even at night, their sinewy forms could be appreciated. As we drew closer to the house, I found myself anticipating her response, though I reminded myself that this place was so close to my heart, anyone's dislike of it would feel personal. My heartbeat picked up its pace and I couldn't stop myself watching her with little sideways glances as we came to a slight turn in the road.

Fen settled his hand on my shoulder and said, 'Slower. Give her chance to take it in.'

There was a generous lake in front of the house which spanned its width. My building was essentially rectangular, but broken up by six substantial window bays that stepped forward from the main line of the house. Each window bay had a solid cedar frame around its perimeter and up its corners. I'd had the wood hewn rather than machine cut so that its lines were meandering rather than crisp, retaining reference to its origins. If we'd arrived earlier in the day, she'd have been able to see that the surface of the wood glowed satin-like from endless sanding and coats of linseed oil. I wished she was seeing it with the rising sun rather than when it was almost in bed. As the beams of wood moved up towards the top floor, they parted ways and joined the roof at tangents. At ground level, the glass was clear with large panels, but as it rose up the building, its colour began to change. Subtle at first, then by the time it was on the top floor, it was an orchestra of stained glass: rich blues and greens mingled with touches of yellow and orange spilling between the arms of the beams.

'Oh, it's beautiful,' Abigail breathed. 'Who could have created something so spectacular?'

'Is that a joke?' Fen laughed. 'It's him, all his work. Don't you know he's an architect?'

'I did, sort of, but I thought he was an engineer. Terry told me he built skyscrapers.'

Fen made a noise of astonishment.

'Didn't you think to Google him?'

'Well, I didn't think his engineering skills would tell me much about any murderous tendencies he might have.'

'He's world famous! Have you seen the business district in Milan? The Marchione building has become a pilgrimage site for the world's lovers of contemporary architecture. He's the Frank Gehry of his day.'

'Oh, shut up, man!' I snorted.

'Scoff all you like, but he is,' Fen said, parting his hands and holding them up.

'You need to take a job in my PR department.' I laughed, wishing he'd shut up.

'You have a PR department?' Abigail's eyes were wide.

I tried to make my shrug relaxed. 'Doesn't everyone?'

'You must be super-rich,' she said, and then wrinkled her nose. Maybe she hadn't meant to say that out loud.

I felt a mixture of self-consciousness and pride, as I often did when people saw my home. This place laid out who I was for all to see – I was in every detail of the place.

'Mony a mickle maks a muckle,' I said with another laugh.

Abigail and Fen looked at each other. Fen shrugged and shook his head.

'It means, small savings add up,' I clarified.

Fen guffawed. 'Right, like that's how he built it – by saving up.'

We drove across the lake's bridge, which snaked from one side to the other. As we pulled to a halt, I noted another car parked over to the left-hand side of the drive. Who the hell was this now? It was like the whole world had turned up to invade my peace. I expected it in London, but not here which was over sixty miles from the nearest city.

In answer to my question, the main door opened and out walked my assistant, Savannah, her golden ponytail swinging high and skimming her tiny waist. A rush of wistful regret came from nowhere. I wished I could fall for her; it would be so easy that way. She was followed by a man I didn't recognise: tall, with the kind of hips that should be riding rodeo. Savannah seemed to appreciate her escort as she threw back her head and laughed at something he'd just said, revealing her long neck which I knew ran down to a deep cleavage.

I heard Abigail's breath catch in her throat.

'David,' she murmured, unable to drag her eyes away from the scene in front of us, 'and Terry!' Her voice rose in excitement as Terry's stocky form came out of the house and leaned against the doorframe. He lifted a hand up in greeting and nodded at me, but I couldn't reciprocate. I was finding it hard to take my eyes from David. The bastard was pretty much perfect: a combination of boy-next-door but with LA style. I couldn't stop myself looking at Abigail. Was she pleased to see him? It had only been a couple of hours since her pulse had been quickening at my touch. I stamped down on that thought.

'Well, we can't stay in the car all night.'

I was so deep within my own thoughts that Fen's voice made me flinch. Abigail too jerked into action and scrambled out of the car, leaving the door open. She ran across the stones to David, who met her with a broad smile and trapped her in his arms as he kissed her the way I wanted to.

I felt as if I'd swallowed a rock. Then I felt Fenrear's supernatural touch, like the twang of a guitar string, in my mind.

'You bastard, Fen. Out of my head!'

Fen sat back in his seat and his smile was that of a man who'd just tasted something particularly delicious. 'I pity you, Robert: conflict and pain. Don't look so indignant. I would have worked it out anyway,' he said with a shrug. 'Oo, but what a devious hypocrite you are, and I never knew that about you. With so much in common, we could be much better friends than we are. That noble Scottish brow and those dirty depths are just what I look for in a friend.'

'We are not friends!' I said, speaking through clenched teeth and holding fast to the desire to drag Fen from the car and beat him bloody on my own driveway. Instead, I got out, and couldn't help staring over at David's arms draped over Abigail's shoulders as she talked to Terry. Remi had already hopped into Abigail's empty seat and freed himself through the open door. I moved around to the boot of the car, limping – my toes were throbbing where that brute in the pub had crushed them.

Fen followed me. 'You're one of them.'

I slammed the boot shut and stared down at him, feeling myself about to lose control. I spoke slowly. 'I don't have to justify myself to you.'

As I was about to step away, Fen's solid hand shot out

and gripped my arm. I went rigid as the impulse to swing and let a left hook go tore through me.

'Oh, but you do. You know what the Underworlders will do to you if they find out you've betrayed one of our own.'

'I don't need you to remind me of that. Whatever you glimpsed, it wasn't the full picture. I have my own reasons for being involved with The Golden Illuminati. My situation enables me to help one of my own and I wasn't about to turn away from that.'

Fen looked at me, unsure, and let go of my arm.

'She's your match, you know – your abilities are similar. Do you know how often that happens? A physical and psychic connection? Let me be your big brother here – don't take that for granted.'

My anger flared. 'You're not here to be a friend to me, or her, so don't pretend you are, man. If I want to pick out a hat, then I'll consult your advice,' I said, turning. I wanted to stride away, but all I could manage was an angry limp.

'You're a fool.' The words wormed their way into my ears and then took root in my mind. I tried to push them out, but like parasites, they latched on to other thoughts in my head and settled in.

As I reached the house, Terry stepped forward. I dropped my bags. He went in for a tight hug: I couldn't help the squawk that escaped me. I drew back, rubbing my ribs.

Standing back, his eyes ran down me, 'What's up with you?' He laughed, slapping me on the shoulder which made me wince.

'Bit of a skirmish on the road,' I said, glancing at Abigail, who raised her eyebrows.

'Been fighting the Red Coats again?' Terry's jokey smile faltered. He turned to look at Abigail, 'You are alright?',

She gave a slight nod, but avoided his eyes.

Fen trotted up, interrupting, and clasped Terry's hands. There were even a couple of back slaps for him. 'Nice to see you, again, Terry,' Fen said with a wink.

'You're looking a little bashed up as well, Fen. What did I miss?'

Fen opened his mouth to reply, but I cut in, 'Do you mind if we fill you in later, Terry? Just need to get settled in and take a handful of Ibuprofen.'

Terry nodded. 'You have quite a hoard of visitors tonight.'

'You're the most welcome,' I said with a sideways glance at Fen, 'I've always wanted you to see the collection of paintings I have here.'

'I thought I might be some use to you and Abigail, and I hope you don't mind, but I brought my nephew David with me – I knew Abigail would be pleased,' Terry said, winking at her. Abigail looked a little flushed.

Fen's expression was devilish. 'Almost like it had been planned. Uniting to help Abigail in the wilds of Scotland. An army against an army is a fairer fight, though I think, technically, we need twelve Highlanders and a bagpiper to count.'

'I think calling yourself, Terry and me an army is reaching a little?' I said.

'But you're not considering Savannah. I'd call her a one-woman army. Ah, Sav.'

She walked the few steps into Fen's open arms and shook her head a little at him as she smiled.

'Looking divine as ever.' He kissed her cheek. 'You agree with me, don't you, darling? The more people to help Abigail, the more people to fleece at poker?'

I knew her well enough to know the battle that was being fought inside her. She hated being up here. It was too quiet for her extrovert nature – alone in the wilds, as she called it – so more people would be exactly to her taste. And yet, she didn't want to encourage Fenrear, as she knew his capabilities and the implications.

'I think there is someone who might disagree, David, here,' said Terry. 'He doesn't like our plan. He wants to whip Abigail away to LA.'

Abigail, who had been pulled across under David's arm, rolled her eyes.

'Nothing new there, then. He thinks LA is the answer to all our problems,' she said.

Could the man make it more obvious that she was his, with his arms practically squeezing the life out of her?

'Maybe it is,' said David. 'Shoot me for thinking you are safer with me than with—' His eyes pressed upon me. The implied word – him – trembled in the air between us. 'Than you are here.'

I was finding it hard to swallow down the dislike I felt for this man whom I hadn't even been introduced to yet. Trying not to let what I was feeling spread across my face, I put out a hand for him to shake, though my honest inclination was to kick him in the groin.

'I see you've encountered the charms of my dazzling assistant, and bodyguard. I hope she provided you with every attention while you waited for us.'

Savannah raised her eyebrows at my comment, but I pushed past it by introducing Abigail to her. The girls exchanged nods and Abigail smiled.

'You didn't tell me you were his bodyguard,' David said to Savannah.

'Yes, I am, so don't go upsetting me,' she said, her eyes offering a challenge.

'David, is it?' said Fen, thrusting out his hand. 'Just don't be too hasty. This can be a short-term experiment. Give us a chance to help her, and if she feels there's no progress, then whip her away to LA with our blessings. Look at it as a break in the beautiful Scottish countryside.'

'Progress isn't my concern,' said David.

'Of course, of course,' Fen clucked and put an arm around David, guiding him towards the house, 'but there are lots of means and ways. We need to be tactical. She is not alone in being unusual, but the key is that if she is not gifted in the way The Golden Illuminati think, then her usefulness to them is no more and there are diplomatic routes to diffuse the situation. Channels that can be opened. It doesn't have to be guerrilla warfare.'

'And if I am what they want?' Abigail said, following Fen.

Fen turned and gave her a wry smile. 'Well, that changes the game entirely. You become much more important to your own kind.'

'Kind? She's not a polar bear.' David laughed.

'An alchemist would be very well protected by our kind,' said Fen.

Terry and I were right behind them as we were about to enter the hallway. David stopped without warning and stepped back, pressing his heavy size elevens on my already injured toes. Choice curses filled my head and I exerted every inch of restraint at my disposal not to weep like a little girl.

He glanced at me, unconcerned. 'Oops, sorry – just realised I left something in the car.'

'Wow, look at that.' Abigail stood at the base of my mighty spiral staircase, looking up. She shook her head, wonder in her expression, and then looked directly at me. 'Reminds me of a tornado, getting wider as it rises. That means I'm standing in the eye of the storm.'

I almost stumbled. It wasn't from the pain still throbbing in my foot; it was my resolve shifting again. I was being tilted forwards this time, towards her.

'Savannah!' I barked. 'Can you take care of everyone? I don't want to be disturbed.'

I moved off towards my study, trying not to hobble.

## 7

## ABIGAIL

Savannah showed David and me to our room on the first floor.

'You're at the front of the house, as you can see.' She pointed at the view. 'My apartment is on the mezzanine, which is at the back of the house, if you need me.'

David smiled his thanks, and Savannah, ignoring me, gave him her million-dollar smile. She flicked her head a little as she turned, making her long ponytail swing after her.

I looked at David and pulled a face.

'What?' David mouthed. 'She's nice.'

I pretended to put two fingers down my throat.

'Very mature,' David said, shaking his head at me with a grin.

David and I stared around the interior of the room as Savannah's footsteps faded. It had the flavour of a Danish hunting lodge. The floor was maple, which was clearly a theme of the house, but had a washed-out blue rug covering much of it. The walls were painted a similar chalky-blue. The bedside table was crafted from tree branches, and the maker had chosen to retain every notch and blemish on the lengths. The table legs wiggled and meandered between their perfect points of contact with the floor and surface. There was a stone chimney breast with gargantuan rough blocks of weathered stone piled one upon another and a window seat that ran the length of the window. It was piled with cushions and gave a view of the lake.

David dropped his bag and walked over to the bed, jumping on to it. He rolled over on the white sheets and stretched out.

'What a dump!' He gave me his most appealing and mischievous smile. 'Come over here,' he said, stroking a deep, furry throw.

Trying to suppress my smile so as not to encourage him, I stayed with my back pressed to the door.

'David, you should be in LA. Safe in LA. What are you doing here?'

'I wanted a *vacation*,' he said, giving the word an American twang. Then his expression changed; he turned on to his side. 'What? Are you not happy to see me? You haven't fallen for the scowling Scot, have you?'

His eyes twinkled, but I felt my insides squeeze a little. I looked at the floor.

'I thought we agreed to take a break.'

He exhaled and laid his head down, speaking to the ceiling. 'Don't you know me by now? I'm like Toad in *The Wind in the Willows*. I will agree to anything, but then I change my mind right back again the minute it suits me.'

I looked at David sprawled over the bed. I'd missed him. My feelings for him were beginning to break out of the little box I'd locked them in and spill all over my heart again. We hadn't broken up because we'd grown tired of each other. You couldn't not be attracted to David: he had a pre-teen sweetness in a very sexy grown man's body. He exuded a carefree youthfulness which I'd desperately needed in those months after I'd escaped. But, I'd wondered often, if there'd been no Golden Illuminati, would our paths have run together for as long as they had? At this moment though, all the reasons why we were good together were jostling out any doubts I'd ever entertained and even seeing off my fears for his safety.

'Come.'

He beckoned. I walked slowly to the bed and climbed up, nestling my head on his shoulder and laying my arm across his chest. The heat of his body seeped through into my hands. He put his hand down to stroke my hair. It felt good to be held. He always made me feel better. His boundless optimism wrapped around me like a warm blanket. The day's awful events were eased by being in his familiar embrace.

I closed my eyes, enjoying the comfort of his arms, but the scene of the tattooed man falling beneath the flames played out behind my eyelids. I shuddered at the thought of the way he'd died. The exhilaration I'd felt was long gone, leaving a chilly regret that I hadn't contemplated any other options.

'You have it all wrong in your head, you know. I'm not with you out of some sense of guilt that I can't break off with you because of the danger you're in. I'm here for the right reasons.'

'If you're with me, they might take you.' My voice was pleading. 'That's how they work. I couldn't live with myself if they did. Really, it would be the end for me, too. If you love me, even a little bit, you must leave. Then we both have a chance.'

'Yeah, I hear you as I did the other million and two

times, but like I always say, it might never happen. Plus, you keep forgetting that it turned out that you were the badass after all, and not them.'

I turned on my front to look into his grey-green eyes. 'David, don't even joke about that. Today, I did something else terrible. We were attacked in the pub that we stopped at.'

'What?' He sat upright.

'With Fenrear and Robert.' I hugged my legs and laid my forehead on my knees so that I didn't have to look at him. 'There were three guys. Everyone was fighting, and it looked bad. One of them had a gun, and suddenly, I just knew what I needed to do.' Tears fell from my eyes and ran down my legs at my rash and extreme actions. It was hard to speak. 'I set two of them on fire. I may have killed one of them.' My chest rose and fell, and then there was another swell of tears as I fully acknowledged the reality of what I'd done.

He let me cry on for a little while. When I began to calm, he put his hand out to me and clasped my fingers. I turned my head so I could see his face.

'Not quite sure how to react to that, but in some respects you're proving my point. I'm backing the pyromaniac, she's clearly the winning horse. Blazes a trail.'

He gave me a tentative smile. I'd shaken him; David was never tentative.

I sniffed and rubbed my nose with my hand. 'You've got to take this stuff seriously. Look at what I'm turning into. Think what sage advice your mother might give you. Stay away from the psychotic girl! And these people, if they caught you, would torture you slowly to death in front of me to get me to do what they want, and whatever I did, they'd still kill you.'

'Were these guys Golden Illuminati?'

I shrugged. 'Not sure. I don't think so. Robert says they weren't.'

'Well, he should know,' said David, settling back down on the bed. 'Explain to me again why we're here. Terry filled me in on the journey up, but truly, I don't get it, and even less so now that I've met Robert. The way he looks at you is weird.'

'I can't say I feel particularly safe, but Terry probably didn't tell you that Robert and Fenrear are like me. They can do things ... they shouldn't be able to do, and I need to explore that part of myself.'

'Ahh, so that's what Fenrear meant by our kind.' David's eyes rose to the ceiling; he swallowed down what he was about to say next like it was a particularly unpleasant mouthful.

He was trying to avoid an argument. Over the last several months, whenever we'd touched on the subject of my gift, which he didn't believe in, shouting almost always ensued. He had a proof-orientated mind, and I had shown him nothing. It didn't help that he'd found me in pools of blood more times than I'd like to admit. I'd tried to explain that it was an essential part of the alchemical transformation, but it rang hollowly in his ears. He thought I was looking for an escape from last year's traumas, and I was in a way, but not in the way he believed.

He swivelled position on the bed and brought his hands to my waist. His strong arms lifted me towards him. He brought my mouth to his and held nothing back as he kissed me, and I heard his message loud and clear: I love you.

Another twinge of guilt soured the perfection of the kiss. What had happened in the pub bedroom with Robert had been unexpected, but I hadn't run from his touch when I'd realised it was him. In fact, I'd longed for it.

I pulled away and gave David a thump on the chest, and then collapsed down on to it, groaning.

'Damn it, David, we broke up! You have the hide of a rhino. Can't you take a hint?'

He kissed the top of my head, and then, with one of his signature moves, he rolled me over so that he was on top and I was trapped beneath him.

'Opposites attract.' He kissed me again, playfully this time. 'You should know that, being a chemist. You can't fight science, baby.'

## 8

## ROBERT

I closed the door of my study and leaned against it, so thankful to be away from people. Even though my mind was back on track, my heart felt like it had taken as much of a pummelling as my ribs and toes.

Remi scratched at the door.

'Go away, Rem.'

Remi scratched again. I took a deep breath, ignoring the noise.

Another scratch.

'Damn dog,' I said as I wrenched open the door with such force, I flinched from my sore ribs. This time when the door closed, I slid down to the floor with my back against it. Remi looked me in the eye before licking my ear.

'Enough, settle down.' I pushed him gently away. Remi had badly done-by dog down to a fine art. He turned, walking across to a beaten-up Chesterfield which I'd bought at auction in my first year in university. The sofa's surface had been scuffed and polished by constant use and the colour had faded to a pale tobacco shade. Remi leaped up and settled down on it, giving me a martyred glance, which hit its target.

I got up and joined the dog who, mission accomplished, forgave me and laid his head across my lap. I let my own head fall back on the rest; I was worn out by the day. Abigail's perfect boyfriend turning up was a good thing, I reminded myself, ignoring the yearning sensation that had settled in my chest. It made everything easier, in fact. Abigail was not available to me, even if I wished her to be. Now I could focus on what had to be done and get back on track.

My eyes fell on Da's diary housed in the tall bookcase. That was why we were here – to set history right, not to give way to some twitch in my pants.

I didn't need to take down the diary to leaf through it. Every page was a childhood memory. It contained countless sketches of the jewels and their unique details, and snippets of information about the family legend, too. It was all etched into my brain.

My da' had never seen his preoccupation with finding the jewels and solving the mystery of what had happened to his father as an obsession, but it could be called nothing else. I suspected it was the reason my mother had left us. Da' had always referred to her as the-bitch-that-went, which I'd subscribed to while I was too young to understand the complexities of human relationships. But the puzzle pieces had eventually moved into a comprehensible picture as I'd matured. After she'd gone, he'd had no-one else but me to talk to about it all, and so he'd brainwashed me with the minutiae: the provenance of each stone; how their cuts were unique; how they were a feat of engineering, as well as design, because each different element was made like a

Chinese puzzle – each piece slotted into the next and was self-supporting without the need for physical fixings.

The resentment of all that my childhood had not been welled up inside me and threatened to burst its banks: something that only ever happened when I was under pressure. Fenrear's words needled me.

'*She's your match.*'

She couldn't be. It wouldn't make sense for that to happen when fate had given me a clear run at this. I'd been brought up without religion to taint my thinking. My da' had often bragged about it as if that had been his biggest achievement as a parent. But the way opportunities had opened up for me was beyond coincidence and I'd begun to question whether there wasn't more to life than a beginning, middle and end as my father had seen it.

After Da' had gone, when the grief began to settle, I'd found something I hadn't expected to find within myself. There'd been a quiet relief sitting at the back of my mind. I had an opportunity to let the quest for the jewels and my grandfather die, too. There was no-one else left who cared. No-one to reproach me.

I had been at the handover stage of a four-year project in Milan. I'd become friends with my client, Domenico Milliardo: an engaging and intelligent man. Just as I was beginning to appreciate all that letting go of Da's mania had to offer, Domenico had mentioned The Golden Illuminati and presented my invitation. Could the name of that secret society have been more familiar to anyone other than me? I doubt it. I found myself accepting without hesitation. Immediately, I felt a sense of peace, as though I was back on familiar ground. I'd stepped off the right path just for a moment and this was the course correction I'd needed.

A knock on the door shattered my thoughts and I jerked

upright, startling Remi. Savannah opened the door and her clear blue eyes made their assessment.

'I know I'm interrupting – everyone is settling in,' she closed the door, 'but I have a couple of questions for you. Why are there so many people here? And particularly, Fenrear Leighton? Need I remind you that he's one of the only people in the world who can discover your plan with almost no effort on his part?'

I stared at her slender figure standing on the vintage silk rug. I thought back to when I'd found it at a little street market in Milan, near the building I'd created.

'I'll admit, it's not ideal, but there is something to what Fen says. The more of us that can help Abigail, the more likely her gift will surface.'

She walked across to me and knelt down on the floor so that I was staring into her eyes. 'If he finds out you are intending to betray an Underworlder, the penalty is death and a confiscation sentence.'

I nodded. 'Ironically, that's not my biggest problem right now.'

Savannah studied me. 'I think I can guess,' she said, getting to her feet and wandering over to the bookcase. 'You like her, don't you? She's your type: doe-eyed and vulnerable.'

I couldn't help smiling at the derision in her voice. It was easy to underestimate Abigail – she did come across as Sav described, but I thought about the fire she'd set over the man's head in the pub. The reality wasn't quite that way.

'So, what are you getting all tied up over? Tell them she's a dud. Live happily ever after and have alchemist babies together.'

I shook my head. 'Not that simple.'

'You're not worried about the boyfriend, are you? I'll

agree that he's hard to improve on, but I could get rid of him for you.' She dropped her head and looked up at me from under her lashes. 'Wouldn't be the worst job I've ever had to do for you.'

I rubbed my eyes. Tiredness was invading my mind, 'I think betraying her is probably enough. Do we need to steal her boyfriend too? I think that would count as petty.'

Could I talk to Sav about this? Our relationship was a personal and professional blur. We were friends first, then I'd offered her the job. There had been nights shared, but neither of us had the heart for love. Sav had never talked about her past, but there was something very dark there – a wound so deep, it might never heal. She regularly took partners in any interludes we had and made no excuses to me about it.

'We'll have to take our chances. Fenrear has glimpsed a snippet. I let my guard down for a few seconds, but he didn't get much. Anyway, there're things I know about Fenrear that he wouldn't want anyone to know. He won't cross me.'

Savannah put a hand on my leg. I stared at it in surprise. It was a gentle gesture, not something she was known for.

'When the time comes, let me report her, not you. Then the Underworlders can't punish you. I'm not one of them so the same rules don't apply.'

I smiled and felt my heart swell for the real friendship that existed between us. 'It's true that the same rules don't apply, but I can't guarantee they wouldn't make a strike against you. Underworlders tend to be vigilantes.'

'I can take care of myself.'

'I know you can, but I wouldn't want you to live like that for me.'

'I'd do it.'

I squeezed her hand and pressed it to my chest, shaking my head.

'I know you would, Sav. What I will ask you to do is to keep me on track. It's so important that I do tell them the truth – whatever that truth is. I have a lot to lose if I don't, and there're other complications, too.'

I thought about Abigail lighting that alcohol as she threw it across the man, and the Society members wanting her for the murder of Pierro.

'And, if you can't? Then would you let me step in?'

I hesitated only a moment. 'Yes – I'll make you that promise. The only time I'd ask you to help would be if I was unable to do it myself.'

She nodded. 'The hardest thing in life is to know which bridge to cross and which to burn.'

I looked at her in amazement. 'I've only ever heard you quote Bart Simpson.'

She pursed her lips and stood up, unhurriedly. Then like lightning, she gave me a solid downward thump on the arm, before striding off towards the door. I swore.

'It's my trademark, being underestimated.' She glanced back over her shoulder, giving me a superior smile. 'Don't torture yourself, Robert! Focus on the outcome – what all this will do for you.'

As she closed the door, I swore again and rubbed some circulation back into the numb patch on my arm. Sav's words hovered for a moment in the air, but rather than what it would do *for* me, all I could think about was what it would do *to* me.

9

## ABIGAIL

'I'm going downstairs to forage,' said David, shouting into the bathroom. I was enjoying the deluge of hot water from a shower head that was twice the diameter of a dinner plate.

I put my head out of the glass door and extended my hand out to him. 'Wait! I was hoping we could explore the house before we eat. Can't you hang on?'

David hovered in the doorway again and gave his head a very slight shake. 'Er, I've actually seen it. Savannah showed me around before you arrived.'

I felt a clout of disappointment. 'Never mind,' I said, dropping my hand.

He came forward and opened the door of the shower wider. 'I'm sorry,' he tilted his head to read my expression, which I tried to hide by pushing my face into the water.

It was so ridiculous, but I felt unbelievably jealous. I'd been anticipating discovering the house with David, and I felt like Savannah had stolen our moment. A smile would have been impossible, but I managed a little shrug.

'Beat it! You're letting all the chilly air in.'

His eyes followed the tracks of water running down my body and he half leaned into the shower. For a moment, I thought he was about to join me, fully clothed. Then his stomach made a loud gurgling protest.

He looked down and then up and rolled his eyes. 'If only I had eaten more than a measly croissant today. I'll see you downstairs.'

I got out soon after he'd gone, pulling on a pair of old tracksuit bottoms and a vest top. I raked through my hair with a comb and rough-dried it, but couldn't see a hairdryer in any of the drawers.

While David was gone, I needed to do some house-keeping on my hands – if he saw me doing it, he'd berate me for the damage I was doing myself in the pursuit of what he believed to be madness. I couldn't help feeling betrayed by his attitude, but at the same time, I couldn't really blame him for not believing in alchemy. What rational person would? David's viewpoint only served to prove how successful The Golden Illuminati had been in their mission to wipe the world of any trace of alchemy.

I got out my first-aid kit and sat on the bed. My phone beeped and I leaned across to the side table it sat on. It was another message from my mum. She was averaging seven a day, but no amount of reassurances could settle her. She hadn't wanted me to leave again, not after what happened in Italy. My parents didn't even know the whole truth, mainly because I didn't want them to look at me the way David and Terry did when I'd told them: meshing pity with incredu-lousness and forever tossing glances to one another that questioned my stability. It had been easier to tell them a plainer version of what happened: Thérèse and I had been kidnapped by Pierro, and I had been luckier than Thérèse.

Mixed in there too was my guilt and grief about my role

in my friend's death. Something as simple as telling the truth seemed to twist and struggle in my mind, not wanting to be revealed to anyone. Blaming Pierro was so much easier than implicating myself, but I knew a different truth: that I wouldn't listen to what Pierro had told me I was capable of and, in the end, he'd been right. If I'd listened, she would still be alive.

It hadn't even been that hard to hide the truth from them. It might have been if I'd ever been a gregarious, gossipy girl. Everyone in the family, and by extension the foundry, was used to my quiet ways and so I suppose to them, the Abigail that returned from Italy was not so very different than the one that had left them and so they had no need to be suspicious.

I squeezed the antiseptic onto my freshest cut – the outcome of another failed attempt at transforming a tiny disc of bronze from less than a week ago. The skin was only just beginning to knit. I'd exhausted the strategy of repeating the steps that had yielded a tiny nugget of gold to be born in my hands last year. The carved-up state of my palms was the only thing I had to show for all the effort.

I'd had plenty of time to reflect on last year's journey, and for me everything came back to one moment of realisation – that transforming base metal into gold didn't only mean lead into gold. Bronze was also a base metal. Bronze was my metal, or maybe I was its person. It had always been that way for me ever since the first day I'd touched a piece of bronze, when I'd been too small to see over the foundry benches. Realising alchemy might have as much to do with bronze as lead strengthened my interest in it. I'd carried on digging, and tinkering, and discovering.

Anyone else might see details like my blood and the bronze uniting as an unfathomable connection to arrive at, but to a patineur like me, whose whole career was about the fusion of chemicals with bronze, it wasn't so great a leap. What made me want to give myself a good shake was that my skin, with its constant irate psoriasis, had been shouting the answer at me the whole time. The irony was that the medical profession kept telling me I was allergic to metal, but although the evidence of my inflamed skin seemed clear to the doctors, it had never convinced me. How could I be allergic when the only time I felt utterly, joyfully at one with the world was when I was touching metal? In fact, in hindsight, my theory was that my skin was having a tantrum at only being allowed to touch it. Nothing less than uniting with metal would satisfy its deep desire, and this is where my latest problems stemmed from.

With last year's transformation, something had shifted in my relationship with bronze. Everything had intensified to what might be best described as an obsession. Contact had always fed something in me, but now I just felt hungry all the time for the profundity of the connection I'd achieved and the relief it had brought to my skin, which had cleared completely for a time. This was why I was patching up inflamed skin and butterfly-taping open wounds. There was an element missing: something I'd brought to the table in that cell back in Italy which had escaped me ever since. That's why I had to hold my nerve and deal with Robert, and Fen. The risks were worth it because, captured or not, if I didn't manage to reconnect with the power I'd found last year, the torment would send me insane anyway.

I hoped I'd get a chance to see Robert on his own at some point that evening. I had questions for him – things I should have asked when he'd come to the foundry. The revelation of his ability had scattered my brain, and with my hopes clamouring, I'd forgotten to ask some sensible questions.

I was thinking so deeply about Robert as I left my room that when he joined me on the landing from the floor above, I wasn't sure if I'd conjured him up. I skipped to his blue-hazel eyes and couldn't help a moment of admiration: they were beautiful. The memory of his silky-soft touch at the pub came back to me. I wondered if he was thinking about it too.

Wrong footed, I blurted out the first thing that came into my head. 'I need a hairdryer.' I tugged at my wet hair.

He gave a laugh that was closer to a bark. 'Let's see what we can find. Sav will know.' He gestured towards the stairs.

Different types of emotions seemed to be scrapping in my stomach: distrust and attraction striking out at one another. I put my hand out to the handrail, and as I gripped it, all other feelings were drowned out by the sense of familiarity. I knew it before I even looked down – it was bronze.

'What a beautiful handrail. I can't believe I didn't notice it before. Someone very skilled made this.' The handrail was cast in bronze to imitate a woman's hair that had been solidly plaited. I pressed my thumb and fingertips into its grooves and felt my blood sing to it.

'I could patinate it for you.' The words were out of my mouth before I'd given them proper thought. 'It's a shame to leave it to tarnish rather than to show its true colours.'

Robert's face lightened in expression. 'You think my bronze is unfulfilled?'

We began to walk down, but I didn't take my hand from the surface. Distracted, I didn't answer right away. I was hearing something – very faint, but definitely there.

'Sort of. It could be more than it is. Bronze holds the potential to be a whole palette of colours, and leaving it as you have, unfinished, is a bit like not allowing Beethoven a piano.'

'Would it make you happy?' he said.

He had no idea how much. I'd only been gone from the foundry four days, but with no work planned, I was already pining. Missing it so much, I would even go so far as providing my services to one of The Golden Illuminati – that was a depth I never foresaw myself stooping to.

My face must have said it all because he smiled. 'Okay, I will allow you to make my handrail a Beethoven.'

We were almost at the bottom of the stairs now, and as I caressed the curl at the end of the banister, I closed my eyes for a moment. Two words floated like feathers into my mind.

"Choose me."

I had no idea what that meant.

"Choose me."

It said it again. Robert cleared his throat and I realised he was holding the hall door open while my mind was elsewhere.

'Sorry.' I smiled, taking my hand away reluctantly. 'No, wait.' I pulled back. 'I need to ask you something. I was desperate to before, but then Fenrear showed up and it didn't seem the right time. I never did find out why you are so invested in bringing The Golden Illuminati down.'

He nodded and let the door go. 'Fenrear knows.' He leaned against the doorframe. 'My grandfather was a jeweller in London. He had a shop in Cheapside. There's a lot about him in the V&A Museum because he designed a jewellery collection which was displayed and widely admired at the Festival of Britain. While at the exhibition, he met a wealthy patron, and for a time was commissioned repeatedly by him. When he was fifty-nine years old, my grandfather disappeared without a trace, and along with him, his jewellery. The police could discover nothing. His wife and children were left to fend for themselves.'

'And you think The Golden Illuminati took him?'

He nodded again. 'It was my da's theory, he pieced the whole thing together. A short while after he died, I was given the opportunity of membership, and on my initiation night, I saw part of my grandfather's jewellery collection displayed in their exhibition hall.'

'But they must have known you were related?'

He shook his head. I could see sadness in his eyes, possibly grief. Was that for his father?

'They don't know. My da's name was changed.' He swallowed, and before he could carry on, a blast of laughter hooked his attention. It echoed around the hall, and his expression wiped so completely, it made me wonder if I'd imagined the pain there.

'Shall we join them?' he said, putting his arm out to indicate I take the lead. His explanation would have to be enough for now.

## 10

## ABIGAIL

Following the noise from along the corridor, we passed a door on the left which was ajar. From inside the room, I could hear a phone ringing.

Robert made a tsk noise. 'I'd better get that. Go along – I'll join you in a minute.'

I saw a brief glimpse of a study as he entered, but bullets have left guns more slowly than the speed with which he shut that door on me. I eyeballed the door. He was either very private or very guilty. Could be either. Only the first day, and I was already getting weary of guessing which side of the line he stood on.

I carried on down the corridor, entered the open-plan kitchen and discovered Fen and Terry sitting at a table made of polished concrete, pigmented white. They were sharing a bottle of wine. The space was distinct from the design of the rest of the house, like walking into an iceberg – all its features were white, crisp, highly polished and glossy. White units ran floor to ceiling around three-quarters of the room.

There was a cook's island in the centre of the room made from a solid slab of Carrera marble. Savannah and David stood shoulder to shoulder there, both holding long knives and chopping vegetables.

'Hey, Abs, turns out that Savannah and I have the same superpower. We can both dice vegetables at the speed of light. Cool, huh?'

I nodded.

'Is Robert not with you? I texted him to come down,' Savannah said in an irritated voice.

'He's just taking a phone call.'

Savannah placed a manicured hand on David's suntanned forearm. He was wearing a short-sleeved fitted T-shirt so you could see his muscular torso, the charcoal grey shade emphasising his unusual grey-green eyes.

'Let's have a race.' She looked up at him, laughter bubbling from her mouth, then shot over to the fridge. Pulling out two cucumbers, onions and lettuces, she placed them in front of the chopping boards. She took another slug of her wine and tilted her neck this way and that, lifting her shoulders up and down like she was about to vault on to a set of parallel bars.

'On your marks,' she giggled, and David lifted his knife, 'get set ... GO!'

The pair tore into the vegetables. In seconds, they were dicing them into ribbons. Savannah finished a moment or two before David and slammed down her knife, her eyes sparkling. There was a spontaneous round of applause from Fenrear and Terry. I was unable to relax and let go, so joined in a little late.

David pretended to be disappointed. 'Bravo, well done. I am defeated. You are a worthy winner, but I demand a rematch tomorrow night,' he said, giving over his hand to her to shake. Savannah looked like she couldn't wait and flicked her perfectly straight hair, reminding me that I needed a hairdryer and also a hairbrush.

'I must admit, you two are impressive. If the world is ever invaded by a giant bell pepper, we'll know who to call,' Fen said, winking.

How could Fenrear be so jolly after what had happened only a few hours ago? Robert said he didn't have a conscience; maybe he was right. Flashes of the man with the tattoo falling beneath the flames kept tugging my attention away from the present.

David proceeded to tie a tea-towel around his neck like a cape. 'I'm Vege-Man,' he declared and pretended to fly across the kitchen towards me. Savannah turned away to check the fish in the oven.

Catching David by the cape as he circled my chair, I said, 'Come on, let's lay the table, Vege-Man.'

'No, Robert can do that when he's finished his call,' snapped Savannah. 'He knows where the plates are.'

'What work do I have to do now, woman?' said Robert, entering the kitchen and overhearing Savannah. He only narrowly missed colliding with David, and both men, almost of equal height, found themselves eye to eye just inside the threshold of the kitchen. They stepped around each other, neither one seeming to want to break eye contact.

'How was your phone call?' asked David, going from silly to serious in a nanosecond.

'Fine,' said Robert, face deadpan. 'Anything else ya'd like to know?'

'Yes, who called you?'

'Err, David,' my voice trilled, though really, he was only saying what I was thinking. 'Come on, let's sit down – I'm starved.' I pushed against his body to snap the two out of their standoff.

After a long moment, Robert turned away and pulled a chair out for me to sit down. 'See if ye like my table. It's unique – I designed it.' Instead of the open space usually provided beneath a table, this one had cored out alcoves like each pair of legs had their own cloister.

'What are we eating?' I asked, tugging at David's wrist to sit down.

Fen tipped more wine into Terry's glass. 'Salmon and salad. Apparently, it's good for us.'

Robert handed out the plates and Savannah doled out the salmon and everyone settled down and took their places at the table. David offered me the contents of the mighty salad bowl, and I was picking up my fork to scoop some out when Savannah squealed.

'Wait! The sprouted greens and roasted hazelnuts. You can't eat the salad without them.'

My fork paused in mid-air. Fen caught my eye and we exchanged a look before he turned to Savannah, keeping his voice serious.

'So, Savannah – you prefer your nuts roasted, do you?' He flicked one eyebrow skywards at me.

I felt laughter kindle, but almost instantly it was doused by a flash of the expression worn by the man in the pub as he turned into the fire I'd thrown at him. I dropped my knife and it made a clattering sound against my wine glass, making everyone jump.

'Sorry,' I said, as everyone stared. 'Clumsy.'

Savannah looked me over as if I was a bluebottle near fruit.

'If you'd like to borrow some clothes, Abigail, I've got a whole wardrobe full that I don't use.'

I flushed, feeling a cascade of insecurities run the length of my body. 'Thanks, Savannah,' I mumbled. Now everyone must be aware of my vest-top that had been through the wash a thousand too many times.

Savannah brought a breadboard to the table with two loaves: Irish rye with walnuts and fig, and a plump white bloomer. Fen sank his nose down to the bloomer's crust and inhaled deeply. Savannah elbowed him hard in the side, and though he flinched, he caught my eye as he lifted his head and gave me a wide-toothed grin. I wanted to respond, maybe roll my eyes at how serious Savannah was being, or make a crack about how the sprouted greens and nuts she had added made the salad look like it was wearing a wig, but it was like I was behind a sheet of glass: visible, but only able to press my face against the glass, unable to engage and enjoy something as simple as a meal. This was what The Golden Illuminati had done to me.

'I never used to get the salad thing until I was in LA,' David said, heaping it on to his plate. 'I was always more of a hot veg guy. They've made a fine art of salad over there, and after two weeks, I was completely hooked.'

Savannah leaned across and lifted the bottle of white wine from the island counter, asking David with a tilt of her head and deepening of her cleavage whether he wanted topping up.

'I prefer curry, really spicy curry,' Fen said, 'with a nice sweet naan bread, spicy potatoes, daal.'

'Oo no, I hate curry. You can tell a person's eaten it days after.' Savannah pulled a face.

I officially disliked her. I'd tried not to go by first impressions, but I couldn't see anything likeable in her, and my impressions were getting into double digits by now.

Terry passed the bowl to me. 'Did you know that Fen

was instrumental in starting my career? He spotted one of my paintings in a tiny exhibition in Venice. That was one of the earliest bits of traction I had. Fen's an art dealer.'

'I am, sort of,' said Fen. 'Really, I make introductions. I bob and weave through the art world, connecting people.'

My mind was shunted back to Pierro, who'd been described to me in not dissimilar terms, and I shivered.

'Abigail, I promised I'd find you that hairdryer. You're cold,' said Robert. 'Do you need a jumper?'

'No, no, I'm fine—' but Robert was already taking his own jumper off. My eyes flew to David's as Robert handed it over. I felt my face flush. David was looking at Robert as if he'd just said he didn't like the salad.

'And who pays you, Fen?' I said, the awkwardness of the situation forcing me to smash through that glass screen and speak. I draped the jumper over my shoulders rather than putting it on fully. As if that was better.

'Good question – I can tell you have a business head on your shoulders. I have a very nice arrangement, now that you ask. Both sides pay me. If the artist gets a show from the introduction, or even a decent sale, then I get a fee. If the gallery likes the artist and wants me to sign them, then they pay me a fee, too. Then after that, I consider them free agents. I'm not a leech sucking on them for ever.'

'I wouldn't say that. You've been sucking on me for years,' said Robert.

'But look at the marvellous talent I've introduced you to. I know your tastes and I've made you very happy, and also very rich. I have a great insight into what's going to go bang in the art world.' Fen tapped his nose and winked. 'Insider knowledge, you could say.'

'You're all bum and parsley, Fen!' said Robert. 'You braggart.'

'I can't be blamed for what God gave me,' said Fen, smiling at Robert's remark. 'I just like hanging out at art auctions, what can I say?'

I imagined that with his abilities, he could glean a whole lot about the tides of the art market from a bit of "hanging out" at auctions.

'But, Abi, I'm very worried about this chappie,' Fen said, patting Terry on one shoulder while keeping his fork in his hand. 'He once was a solid income stream for me, but now, *nada*. We have to encourage him to paint again, for my sake.'

I looked at Terry and felt guilt trickle down my neck and around my throat, mimicking the noose that The Golden Illuminati had put around his wife Thérèse's neck. The grief had corked his creativity and he had produced nothing in the nine months since her death.

'Don't hold your breath, Fen. I have only one focus now and that's bringing down The Golden Illuminati,' Terry said, lifting his wine glass towards Robert's and clinking it.

Fen's eyes were on Robert and his expression was thoughtful as he took a sip of wine. In that instant, I wished for Fen's gift. How divine it would be to saunter into Robert's head and hear his thoughts. As it was, I could only guess at them, and my hunch was that I was not the only one who had some doubts about Robert.

Fen put down his glass. 'I know that the vigilante in you is out for blood, but really, Terry, man cannot dine on revenge alone. You are not a better foe by denying your soul art.'

'No, that's true, but I'm dry, Fen. There's nothing left of my soul but ash.' Terry rubbed his large hand across his ex-boxer's face. With a squashed nosed and half an eyebrow that would never sprout hair again because of its scar, he could never have been called handsome, even in his heyday, but grief had stripped him of his colour, too. Where before his shades had been ruddy, now he was grey like a ghost, both in the tone of his skin and his hair.

Fen nodded. 'Maybe from the ashes will rise a phoenix, otherwise we may find you a new career as a poet. The best ones never recover from broken hearts.'

David cut some bread, then looked up at Robert. 'So, these bastards – Terry's words, not mine – they don't have any idea she's here?'

Robert locked eyes with David for the second time that night. 'No, they don't.'

'They would be pretty upset, I imagine, if they discovered the truth. You are taking a pretty big risk, knowing as you do what they are capable of.'

Robert looked annoyed. I could see he was struggling with how to continue the conversation.

'I infiltrated them nearly four years ago. During that time, I haven't seen anything particularly terrible go on. Though there have been a few bad speeches.' He smiled, and Savannah tittered.

'Nothing terrible apart from Abigail's kidnap and Thérèse's murder, you mean,' David shot back at him. The room seemed suddenly charged, as if every atom was standing to attention.

'Well, within the Society, the word is that Pierro acted without authorisation. They say he had something to prove.'

'Are you defending them?'

'No, I have my own reasons for wanting to see them fall. Historic grievances, you could say, but it's no good exaggerating what I've witnessed.'

'Why should we believe you're not working for them, and about to manoeuvre Abigail into the perfect position to be captured?'

Even though David was only voicing my own fears, I would have kicked him if it wasn't for the design of Robert's unique table that had my legs cocooned. There was no point in baiting Robert; he wasn't about to admit to David any secrets he might have.

Robert picked up his wine glass. His eyes were fixed on David. Without hurry, he inclined his head slightly towards him. '*Slàinte*,' he said, before taking a sip. 'Actually, I-have-her-in-the-perfect-position-now.'

There was an intake of breath from David. He crossed his arms and looked around at the rest of us with his eyebrows lifted.

'If I hadn't just seen you be so concerned for the welfare of my girlfriend, I would believe that. Can't say you've really put my worries to bed.'

Robert shrugged and took another forkful of fish. The two men stared at one another, neither willing to look away. My gaze bounced between them. Even disregarding the circumstances that had brought them together, it was no wonder they didn't get on – David and Robert were about as unalike as two men got. David was an open book, all smiles, hugs and puppy-like over-exuberance. Robert came across as worldly-wise, intense and a loner. Both were super-smart in their own ways, but with little understanding of each other's lives.

Savannah stood up, placing her hand on David's shoulder momentarily as she did.

'Who needs water?' She took a glass jug from the counter and filled it. The tension dissipated as Savannah returned to the table with the heavy jug and moved between everyone to fill their glasses. 'From here on in, I'm going to forbid any talk of Abigail being recaptured. It will be an offence to say the word in this house, do you understand? David, in particular?'

She settled back down into her seat and turned her body towards him, giving him a school ma'am stare with a bit of crackle. 'I've spent my life fighting people, and I'll tell you something I've learned. It's all about mindset. Abigail, tomorrow we'll start doing some training together, but your first lesson starts here: I absolutely forbid you even to think about the possibility of being captured. Terry, tell me, when you used to earn your living in the ring, did you ever go in thinking, yeah, he might beat me?'

'No, but I was an arrogant young so-and-so. It's not an easy thing for Abigail to do after what she's been through,' said Terry, buttering himself some bread.

'Mindset is everything in a fight. It's the same in sport. It might be easier for you, Abigail, to relate to tennis players or golfers. They have to believe they'll win before they do it. It's a faith mindset, but it's absolutely vital to success, and for you to ensure that you won't get captured.'

Fenrear made a huffing noise. 'Oversimplifying, aren't we? No-one aims to be captured.'

'I can't make you take my advice, but it's probably as valuable to you as the practical skills I might be able to help you develop.'

I couldn't think of anything I'd like less than to train to fight with Savannah, but all the men seemed to be nodding their heads.

'I'm sure Terry can teach me the basics,' I said, giving Terry a look which I hoped plainly said, 'Help!'

'You'd be better with Sav, Abi. She's more your build than I am. Also, I'm very old-school – fight just with my fists, use my bull strength, but that won't be your way. I'm sure Sav will have a combination of tricks that I can't teach you.'

'Will you come along to the sessions and help, at least?' I gave Terry a begging look.

He nodded. 'Of course, if Sav doesn't mind. In fact, I might be useful – if a little thing like you can get through me then you'll be well on your way.'

Savannah smiled. 'Yes, nice idea, and maybe we can do a little sparring, Terry – brawn against—'

She paused, looking at him with precocious eyes.

'Don't you dare say brains!' he bellowed.

She sat back in her chair and pouted. 'Well, am I allowed to think it?'

Terry laughed out loud, a great bear-like guffaw, and it took me back to my childhood. It had always been a part of Christmas dinners and big family events. Terry laughed so often during the months I'd spent living with him in Venice that I'd stopped noticing it, though its raucous echo wasn't something that was easy to ignore. I felt my heart swell.

Everyone had finished their meal now and they were sitting back. Savannah was saying something to David. I would have to ignore the eleven times Savannah had touched David during this one meal and be determined to like her. Anyone who could help Terry to wake up out of his grief needed to be embraced, and I should be grateful for her offer of help, too.

I lifted my glass up. 'To Savannah. Thank you for a lovely meal and sage advice.'

Savannah looked a little surprised, but pleased as everyone chorused her name.

**11**

---

## ABIGAIL

The next morning, I was feeling less altruistic. Nerves and my aversion to Savannah were not a happy combination, and my stomach churned.

I let myself out of the back door of the house, just past the kitchen. It opened on to a wide courtyard with stone buildings surrounding it. Only one had lights on and I could hear a radio playing inside. Pushing the door open, I saw Savannah inside. She was skipping with a rope in front of a wall clad with mirrors. The room was spacious and about half of the floor was covered in gym mats.

'Come in,' she said, lifting her voice above the music. I moved inside the room. There was a punch bag strung up and pads on some shelves.

'Feel like I'm a fish out of water here,' I said, staring at a wooden post with boxes at various heights which I presumed were targets. The wood looked mean and tough; I hoped I wouldn't have to hit it.

Savannah kept skipping, not attempting to put me at my ease with small talk. I continued to prowl around the room. There were some prints on the wall.

*Fall Down Seven, Get Up Eight.*
*The Hawk with Talent Hides his Talons.*
*What Does Not Kill Me Makes Me Stronger.*

'You kind of forget the philosophies when you're down on the floor with blood in your mouth,' said Savannah.

'I hope that's not your lesson plan for today. Get me down on the floor with blood in my mouth?' I tried to laugh, but the ball of nerves in my stomach made it hard.

'It's very likely to happen. We aren't here to play tiddly-winks,' said Savannah, stopping skipping. She walked over to the shelves, tied the rope and laid it down. The way Savannah moved was so graceful. She looked more like a dancer than a fighter.

'Are you an Underworlder?' I asked.

'No, but my brother is.'

'How does that work?'

'It's genetic – it misses some members of the family. Recessive genes, I suppose. He was always getting into trouble as a teenager for zoning out, as the teachers would call it. They gave him hell and he got bullied. He never would fight back – it's just not in his nature. So, I learned to fight to protect him. Eventually I realised that it was what I was good at, and most naturally inclined towards, and I'm always underestimated.'

If gifts were a genetic trait that must mean there was someone else in my family with the ability I had. I supposed something like alchemy might not be that obvious to a person, but as far back as we had traced, my family had all worked with metal.

'What is his gift?'

Savannah wrinkled her nose. 'He was a whisperer, like Fen.'

'Fen's a spook, he told me.'

'Fen's a mixture.'

'Like a horse whisperer?'

'No, whisperers hear things – snatches of conversation float into their minds, sometimes from miles away.'

'Is it like having incredible hearing?'

She shook her head. 'No, and it's not telepathy, either. He didn't necessarily know who the person was that spoke the words. He just heard it – it was very often useful information, but useless to him if he didn't know who it related to.'

'You said, was?'

'He's not dead, but he's ... disturbed. He had a particularly horrific experience with some Mexican mafia guys who thought he would be able to tell them about business dealings of a rival group. He couldn't, of course – it doesn't work like that. They were pretty cruel; he's never been right since.'

Savannah shrugged. I tried to catch her eye, wanting to show how sorry I was, but she wouldn't look at me. My mind skittered back to the pub. This morning after some sleep, my feelings about what I'd done were less raw. Savannah's story only reminded me that protecting myself was essential, and that trying to do it neatly wasn't guaranteed. If I was going to be able to get on with my life, I'd have to accept this blunt truth.

'Savannah, can I just ask one more question? How do they not get noticed by people?'

'It's not like they wake up one morning and suddenly they can do something. It emerges little by little, and as it tends to run in families, there'll be someone who can guide them or some family history about it. And then there's the Collectives.'

'What are Collectives?'

Savannah shook her head. 'I'm not here to give you a history lesson, enough with the chatting. Now, if we had endless time, I would start you on the basics. Strength training, some martial arts, and go from there, but given your situation, I think we'll just stick with the down and dirty moves that might be most useful to you. After all, fighting will always be a last resort, given your inexperience.'

'What sort of thing is down and dirty?'

'Genitalia, knees, noses, and maybe eyes. Whenever there's an opportunity, they are your bullseye. The advantage we have, being smaller than most men, is that we are the right height to strike the most painful blows. There's a variety of moves that can inflict serious wounds. What you need to remember is that these will be no help to you if you do them in isolation. It's momentum that will make them devastating.'

Savannah held out her arm and guided me over to the other side of the room. Damn her, if she didn't stop at that wooden post I'd been eyeing with dislike moments before.

Savannah began to demonstrate kicks. Was the woman superhuman? Whenever she connected with the wood, she didn't flinch. I copied her as well as I could, but when I made contact, I couldn't help yelping and limping immediately afterwards.

'Flex your foot so your toes are back. It's a stamping down kind of motion. You should be hitting the target with the ball of your foot,' she said, annoyance written into her brow.

I tried again, but knowing it would result in pain, I couldn't help slowing down fractionally before making contact.

'Don't hit the target; you need to be thinking about a point inches behind it. Also, I'm standing to one side of the post. You are a bit too face-on. If we are going for the knee, then you need to make contact from the side, not facing the target.'

The pain was getting to me, and I felt the part of myself that I wanted to stay as far away from as possible stirring. This was such a bad idea – why hadn't I realised it last night? It was crazy to feed me with anything that might strengthen that side of me. Of course, this kind of training would lead me to engage with it.

After she'd repeated the same instructions in a half-dozen different ways, her voice became shouty.

'I thought you had brothers?'

'I do, but there was never much violence. They were always too busy doing their own stuff to bother tormenting me.'

'Shame, it would have come in more useful if they'd sat on you on a daily basis. Your mindset has to be nastier, otherwise you're wasting your time.'

Nastier than a double murderer? Doubtful.

'You've got to realise that these guys who are going to try to take you will have all of the cards. You have to find some.'

There was a knock at the door and Terry came in. 'Hiya, love.' He walked over and kissed my hot cheek.

'She needs to get meaner, so none of this hugging and kissing stuff,' said Savannah to Terry as she picked up her bottle of water.

'Something I sense you have in spades, Savannah.' Terry's eyes almost closed when he smiled.

'I certainly do, which is why I'm a cat with nine lives.'

'Look, this really feels like a waste of time,' I said. Savannah rolled her eyes and didn't exactly tut, but I could tell she wanted to. 'No – I've had enough. The ball of my foot feels like it's dented already. I'll be easier to catch if all I can do is walk with a cane.'

'Abigail—'

'Savannah, stop pushing me!'

Terry intervened. 'Sav, maybe just change exercises. It's her first day, after all.'

Savannah made a non-verbal noise which somehow expressed precisely what she thought of me, but complied.

'Okay, noses. Stand here, Terry. Now, noses are a small target – same with gouging eyes, but people often leave their faces exposed, and if you're quick, you can deliver a punishing blow.'

Terry stood in front of Savannah as she demonstrated how to cause real damage by hitting someone with the heel of her hand to the base of his nose. Fortunately for Terry, Savannah didn't actually make contact.

'Come on, Abi. Take my nose off,' said Terry, turning to me.

I tilted my head at him. 'Okay, but only because it's you.'

'Ahh-err.' Savannah shook her head. 'You've got to work on intent. Go for me instead of Terry. You won't want to hurt him.'

Savannah and I circled each other. I threw out my hand every now and then, but never got anywhere near her. Savannah upped the pace and I followed step. The two of us were moving around so fast that I felt the room begin to blur.

Suddenly, Savannah stepped in and threw a punch at exactly the same moment that I stepped forward into her oncoming hand. The pain was searing and blinding, but most surprising to me was the fan of blood that sprayed out from my nose. There was a throaty noise, but it was not my own. It came from Terry, who was staring at me and the blood with the oddest expression on his face.

'Excuse me,' he said, and dashed out of the room.

I sank to the floor, holding my nose. Savannah stared after Terry.

'Surely, he's not squeamish? Doesn't look the type. Head back, head back,' Savannah bossed, leading me out of the room. 'Just stay here a minute, you might feel giddy. We'll go over to the kitchen in a bit, there's ice there.'

Five minutes later, Savannah propelled me across the courtyard. I felt like my nose had a red-hot poker stuck up it. As we arrived in the kitchen, Terry was standing at the counter. His hand clasped charcoal and he was moving it over an A1 pad with lightning speed. As I got closer, I could see he was drawing the two of us circling each other: Savannah's face was predatory, mine wary. Though much of it was abstract lines, he had our pace precisely and the individual curves of both our figures. The momentum of the blow was there, and the fan of blood which swept around me.

'You're a genius,' said Savannah, who'd completely forgotten about getting me ice.

'Haven't picked up a pencil,' he took a shallow breath, 'since Thérèse died.'

I laid a blood-smeared hand on Terry's and squeezed it. 'She would have hated that, you know. She loved your art.'

'My art was all about her. When she was gone, there was nothing left for me to paint.'

'You painted before you met her, remember? I grew up looking at your paintings hanging in our house.'

'But it was her face that made my art famous. People bought her.'

'They bought how you saw her. They'd buy how you see other things, too, if you gave them the chance.'

Terry swallowed and made some further sweeps with the charcoal. 'I need to work this up properly and charcoal is the wrong medium, but it's the only one I have here – just in case. I need oils and canvas to do it justice.'

'I can get you any supplies you want by this afternoon. Glenkubright has a great art scene and there's a good materials shop on the main road . If you come to my office now, you can tell me what you want. You can sort yourself out, right, Abigail?'

I shrugged. 'Sure.' Better without you, in fact. As I squeezed my nose with my fingertips, it felt like the size and shape of a potato.

'Will I see you tomorrow, same time?' Savannah said before leaving the kitchen. I paused to think this over. Was there any point? Then I looked at Terry's drawing.

'I'll be there if you promise to come with your sketch-pad, Terry.'

He looked up at me and I saw the struggle, pain and potential behind his eyes, but he gave a brief nod.

**12**

---

## ABIGAIL

I got myself some ice and plodded to the hallway. Staring up at the sweeping spiral staircase, I had to lean against the doorframe for support. It must be the loss of blood that was making me feel dizzy, or the strain of forcing myself to do as Savannah directed, knowing that it was futile unless I engaged with the other part of me that scared everyone else.

I needed to sit down somewhere for a while. The door next to me had a small cut-glass viewing panel in it and I looked through it down a short corridor to see a floor to ceiling mural of a girl's face in profile. I pushed open the door and immediately felt a cool breeze as I moved towards the sepia shades of the portrait.

The girl was gasping; her eyes were fixed on something in the distance and her hand was almost at her chin, about to cover her mouth. It wasn't a glamorous image. The girl had her slightly wavy hair tied back, but her face was so captivated that she made me forget my sore nose and drew me towards her, which was clearly the artist's intent. As I moved along the corridor, I saw that the wall she was staring at had a break in it, though it was cleverly done, with no architrave, so it wasn't immediately obvious to the eye.

I turned through the opening and found myself mimicking the expression of the girl in the mural as sunshine cascaded over me. The high glass of the window bay was open, revealing the exquisite wild view of the lake, the mountains beyond it and the epic skyline. The whole space was a viewing platform, with a variety of comfortable-looking, well-worn armchairs, all sporting warm woollen rugs and footstools nearby like doting dogs. I walked outside to the brink of the decking and took in a deep breath of the crystal-clean air.

The lake was spectacular, reflecting the natural shades of the mountains and trees surrounding it.

'Wow,' I said aloud.

'Special, isn't it?'

I jumped at the voice and turned to see Fenrear sitting in one of the armchairs to the far left with a book on his lap, feet up, a blanket over his legs and a teapot with cups next to him on a small side table.

'What on earth has happened to your nose?' he said, sitting forward and looking thrilled.

'Savannah happened,' I said, throwing myself down into one of the other armchairs, which had carpet cushions and leather padded arms. 'She is not my favourite person.'

Fen poured me a cup of tea and passed it across. 'It's Lapsang. Shall I tell you who is my new favourite person? It's Mrs Baines, Robert's housekeeper. She just brought me this pot of tea, delightful woman.'

I sipped the smokey tea. 'Now Savannah has drawn blood, I imagine it will be the aim for every session.'

'Why do you think that? Savannah is divine.'

'She's not my type.'

'Well, darling, nobody is asking you to sleep with her. Just learn.'

'She's like mercury – cold and beautiful. Not a metal I'm drawn to,' I said, relaxing back into the cushions.

'I would have thought it one of your favourites. I hear you're quite the professional poisoner.'

So, he knew everything about me, even how I'd murdered Pierro. 'Wouldn't have been much good to me last year. Mercury is a slow killer. It percolates into people and shuts their nervous system down bit by bit.'

'Judging by your work at the pub, slow isn't your style.'

I felt a bullishness emerge at his words. 'Murdering, fast or slow, isn't my style. Last year I was fighting for my life. Pierro would have killed me – there's not the slightest doubt in my mind about that. I didn't intend to murder anyone in the pub.'

Fen put his tea down. 'You're a funny thing, Abigail. I see the alchemy in your personality now that I'm getting to know you a little. Tell me how it happened last year – the real story.'

I shook my head and pulled a rug from one of the footstools to drape it over my legs. 'I'm not going over it, Fen. I wish it hadn't been necessary.'

'I don't mean that – I mean, tell me about the alchemy.'

I closed my eyes for a moment and lifted my face into the soft breeze, hesitant about opening up to Fenrear. Apart from Terry and David, who definitely had nothing to do with The Golden Illuminati, I hadn't admitted to anyone what I could really do. It was one of the few ways I could protect myself. If they knew for certain, there'd for ever be a target on my head. But, with Fen's gifts, it seemed highly unlikely that he had anything to do with them, and I needed help. My instinct was that I could trust him.

I went back in my mind to the incredible thing that had happened last year, trapped as I was in a dungeon cell in Italy. It was a familiar place; I'd replayed it unendingly since then.

'You know, you're the first person to ever ask me that. I told Terry and David what I'd done, and they've never once asked me about the details. I think they don't want to encourage any delusions I might be suffering under.'

'It's hard for those without our capabilities to accept them, and you can't really blame them for not believing in yours. It is,' he opened his hands wide, 'mythic.'

'I'd cut my hands deeply with a knife. I was demented, Fen. Pierro had just murdered Thérèse and I was clasping this metal nugget that I'd been working on for hours, just for show – so they'd believe I was trying. The blood was really flowing, and at one point I thought, maybe, I might just bleed out and die. Then I pushed the world back with my mind and my head sort of caught light and it blazed brightly, blindingly so, and eventually I blacked out. When I woke up, the nugget in my hand wasn't bronze anymore; it was gold.'

Fen sat forward in his chair and the book he'd been reading fell to the floor. 'This bright light – tell me more about it.'

'I don't know what it was – sort of like sunshine, but much more intense. I've tried to summon it again, but it doesn't come on command. All I know is that I was very upset. Thérèse's body was hung a few feet from my window. She was dead because of me. It's possible it was a unique event – a psychic trauma, I suppose?'

'Did you notice anything else about it? Any detail you've not mentioned – or even, have you noticed anything since then?'

I looked down at my hands. 'My hands seemed to like what I did because my psoriasis cleared up completely.' I gave him a flash of both my palms. 'Didn't last, though – they're pretty much as bad as they ever were now. I find my viewpoint sometimes changes, particularly if I'm stressed. I had an odd incident where I moved out of my body when I was still being held in the cell. I witnessed myself being tortured, sort of, by one of the guards, but I was definitely outside my own body.'

'Anything else?' He was leaning forward in his seat, cup now dangling from one finger.

'Yesterday at the pub, I sensed something was happening within the building. When I went to look, I found Robert had projected outside of his body. I couldn't see him, but I knew he was there: I could feel him.'

He nodded. 'Go on.'

'I've always had a sense of understanding metals in a deeper way than other people seem to. It's probably what made me good at my work, but that connection is growing.' I wriggled in my chair and looked down at my hands. 'I sort of hear things now, too ... some metals tell me things.'

Fen clapped his hands and clicked his fingers on his right hand. 'Now we're cooking. Metal whispering, alchemy and astral projection – possibly all part of the same gift. The latter is something I can help you with, though maybe Robert is more your man in that regard. It'll be a very useful part of your capability, if you can master it. I can't help you to be an alchemist, but I suspect if you gain control over some parts of this gift, then you will have a greater chance of connecting with the other parts.'

He sat back and gazed out over the view, taking in a big lungful of the nourishing fresh air. 'I'm grateful you told me the truth. I must admit, I've never exerted more restraint in my life than not hopping into your head when we first met.'

'Why didn't you?'

'I wanted you to trust me, Abigail.' He dropped my eye contact. 'Plus I'd have only caught a glimpse; I never get more than that. Knowing who to trust must be hard when you've had such a messy ride, but it's my turn to be honest with you now.'

I'd been beginning to feel relaxed with Fen. It was good to talk to someone about the strange things I could do, but as if we'd just gone over an unexpected bump in the road, I felt my insides flip over.

He wagged a forbidding finger at me. 'No. Calm yourself – I'm nothing to do with them. It's to do with our culture as Underworlders. What you need to remember is what I told you en route to the pub – you are not unusual in having a group a little too interested in you. It's always been so for our kind, and to protect ourselves, we have something called Collectives. They were formed with the aim to serve and help our kind. Although it's true, I did run into Terry in London, I engineered it. I already knew about you because you had come to the attention of the Collective I am part of.'

'But how did they know about me?'

Fen shrugged. 'Collectives are made up of people with special gifts. We know all sorts of things that we shouldn't know, which is why we are so often targeted. Then there's the possibility of leaks within The Golden Illuminati ranks – bragging about what has gone on, perhaps. Secrets always slip out, and the Collective's *raison d'être* is to gather information in order to protect us. Let's not get too focused on that right now. There's very little you can do about it, but I was nominated to come and meet you and see if I can help you.'

'Why me particularly? Surely, if what you say is true,

there are lots of Underworlders that need as much help as I do – ones like Savannah's brother.'

He glanced down at his feet and twitched his mouth. 'He isn't special enough,' he said in a small voice. Fen gave a slight shrug and his mouth pursed like he'd tasted something sour. 'The Collectives protect Underworlders, but they don't usually get involved in aiding the development of their gifts. You are a special case.'

I shook my head.

'Let me explain how Collectives work. It's a voting system. Some Collectives have a higher rank than others and they get more votes. Your Collective's rank depends on the rarity and power of the gifts within the group.'

'So, it's political?'

'It's not supposed to be, but it is. Your gift is made for a position in a Collective – not only is it exceptionally rare, but it may also yield valuable currency. That's useful when it comes to bargaining and can tip the scales on deals.'

'What deals?'

'Ransoms, in some cases, but also currency helps to encourage other Collectives to vote your way.' He clasped both his hands and they shook slightly as he said, 'If you can master your gift, Abigail, it could change everything for our region. For the first time in centuries, our Collective could be a Primary.'

'This really doesn't sound like my kind of thing.'

'If you were part of a Collective, you would have diplomatic protection. High levels of security just detailed to you. You'd be safe from The Golden Illuminati.'

'I wouldn't need to hide?'

'No, you wouldn't. You'd be safer than most Underworlders ever are.'

My heart leaped at this possibility: safety; a relatively normal existence. All that I'd thought I'd lost for ever.

'I don't know anything about protecting people or politics. It sounds slightly mafia. Do Underworlders pay for this protection?' I forgot my nose was sore and rubbed it distractedly, which made me flinch.

'Yes, they pay a tax which funds the work of the Collectives.'

I was only just getting my head around the idea of Underworlders, but I suppose I shouldn't have been surprised that the group would be organised.

'Tell me more about the Collectives.'

'They are divided into regions – so we have eight worldwide. They are named after the first eight Underworlders that formed the first Collective back in the 1700s, but we also designate them a rank, so primary, secondary and so on. The lower you are ranked, the less power you have. We are all supposed to work together to protect our kind, but really, it's like having eight political parties, all with slightly different viewpoints and agendas. The Collective with the member that has the rarest gift is designated the Primary.

'Why?'

'It's historic – recognition and respect for what makes us who we are.'

'It all sounds very noble.'

'Well, it is and it isn't. Those men who attacked us at the pub, it's very likely that they were soldiers from one of the other Collectives. There are some that stand to lose substantial power if you are what we hope you are. There's a bit of form for this type of thing. Around seven years ago, a young boy in the Devlan region – that's Germany to you – emerged from nowhere with future-sight. Now this is another exceptionally rare gift, and what he did see in his short life was incredibly accurate. No region ever admitted to taking him out, but there was a lot of evidence to suggest it was Underworlders culling Underworlders – awful.'

The taste of fear was suddenly in my mouth from nowhere. Now I had another predator after me.

'Why is it so important to be the Primary Collective in all of this?'

'You're not that naïve, are you? It's about power. The Primary Collective always gives preference to their own region and schemes – they steer the ship, too, as they have more voting power than the others.'

'Surely, you want someone like Robert – successful, commanding, and more importantly, in control of his gift.'

'I've been in politics a long time – our region has been dominated by every other part of the world for as long as I can remember. I'd be very happy to see the power shift to us: the underdog for so long. It would be a lifetime ambition fulfilled.

'Underworlder Collectives are not like regular politics. Robert may be a fine, upstanding man, but his gift is a little,' he glanced around, 'pedestrian. Don't tell him I said that. All Underworlders think their gifts are the most special, but let's just say some are more so than others. Now, Robert, for example, can astral project, but that's it. You, on the other hand, sound as if you have multiple gifts, as I do.'

'What else are you capable of?'

'Apart from being a spook, I'm a whisperer and a no-end.'

'No-end?'

'Yes, in fact, it's being a no-end that distinguishes me and secures my position as a Collective member because it's very rare. I'm older than I look. A lot older. I just stopped aging one day. It's rather annoying that it couldn't have been when I was thirty years younger and in my prime, before everything began to droop, but there you are.'

'Do you mean, you're immortal?'

'No, I mean I haven't aged past sixty-three.'

'And for how long haven't you aged past sixty-three?'

'About eighty-three years.'

A gust of wind blew and I gazed over the fields and trees all around us. Before when I'd looked at the view, the seclusion of this place had settled me; now I felt vulnerable. They'd found me at the pub – that wasn't that far away. Collectives could be sending armies to hide in those trees and march upon us.

I stood up. 'I need to think all this over – it's a lot to take in.'

'Of course,' said Fen. 'The important thing is to begin your training. When do you want to start?'

'Certainly not today,' I said, touching the bridge of my tender nose. 'School's out.'

'Tomorrow, then. We can start with bitching about Savannah and move on to astral projection after that. How does that sound?'

I nodded. 'Sounds good. Fen, does The Golden Illuminati know about the Collectives? Is there a relationship established?'

'Not a current relationship that I know of. There may have been in the past – you're the first one of us that has been of interest to them in my lifetimes. Don't worry about that. We are very good at opening channels.'

'But, why aren't you starting that dialogue right now? You know they want me. We have heard that first hand from Robert.'

'We know all about them, we know about you, but it will

only be if you are taken that we'd intervene. There's nothing to talk about as yet.'

'That's a ridiculous way to go about things.'

'Do you think they'd drop their interest in you just because we told them to? You're naïve if you do.'

I shook my head and let out a breath I'd been holding on to too long. 'If you can get Savannah to move her session to after yours, then you'll have a better chance of me achieving anything. Otherwise, I'll just be bleeding and limping all over the place.' I turned to go. 'Now, I should go find David.'

'Yes, he's a nice boy,' said Fen, picking up the book from the floor beside his chair.

I looked at him. 'Been in his head, have you?'

Fen smiled in a sheepish way. 'Perhaps just for a smidge.'

## 13

## ROBERT

I woke at 5.45am. I was feeling anxious because I'd spent the previous day on Skype and it was clear that my project in Berlin, which I'd left in the hands of two of my best architects, wasn't going smoothly. It sounded like it was down to a very unyielding builder who was being difficult about every small change, changes which always occurred during a build. By the sounds of things, the site was turning into a battleground.

Not that I was the greatest negotiator in the world, but I was good at observing people. I took the time to do it and I swapped the team around if I felt personalities didn't stack. It sounded like the three of them weren't a good mix, and yet it wasn't fair for me to start wading in from such a distance. The team was obviously perplexed that I'd given myself an extended leave period at a critical point in the project.

It was almost light and so I thought I might take Remi out for a walk. Being outside here never failed to give me clarity and freshen my mood. I dressed and headed downstairs to be met by Remi, who preferred to sleep in the cooler hallway than in my room. He was ready to go in an instant.

Slipping into the kitchen to make myself a coffee to go, I was surprised, and slightly annoyed, to find Fenrear had beaten me to it. He was reading on his phone and raised a piece of toast in greeting.

'I don't need to go inside your head to tell you're not thrilled to see me,' he said.

'I was hoping for some time to myself before the day began.'

'Too bad, I beat you to it.'

'Have you spoken to Richard?'

'Yes, it's going as well as an incident like that can. I don't think I need to drive over.' He shook his head slightly. 'It doesn't sound like I'd have much to contribute, whereas here I'm keen to get started with Abigail. I'm going through emails that friends have sent me about their own gifts which are similar to hers.'

'For God's sake, Fen! Tell me you're not letting more people know about her?' Anger fired up as I felt the precariousness of our situation. 'That's the last thing I need, more people getting involved.'

I gritted my teeth. Fen raised an eyebrow at my outburst and shook his head slightly.

'No, I'm just making vague enquiries with others who have traits like hers to help me with her training. Training that you should be a part of, I might add. She definitely sounds as if she's got projection capabilities – the fact that she can sense you outside your body is very exciting.'

'I've got a few things I need to straighten out with work, so seeing as you're here, you might as well make yourself useful.'

There was one particular reason why I was coming

around to thinking that Fen turning up wasn't such a bad thing. The idea of working with Abigail was too appealing. Last night, I'd let my mind roam over the way I'd touched her in the pub and how she'd responded. It hadn't made for peaceful sleep. Any more of that and my resolve to turn her in might cave completely. At present, keeping my distance from her felt like the best course, and with Fen as her tutor, I had the luxury of that option. Just so long as he wasn't too good a teacher. She'd be free for little enough time as it was. There wasn't any need for her to discover herself too quickly.

The door swung open to reveal Terry holding his phone. I turned my body towards the coffee machine so that he couldn't see how annoyed I felt. Was there no peace to be had in my own house?

'Bit early for you, isn't it?' Fenrear lifted his eyebrows.

Terry looked elated. He moved over to my side at the counter. 'Making enough for two there?'

'Sure,' I said, inhibiting the urge to be pissy and tell him to make his own bloody coffee. He exchanged a little banter with Fenrear while I scowled at the coffee machine.

When it was ready, I poured him a cup. 'What's put you in such a glorious mood at this early hour?' I enquired.

'Just received some very good news. Something I've been waiting on for a number of months,' said Terry. 'I'm going for a shower, see you guys later.'

As he walked into the corridor, Fen gave me an expectant look, tapped his temple, then inclined his head in Terry's direction.

I sighed and nodded, grudgingly. 'I'm making an exception, but only one. Other than this, head-hopping is still not allowed.'

Fenrear winked, enjoying my duplicity, and closed his

eyes, giving a subtle shudder before his body went still, like he was suffering with narcolepsy. I waited, sipping my coffee.

A minute later, Fen's body tremored again as he came back into it and sat up. His eyes rolled before they opened.

'Worrying,' he said, picking up his toast again and swigging a sip of tea. 'He's got himself a security job as a subcontractor, working for a firm that have the main contract in The Golden Illuminati HQ, your building in Milan. He'll be handling CCTV.'

'Why would Terry be going undercover now? That doesn't make a lot of sense. He's not likely to be able to record anything useful. Abigail has been the only person of significant interest for many years. Wasn't there more?'

'I only get to hear what people are thinking if they're thinking it, and only for a few seconds.'

'CCTV is not that useful. If he's trying to gather evidence, he'll need sound. There's a possibility things might be discussed there which they wouldn't want revealing.'

'It must be about placing himself in their space and seeing what opportunities arise. What else could it be?'

I turned and looked out over the cobbled courtyard with its high walls, mulling this news over in my mind. 'Could turning her in be—' but I didn't get to finish that sentence. David seemed to materialise from nowhere at my side, and the punch he threw was eloquent enough to ensure I felt his full opinion of me. My coffee flew up in the air and fell like black rain around me as I hit the pale stone floor. I didn't lose consciousness, but I could taste blood in my mouth and my body stalled temporarily. It flatly refused to respond to any signals I gave it to move.

David's shadow was cast over me. I heard Fen's legs scrabble beneath the table and push the chair away.

'What the hell are you doing, you big ape? He's on her side.'

'That's not what it sounded like. You will not fucking turn her in, do you hear me?' he shouted, edging closer to me. Fen threw himself in front of David and pushed him back, but I could see David's feet trying to force their way forward.

'David!' Abigail's voice came from the doorway. She was beside me on the floor in an instant. I felt the light touch of her hand on my shoulder.

'I told you this man couldn't be trusted, Abigail.' David's voice was super-charged. 'I don't like him. Don't you dare try to defend him after this! He's a member of the Society, he even built their HQ, and now I've caught him admitting he's going to turn you in.'

It took every ounce of my will, but I forced myself to roll on to my back and look up over Fen's shoulder into David's furious face. 'You have it wrong, David. We were discussing your uncle. If you hadn't been so quick with your fists, you would have heard me say, "Could turning her in be on his mind?"'

'Rubbish! He'd never do that!' But David stopped pushing against Fen.

'Pass me the tissues, and give Robert some space, David. You've made your point.' Abigail leaned up and over me to take hold of the box of tissues. Her T-shirt rode up as she did, revealing her slender waist. I had the strongest urge to lift my hand and rest it on the curve of her hip bone. Now that would really start a fight.

'Let's make everyone some more coffee,' Fen said, leading David away.

Abigail sat back on her heels and I saw her smile for an instant before her hair fell across her face. 'With your lip and my nose, we make a good pair.' She pressed the tissue to my bleeding lip.

'We do make a good pair.' As I repeated her words, the truth of the statement blew through my mind.

'Come on, up,' she said and slipped her hand into mine. Without thinking, I clasped it to me and held it for a moment. Elation lit a fire through my body. I looked into her eyes and saw her lips part as surprise escaped her mouth, but then her expression lightened.

'Err, I was trying to help you up,' she said, raising her eyebrows. Slipping her other hand beneath my elbow, she gave me a tug.

Realising my mistake, I felt a kick of embarrassment as I rolled on to my knees and, jelly-legged, made it to my feet, but it wasn't too painful. For an instant, she'd returned my touch when I'd squeezed her hand, and my body revved as I thought about even that small response.

I rested a hand on the back of one of the chairs. Fen passed me a new cup of coffee.

David came forward, not looking at me. He put a hand on Abigail's arm.

'Come on, Abigail, let's go.'

As they reached the door, jealousy wiped every other feeling from my brain.

'David, you don't like me because you know I'm a threat, but not in the way you'd like me to be.'

Abigail took one glance at me and pushed him out of the door.

## 14

## ABIGAIL

David stormed up the stairs with me tagging after him.

'Where are you going?' I asked.

'To see Terry.'

I put one hand on the banister.

"Choose me."

The words came through even louder than before. I dropped David's arm and let him forge forward, laying both hands on to the bronze's surface.

What did it mean? I closed my eyes and spread my fingers out across the solid pinkish metal. My hands began to throb. I felt a yearning inside them for something just out of reach. The connection between us became more focused as the seconds ticked past. My hearing of the outside world dulled as the sounds of this other world became louder.

"Choose me."

I could hear movement: a rushing, whooshing sound was in my ears, and under my fingers there was a flow like water moving along a stream. My hands cooled and tingled with energy.

Shouting broke through my thoughts. I recognised Terry's voice and let go of the rail, taking the steps two at a time as I made for his room. As I reached the third floor, I realised why the house had a lift – I was gasping as I put my hand on the doorknob. There didn't seem much point in knocking on his door; no-one would hear me through the yelling.

I opened the door and was met by the odour of turpentine. Terry stood in front of a vast canvas that divided him and David. Both heads spun in my direction. David's colour was up, and Terry was leaning over his canvas towards David. He held a broad paintbrush in his hand. If I didn't know how much affection there was between the two, I'd have sworn Terry was about to hit David with it.

'What is going on here? First David and Robert, now you two?'

David moved across to the wide windows that looked out over the land at the back of the house. He put both hands on the windowsill and dropped his head so that he was staring at the floor and took a deep breath in. Terry sat down on his seat in front of his canvas, picked up his palette from the floor, and began banging a rusty shade of oil paint on to the canvas with the brush. No-one said anything for a minute and I picked my way across the dust sheets on the floor, which was scattered with all Terry's new art supplies: the ornaments of his craft.

A memory flashed across my mind of Terry spreading a huge canvas out across my mum's living room carpet when my brothers and I were small. He'd handed us fresh tubes of acrylic, brushes and palette knives, just like the ones I was stepping over, and taught us to do what he called blocking in, which meant to fill every inch of the canvas with background colour. My mum had been mad. We'd also managed to cover much of her furniture, too. Terry had given us a quid each as wages.

I collapsed on to the bed and had to pull out a roll of masking tape from under me. I looked between David and Terry.

'So, what just happened? I feel like I've completely missed a step.'

David huffed and crossed his arms, continuing to stare at the floor. 'I heard Robert say he was thinking of turning you in, but Robert denies it. He says, *Terry*, wants to turn you in which is ridiculous!'

I looked at Terry, who refused to look up, staring mulishly at his canvas.

David spun round. 'That man is manipulating us! He's playing us off against each other.'

'Why would he do that? It doesn't make sense.'

David let out an exasperated sigh. 'I can't believe I am the only person that doesn't think the sun shines out of his backside!' He held up his hand. 'One, he's a member of The Golden Illuminati. He says he has a grudge against them, and yet he hasn't acted against them at all since he joined them. Two, he built their HQ, making shed loads of money from them, so why would he want to rock the boat? And three – I don't like him.'

This time, Terry did look at me over the top of his canvas and raised his eyebrows.

David caught the look. 'Okay, I will qualify that by saying it's not jealousy of this spectacular house; it's because he's so closed. Good luck to any woman that tries to prize that clam's heart open, and there'll be a reason why it's so tightly shut: glued up with secrets and lies.'

'I didn't tell Robert that I was thinking of turning Abigail in,' said Terry to his canvas.

'So I'm right – he lied about you. I don't get why you are defending him, and it might sound childish, but I want you to believe me over him.'

'That does sound childish,' snapped Terry.

I was looking at Terry. There was something in the ring of his voice that sounded tinny when he said he hadn't told Robert. It wasn't a denial. Suspicion crept across my mind. When I'd entered the kitchen, Fenrear had been restraining Robert. Fenrear, the mind-reader.

I'd told David that Fen and Robert had abilities, and I'd presumed Terry knew, but maybe he didn't. I hadn't been specific with David, either, because it was such a taboo subject between us. Judging by David's behaviour this morning, he'd go stratospheric if he knew about what Fen could do.

David shook his head and stared at Terry for a moment. Terry went on covering his canvas in background colour. I stood up to go over to David, but as I did, he stiffened and set off for the door, closing it more loudly than was necessary.

Terry threw down his brush as David left. I moved over to his side of the canvas and knelt down, taking his big hands in my small ones. How was it possible that his mighty paws seemed just as awesome now as they had done when I was a mini six-year-old being swung between him and my father as we'd crossed the foundry yard?

'It's not like you two to argue. Tell me the truth, Terry – what's going on?'

He looked at me with an uncertain expression. 'I have something to tell you that I haven't told David.'

'Yes?'

'I've been trying for months to get a position inside The Golden Illuminati HQ building in Milan, and this morning I heard word that I've managed to pull it off. It's the start of the plan I've been putting together.'

'What if someone recognises you there?'

'They won't. It's a huge place. I have a false identity and it's watertight. I'll be in the background, but there will be opportunities there. Exposing them will be impossible if we are always on the outside looking in.'

I sat back on my heels. 'Terry, I don't want you risking your life for me.'

Terry shifted in his seat and lowered his voice. 'I'm not doing it for you.'

'It won't bring her back, Terry.'

He sat up and took a deep breath, looking into my eyes. 'I'm not sure at all how it was figured out, but what he said to David was true. I do want you to turn yourself in to them.'

I reeled back and met the floor. I put both my hands up to cover my eyes, wanting to shut the whole world out. Yesterday, I'd found out the Collectives wanted me, and now Terry – always-on-my-side Terry – was throwing this bombshell out there. It was too much.

'Why would you ask that of me? What are we doing here if that's the plan all along?'

'We are here to help you get some idea of what this thing inside you is. If it's real or imagined. We are here to rest in a safe place for as long as possible before jumping out of the frying pan and into the fire. But I wouldn't ask you to do something that would put you at risk if I didn't have a solid plan to get you out, and a really good reason. We need evidence, Abigail – to expose them. We have nothing to prove what happened to you or Thérèse last year. We need actual footage of you being held against your will, and I will be involved with CCTV.'

'Robert's one of them. Why can't he get evidence from archives about other people that were held?'

'I've asked him about that possibility in the past. He's a relatively new member – he would never be given access to anything that might incriminate them.'

'You're assuming they'd take me to the headquarters. They could take me anywhere. Do anything to me. How would you know where I was?'

'Robert could help with that. There'd be whispers among the members, gossip and excitement at you being taken. But I'm betting that this time they will take you to the HQ, and I'll be there working for security and able to get all the evidence we need. I know it's an enormous risk, but Abigail – look at our position. There's just no way that you can have a normal life as it stands. We don't have to do anything this minute, but please, think about it – please. Robert will help us if I ask him.'

I shook my head at him, feeling resentful. 'I barely got out with my life last time and you're asking me to go voluntarily?'

'If they believe in your gift, you'd be too valuable to them to hurt you.'

'But you, or my family, or David wouldn't be too valuable to hurt. Do you really want a repeat of what happened to Thérèse on your hands? Please don't ask it of me, Terry – I couldn't go through it again.'

Angry tears sprang to my eyes.

'If we can get evidence, it will mean justice for Thérèse and all the thousands of other people whose lives have been damaged by these extremist crazies in the past.'

'Don't put that on me! I have enough to deal with. I'm not taking on other people's injustices, I've got enough of my own to handle. David will never forgive you if he finds out.' Trying to pull myself together, I stood up. 'I have a session with Fen to get to.'

I paused at the door and looked back at Terry. He'd picked up his brush again. The room was about three times the size of mine and David's, and was bathed in natural light.

'It feels like a real studio in here. Why don't you let the vengeance go and become Robert's Artist in Residence – lean into this other world that's open to you? I'm sure it would make you happier.'

Wistfulness passed through Terry's eyes for a moment, but then he shook his head.

'You don't know me, Abigail. I'm going to kill every last one of them for what they did to her.'

**15**

———

## ABIGAIL

Moments of certainty had been few and far between since I'd been taken by The Golden Illuminati, but as I walked down the stairs away from Terry's room, I had two back to back. Firstly, there was no way that I would even contemplate Terry's suggestion. That door was shut; he would have to find another way.

Secondly, I knew what the handrail's message meant. It was begging me to try again – the same way my hands were, but I wasn't going to do it. I wasn't going to yield to their desire until I had got the help that Fen and Robert might be able to give me. I had cut my hands to ribbons over the last several months and shed more blood than I should ever have had to. So as not to be tempted, I wouldn't even allow myself to touch the handrail – no matter how much I longed to.

I made my way downstairs. Fen had arranged to meet me in the book room, which was the first door off the hallway. Looking inside, I saw Fen sprawled across an L-shaped suede sofa with his feet on a substantial wooden coffee table which was home to a couple of flowering pot plants. He had a newspaper on his lap.

'I was just about to come and find you. You're late.'

I nodded. 'Had a few things to take care of,' I said with a sigh, and dropped down next to Fen.

'How's Muhammad Ali?' he asked.

I laid my head back against the cushion. 'Angry, and I suspect it's your fault.'

Fen turned innocent eyes on me.

'Don't give me that. Terry said he told you nothing, so that means you found out another way.'

He held up his hands. 'Robert told me I could,' he said, defensively.

Robert was clearly not above using Fen's gifts when it suited him. That was something to keep in mind.

'Putting aside precisely how you discovered it, in a way, it's a good thing. It's flushed Terry's real intentions out – he wants me to hand myself in to The Golden Illuminati, so he can get CCTV footage proving they're holding me against my will. He thinks it will be enough to open up a proper investigation into them.'

Fen sat up quickly from his languid position and the newspaper he'd been reading dropped to the floor. 'Well, that's the stupidest idea I've ever heard. What a selfish moron! Isn't he supposed to be your guardian angel? With angels like that, hell is only around the corner. I hope you aren't idiotic enough to listen to that load of old clap-trap! If you are, you deserve what you get, is all I can say.'

He folded his arms, turning away from me in a huff. Seeing him in such high dudgeon brought one of the first smiles to my lips since I'd arrived at the house.

'Don't worry, Fen. I was very clear that I wouldn't entertain the idea. I've pointed him in Robert's direction if he wants to go digging for evidence. I will say one thing, though – Terry's not the only one keeping secrets. It's only fair that you disclose your abilities to Terry and David.'

'Not ruddy likely after seeing David's left hook. You can tell he's related to Terry – boxing must be in his genes.'

'Fighting is not like David at all. David's very mellow, usually. Robert brings out the worst in him.'

'Hmm, I wonder why?' Fen said, raising an eyebrow.

Not wanting to speculate about that with Fen, I looked around the room, taking it in for the first time. All the furnishings shared a soft palette of brown with warm touches of orange. There was a wall of books at the far end that rose from the ground floor up to the lofty ceiling. In front of it was an elaborate staircase in polished wood which rose up to the first level, then split so you could walk in either direction before meeting another flight of stairs at each end. It was highly decorative with ornate carvings and twisted iron spindles, the type of staircase you might see in a grand entrance of a building, but here it appeared to have no other purpose than enabling a person to browse the spine of every book on the wall.

'Can you imagine living in a place like this?' I marvelled.

'It's pretty spectacular. Most Underworlders are nomadic, it's safer that way, but this place could persuade me to stay put. I can't get enough of this room – stayed in here with the wood burner on last night and read till late. Filled my soul right up.'

'I wonder if I'll ever be able to have something as normal as a home?' Between the threat of The Golden Illuminati and rival Collectives, that didn't seem likely. I was better off not thinking about the future.

'Ready to get going?'

I nodded, a spark of excitement kindling in my stomach.

'Maybe I need to be in immediate danger for any kind of ability to surface. Nothing has happened at all since I've been safe.'

'I think that's unlikely, so let's forget about previous attempts for the moment. We don't need an alchemical epiphany right away. I'd just like to see if we can experiment with simpler things to start with – a little astral projection. For me, there is a sweet spot in my head, and that's what you need to find if you can. If you want to leave your body, you can't just jump out. You have to go through the trapdoor and that's the sweet spot. It's like a keyhole where your consciousness can slip out and in, and soon you don't even have to find it. You just feel for it and off you go.'

'So how do I locate it when I don't know where it is?'

'Well, you just have to mosey around your head a bit. Close your eyes; sense it. There might be something that feels familiar about how you did it last time, or you could look for those lights that you described to me. They're still in there.'

'It happened when I began with a form of meditation and pushed the world away from me.'

'And what you probably did was fall out through your sweet spot that you didn't realise you had.'

'Are you saying that when I transformed that metal, I wasn't in my body?'

Fen chuckled. 'Well if you don't know, I certainly don't. All I'm saying is today, let's explore. Close your eyes, look for the trapdoor, Abigail, and then we will go for an adventure.'

I closed my eyes and steadied my mind. I played with the technique that Father Christopher, the priest in Venice, had taught me. This was a technique that had evolved. First, I concentrated my mind, quietened it down, and then I began to step back in my mind as if I was in the centre of an endlessly large, empty room. As I was stepping back, I looked for a glimmer of something unusual, just as Fen had suggested, but there was nothing.

The more I moved around my head, the more frustrating it felt. Instead of pushing the walls away from me, I let them close in on me so that the space around me was tiny rather than huge. Then I leaned against the walls in my mind. It was a strange sensation, like pushing into a dense blackout curtain, but everything seemed to hold.

'Fen, I don't think I'm in the right frame of mind. David and Terry were at each other's throats and it has me all wound up. I can't—'

'Shh, try again,' he said in a severe tone.

Next, I tried to lengthen out the walls bit by bit, like smoothing out wrinkles on fabric. Though I don't have hands in my mind, as soon as I thought about feeling my way rather than seeing it, it felt more natural. Now the sensation was one of silk over skin.

It was the smallest tingle I felt in my fingertips at first, and then a flash, there one moment and gone another. A trill of excitement ran through me and energy started to buzz around my stomach. The flash happened again. At the moment it flashed for the third time, I reached out into the light and the sense of myself began to disappear. It felt as if I was dissolving into the light, fragment by fragment, until I was outside of my body – feeling slightly dazed.

Fen stood by the wood burner, made up of an opaque and shadowy light. When I looked down at myself, I was brighter than he was – more flame-like. Fen pointed at our unconscious bodies still on the sofa. The oddest thing was how silent everything was. It was like I was in a vacuum. I must remember to ask Fen why I couldn't hear anything; the last time I'd had an out-of-body experience, I had been able to hear, but it hadn't felt like this. I felt disconnected from the world, like I was looking in on it.

Fenrear smiled at me and motioned that I follow. He walked through the door without opening it. I stopped – this would take some shift in mindset for me to do. It wasn't the idea of passing through something solid that made me hesitate; it was the passing through wood specifically that made me feel strange. The idea of going into or through wood was about as appealing to me as jumping into icy sea water.

Gritting my teeth, I propelled myself through it and into Fen's pale opaque light. I felt nothing worse than a cool sensation run through me, like tasting spearmint. Fen raised an eyebrow, probably at my expression.

We walked into the hallway and stopped at the very next door we came to. He moved through it and I followed, finding myself in Robert's study. He was lying stretched out on an old Chesterfield sofa, gazing out of the window beyond his feet. On his lap a sketchbook was balanced. Remi lay by the side of the sofa and Robert's hand rested on the dog's back. Remi looked up as we entered.

Fen walked along the painted bookshelves which ran along one side of the room, and I moved across to Robert and looked down at what he was drawing. In fact, the page was blank. I knelt down on the floor and looked up at his face. His expression was sad. He didn't seem to sense me the way I had sensed him when we were in the pub, but suddenly the pencil in his finger twitched, and he lifted it to the page and began to draw.

I was expecting him to draw some abstract outline, one that would come together as a futuristic building. Instead, he drew a face, beginning with the shape of the eyes and the swell of lips. His pencil moved faster and the image became more definite as the seconds ticked by, and it wasn't long before I could see that I was coming alive on the page in front of him.

Fen walked across and peered over my shoulder. I glanced up to see Fen with his eyebrows raised. An uncomfortable ripple of embarrassment shimmied through me. Fen beckoned me to follow him, but really, I wanted to stay. To sit by Robert's side and just watch him draw me. Every detail of my face was there – how was he able to remember it so clearly?

Fen walked off through the door, forcing me to follow. He walked up the spiral staircase, turning off on to the first landing and into Savannah's room. She was dressed in only a bra and panties, and lay on the bed, talking to someone on her mobile phone.

Her body was gorgeous – lean, long and toned like a fit racehorse. Her skin had a healthy hint of colour, but not too much. I turned to look at Fen, whose gaze seemed to be stuck on her backside. This was surely nothing more than perving on a grand scale. Fen seemed to be noting every dimple and freckle of her skin. I felt uncomfortable and was about to turn and leave the room, but Fen wagged a finger and moved even closer to Savannah. I thought he was about to look down her cleavage, but actually he was looking down at her phone.

Following his lead, I looked down to see the name Brandon on the screen. As soon as I'd taken note, Fen seemed satisfied and moved off towards the door. I followed, feeling uncertain about what Fen was trying to teach me.

We walked back downstairs and across the hall, returning to the sofa room we'd started out in, and I discovered that, for me, re-entering my body was much easier than getting out of it.

Fen sat up with an expectant expression. 'So, good lesson?'

I stretched; my body felt heavy and head a little achy. 'I don't think spying on people is a particularly admirable skill to have.'

'Then you completely missed the point of the exercise, so it's a good job I'm here to clarify it for you. We were gathering information. One of the main uses of an out-of-body state is an ability to gather information about people without them realising it. These bits of information can save your life. Practise being observant, and yes, that might seem nosy, but it also empowers you and enables you to be one step ahead of your enemy.'

'But these people are on our side.'

Fen got up and took a deep breath, rolling his neck forward and side to side. I felt a prickle of anxiety: what did he know that I didn't? Why was he hesitating?

'Of course they are, dear, but if you are taken again, they will be your enemy. Why do countries spend vast budgets gathering intelligence on each other? It's because it's damn useful.'

'The last time I did this, I could hear, and also my body wasn't asleep when I left it like it was today.'

'Okay.' Fen nodded slowly. 'Let's take a look at what we learned on our brief walkabout. First, Savannah has a sexy body, tick, but my imagination had already told me that, so, not useful. However, who was she on the phone to? Someone called Brandon. If she were working against you, it may be useful to know who Brandon is. Some connection may come to light which helps you establish a vital connection. Now Robert is an interesting fellow.'

I sat up and folded my legs, squirming in my seat slightly.

'Have you Googled Robert?'

'No. I told you that before.'

'Well, you should have by now. You've had plenty of time. I call it idiocy on a grand scale to go traipsing off into the wilds of Scotland with some man you know nothing about.'

I knew it was idiocy – you know you are in a bad place when idiocy seems to be your only option.

I pursed my lips. 'Yes and no. I thought it was unlikely I'd find anything out about his true character, and I had a character reference from Terry.'

Fen grunted. 'You should always do your homework.'

I lay back against the cushions and stared at the ceiling. This was feeling a lot like a session with Savannah, but Fen had more emotional awareness. He laid his head back on the cushion next to mine and stared at the same spot that my eyes were drawn to on the ceiling.

'Sorry to nag you, but just pick up your phone and do some noodling.'

I pulled my phone out of my pocket and typed in Robert's name. The screen came up with dozens of entries and interviews about his work. Fen leaned over and tapped the images tab. Hundreds of images of Robert whooshed up on the screen, nearly all with very attractive girls at celebrity events. I felt an instant aversion to looking at them.

'Quite a popular man, wouldn't you say?' Fen said, leaning in and scrolling down for me as my hand stilled.

'Do I need to know this?' Looking at Robert with his arm around a ream of beautiful women felt like needles under my skin. I grimaced.

Fen put a calming hand on my wrist. 'I'm saying the public Robert seems to have a very different identity to the man we see here. You saw the shelves in his personal study?'

I hadn't been looking. I shrugged. Fen shook his head.

'If you'd been paying attention, you would have seen that there were no photographs of any of these girls, anywhere. Then he began to draw you. I'm not going to comment on the havoc that that little bit of dynamite could cause, but what was interesting was your reaction.'

'I didn't react, particularly.'

'Ah, but you did. Your lights surged as you realised what he was drawing.'

'No, they didn't. Don't tease me, Fen.'

'I can assure you, they did. I won't speculate on what that means on a personal level, but for our lesson's purposes, it means your power is variable. You are able to be turned up and turned down. Now that is interesting for lots of reasons. It seems that your emotions power your gift, and I'd like to bet that this is the key to developing your power further. I'm very envious, by the way. The idea that your power can be extended is a tempting one.'

'Can't yours?'

Fen shook his head. 'The fact I have more than one gift is rare, but I don't have range within those abilities and I can't say I can think of many of us that do. Robert can't project slightly. He either does it or not.'

'But I can't project slightly, either.'

'But your power varied, and you say last time you had hearing, this time not. It seems likely to me that this will be an interesting area to dabble in – see what more we can get you to do.'

'But aren't they just different components of the one ability?'

'Maybe, but if you can use them independently of each other, then we count them as individual gifts.'

'Thanks, Fen. That was a good lesson,' I said, feeling a

bud of hope sprout inside me. 'I've actually done something. It was a good step forward.'

I looked down at my hands as Fen got up.

'Try not to make assumptions about your gifts, or people. It can lead you astray.'

'I should just have time for a coffee before getting a pummelling by Savannah.' I took in a deep breath and sighed at the prospect. Fen smiled.

'Oo, you're so lucky. Let's swap.'

We stood up and left the room together. I felt a flurry of gratefulness towards Fen.

'So Savannah is your type, huh?'

'Darling, I lean towards beauty in all things, but I'm not fussy if I fall in love with a print or a sculpture. I feel the same about people – it's about the person. I'm very evolved. I believe it will be the way of the future.'

He escorted me towards the kitchen, passing Robert's study door again. Fen paused.

'I know it's none of my business, but I think your future is in there.'

16

———

## ABIGAIL

The days slipped into a pattern over the following week. Some days I hardly saw Robert. He even stopped eating with us – that was probably because the atmosphere between him and David had reached arctic frigidity. I tried not to be disappointed that he showed so little interest in my progress. He seemed to have slipped on his promise to help me engage with my gift entirely.

On the one occasion I did run into him outside his study, I tackled him directly about whether he intended on ever doing any work with me. He rested his wary eyes on me and replied, 'There's no need to rush, Abigail,' and retreated back into his study.

The mornings weren't too bad. I worked with Fen and felt myself gaining ground each day with the astral projection. Now that I could do it to some extent, I was impatient to move on. I only had eyes for the next stage which would bring me back to my beloved bronze, but Fen wouldn't entertain any skipping over elements of his programme.

We were working on being able to travel greater

distances from my body. The further I went, the more effort and concentration I required, but the thing that tripped me up every time was my confidence. Learning to be outside myself was similar to learning how to swim. I'd be doing it fine, but as I became aware of how far I was from the side – or in this case, my body – I suddenly questioned how I was doing it. Then it was gone; I'd lost it and sank back into my head and found myself on the sofa again. I was able to do it if Fen was with me, but not alone. So far, I'd managed it as far as the lake outside, but only once.

Fen tried to reassure me when I became disheartened, but he didn't know the half of what was going on in my head. My biggest struggle was believing this unbelievable thing could be done. I couldn't figure out why I couldn't get past this barrier – I'd seen enough proof by now. I suspected that my doubts on top of a bushel of underlying fears, added with Fen's palpable expectation that I might be the answer to all his prayers, made for an insurmountable hurdle.

I began calling home around midday seeking some childish comfort before my afternoons with Savannah, when I knew I was going to get my arse kicked. I kept the details of my day to a carefully selected few. Mum hadn't understood why I'd wanted to go and stay with a friend of Terry's in Scotland in the first place. My explanation of needing a change hadn't satisfied her, but since Terry and David had joined us, she'd relaxed – seeing it more as a holiday. I told her that Robert's assistant was teaching me self-defence and how tough I was finding it. My mum, an Irish Catholic, had a habit of tacking moral lessons on to every life challenge, and would always leave me with some choice platitude such as, 'For anything worth having, one must pay the price.' Afternoons with Savannah certainly seemed to give me ample opportunities to pay up.

I tried to start Savannah's sessions in a positive frame of mind, but it was hard when she flitted into the gym looking bright-eyed and invigorated from the walk she'd just enjoyed with David. Savannah, who may have been an excellent martial artist and bodyguard, had no teaching experience and was sarcastic and short-tempered with me continually. In some respects, I could see why. My progress was snail-like.

She had three exercises she particularly wanted me to nail: the knee crack, the nose splinter and the throat hack. Each day, we began by breaking these moves down and going over the constituent parts, and then trying to bring the components together. If Terry wasn't getting so much out of the sessions, I'd have been inclined to call time on the whole thing. It was clear that it was an exercise in futility for both Savannah and me, but the amount of work he was producing was prolific. I hoped that he might have ruminated on my suggestion about focusing on his creativity rather than his revenge plan. The way he lost himself in his work, I hoped, was a good sign and might just work some magic, making him let go of what he wanted me to do.

He got most out of the sessions when Savannah was hard on me because it piqued his creative interest. He sometimes guided Savannah in the structure of the lesson, suggesting new moves or ways she could teach me. But despite my hope that he would occasionally intervene when she went too far, that was exactly the point at which he was lost to me completely. It was then that he became entirely absorbed in his sketches, capturing the drama: the arc of an arm or the sag of my body when a blow met its target.

He worked up his drawings on to canvas in the late afternoons when I was usually soaking myself in Epsom salts. Before dinner, the routine was that we all convened to admire his progress. Savannah always looked like a super-hero fighting against me, the unworthy antagonist. His art was eloquent; it said everything about the pain I'd been in at that moment, but with a lyricism that I'd certainly been unaware of at the time. The adrenaline had dropped off by the time I saw the paintings, and by evening, I was feeling pretty low. It was hard to admire the energy and violence conjured by Terry's paintbrush and be as enthusiastic as everyone else when I could hardly breathe out because my ribs were so sore, or see straight because my eye still wouldn't stop watering. I just wished he'd had his artistic epiphany watching David play the saxophone rather than while I was having the daylights beaten out of me. Fen was already on the phone night and day, it seemed, talking to his stable of hungry art collectors.

The most difficult part of all for me was that I hadn't let myself touch the handrail since the day of David and Terry's argument. This may sound like a small thing, but it was as much of a torment as my psoriasis. The longer I refrained from handling it, the more strongly I felt its presence. At first, I just felt a bit jittery, but now it was like the handrail had developed its own body and was following me around the house, whispering 'Choose me' all the time. I was beginning to hope for something to change, though even as I let this thought drift through my head, I could hear my mother warning me against such fate-tempting.

After a taxing morning session with Fen, in which we'd been trying to dial the strength of my projection up and down, I found I had some time to hang out with David before Savannah's lesson was due to start. I texted him, and for once he wasn't out exploring with Savannah, so I made us both a cappuccino from Robert's amazingly cool coffee machine. I took them upstairs to our room, concentrating hard on not spilling coffee on the beautiful woollen runner in the mid-section of the staircase.

David was playing his guitar. The sound drifted down the staircase and met me on the landing. He was probably tinkering with a new creation. Putting the cups down on the windowsill outside our room, I opened the door so as not to disturb him.

I was confronted with Savannah lying across our bed on her front, her elbows digging into the mattress almost at David's lap with her chin in her hands. Rather than tracksuit bottoms, she was wearing her gym shorts and vest top today, and the way she was lying made her shorts ride up her legs a couple of inches, enough to reveal the crevice of one rather choice butt cheek.

Jealousy jabbed me, almost making me drop the coffee. David broke off and stood up from the bed.

'Hi, sweet, Savannah just dropped by.'

I nodded, a bit mechanically. 'I can see that. Hi, Savannah, I wasn't expecting to see you for at least twenty minutes,' I said, passing David his coffee.

'I just popped in to tell David about Brandon White in Glenkubright, but I got distracted when he played me this divine new tune he's composing. Have you heard it?'

'No, had a busy morning.'

'It's been killing me keeping our local music scene quiet from him, but seeing as David's all LA, I didn't want to take him down there until Brandon was around to do it properly. Brandon was the songwriter and guitarist in a rock band called White Stars, one of the most popular during the noughties.' She laughed, tossing her long blonde hair. 'Glenkubright is actually something special. Brandon's still quite the rock star – has a huge following, but these days he says he's more an artist-entrepreneur, which is understating it somewhat. He's more of a social pioneer.'

So this was the Brandon she'd been speaking to on the day I'd had my first lesson with Fen. I sat down on the edge of the bed and Savannah sat up, crossing her legs as she carried on.

'Glenkubright, the local town, was dead before he bought the pub. He started by getting local musicians to gig there and created a really good buzz around Friday and Saturday nights. Then he invited bigger talent to the town, and more people began to come from far and wide to see them. But he saw people couldn't drink much, as they had distances to drive home, so he bought up the empty shops and houses around the pub and converted them into what he calls "hubs".

'There are now nineteen hubs to stay in. They are super-cheap to book, plus there are rooms for artists to exhibit in and social spaces for recitals, theatre and music groups, a library space, and loads more. Every so often, Brandon brings a big-name band in to play on the green outside the church and gets artists to decorate everything with installations around the streets. His slogan is, "Art is the answer".'

'Sounds like a fantastic guy,' said David, looking excited.

'I took the liberty of telling Brandon you were in town and he really wants you to come down tonight and play. Will you come?'

I knew the answer to that. David couldn't resist playing to an audience, no matter how small.

'That would be great. Thank you so much, Sav,' he said, giving her a peck on the cheek.

'Shows you what you can do with art – there's power in it.' She laughed, and her face softened. For a second, even I saw the ice-queen façade slip. 'I go down to Brandon's pub most nights when he's here. You're always welcome to join me. I love the community and the music.'

Jealousy clawed at me again. I could see it now: David would be down there every night from now on, with Savannah, if this Brandon was half as terrific as he sounded.

Savannah hopped off the bed. 'Okay, is it just you and me tonight, or are we all going?' she said, her voice alight with excitement. Nothing in the world could sound less appealing to me, but I was damned if I was going to let my boyfriend out alone with her.

'Of course, we'll all go,' I said. 'Sounds like a great night out!'

'Okay, see you in ten minutes for our session, Abi. Don't be late,' she said, sliding out of the room. I had to exert an enormous amount of control to stop myself putting two fingers up as she closed the door.

David bounded across and picked me up off the floor. He spun around and squeezed me to him, burying his face in my stomach and nuzzling my vest-top up, kissing my midriff. Putting me down, he swept spare tendrils of hair away from my face, and I stared up into his gorgeous eyes.

'It's great about this Brandon guy, isn't it? I was awake last night, thinking whether I might go raving mad here.'

I'd been focusing on how tough the days were for me, so I hadn't given much thought to how hard it must be for David. He always seemed so upbeat – he jogged every day and did what seemed like endless press-ups and hand-stands; wrote music; laughed a lot with Savannah and Fen. He'd even made peace with Terry, though the fact that Terry hadn't admitted his real plan to David meant there was a nuclear-level family feud on the horizon.

'This place really isn't my scene at all – too many rolling

hills and sheep. I checked my Starbucks app – it's something insane like sixty miles to the closest one!'

I smiled at him and stroked his short hair. 'You've changed so much since you've been in LA,' I said, running my hands over the curves of his arms. 'You look great, you know. LA agrees with you – must be all the healthy food and sunshine.'

'It could agree with you too, if you let it.' He caught my frown. 'But I think you've undergone a number of changes, too. Never let it be said that I am not a thorough man. I consider a further inspection is essential,' he said, carrying me across to the en suite bathroom.

'I can't! I have a session with Savannah, like, now.'

'Send her to me to sort out,' he said, closing the door.

I was sure she'd like that!

17

## ROBERT

When Sav proposed the idea of me going, I'd flatly refused.

'What? You don't fancy being in a roomful of people all admiring and clapping for David? I can't believe it!' She laughed and shook her head. 'You know where we'll be if you change your mind.'

It was the last place on earth I wanted to be, but as the afternoon wore on, I began to feel a shift coming on, and by late afternoon I'd decided to go. Over the last week, I'd focused on the Berlin project as much as I could and spent no time at all with Abigail. I'd decided to give myself this bit of distance to let my thoughts regroup, but where I thought a bit of time would toughen me up and dampen my desire for her, instead, the opposite was happening.

It was a new experience for me. I couldn't stop thinking of her. With some women I'd dated in the past, the sex had been so good, I'd thought about it the following day. But that had just been flashes of distraction. Not like this. It was closer to thirst: a basic need bordering on uncomfortable and impossible to ignore, however much I wanted to.

I arrived at the whitewashed pub in Glenkubright, and the buzz of excited people and music met me at the door. There was a band already on stage and the female vocalist was singing classic soul ballads. Her heart-shaped face was framed by a shock of pink hair. The crowd were loving her.

Abigail and David were queuing at the bar. Sav was sitting on the side of the stage as she talked to Brandon. Terry was leaning against a wall with a beer in his hand. He nodded and raised his beer bottle to me.

I'd tackled Terry as soon as I could about his intention to go undercover at The Golden Illuminati HQ. He'd been furious, assuming that I'd tapped his phone, so I'd been forced to tell him about the range of Fenrear's abilities and a little of my own. It was a good job that I'd been able to slap him with my suspicions about him wanting to push Abigail back into the arms of The Golden Illuminati, otherwise I might have had my second knockout of the day. He'd argued and even pleaded with me to consider his viewpoint, trying to convince me of his reasoning. I'd felt the prickle of hypocrisy as I'd pretended to take the moral high ground, knowing that we both harboured the same outcome for Abigail.

'You're in a perfect position to ensure she's safe,' he'd pushed. 'Don't you see? This could be the chink in their armour that you've been looking for.'

If I'd been the slightest bit interested in revenge, he'd have been right, but I wasn't. What had been done to my family was done. I just wanted the jewels back – that was all. Terry's heart was in a better place than mine: his hopes were to dissolve the heinous group that had ruined his wife's life, and those of so many others, whereas mine were purely self-serving.

Sav dived into the crowd and made her way towards me.

David leaned in to whisper something in Abigail's ear. She nodded and they both began to move my way. This was likely to be awkward. David and I had avoided each other as much as possible since our altercation in the kitchen. Small talk was bound to be painful, but thankfully, Sav must have anticipated the situation, which was why she was such an excellent assistant. She arrived at precisely the same moment Abigail and David met me.

David turned his attention immediately to Sav and kissed her cheek. 'I didn't think it was that kind of place,' he said, surveying her outfit of head-to-toe leather.

'I need to go peel down. I came on my bike – leather is safest.'

'Don't peel down – you look divine. You'll have to introduce me to your bike. I have a sweet little sports bike at home, a Yamaha R1.'

Abigail raised her eyebrows at me, clearly not interested in the enthusiastic detail swapping about motorbikes.

'Do you mind if I steal him?' Sav made a pleading face. 'Just for a while. I want him to meet Brandon.'

Sav's golden hair was shiny and poker straight, her make-up was rock-chick, and excitement made her eyes glitter as much as her sparkly eye-shadow. Abigail nodded, and the pair dived into the crowd. My eyes fell on Abigail, who to me looked much more attractive for not covering up her natural beauty with a lot of make-up. We were alone, and I felt my mood surge, but her smile looked tentative.

'Can't say I really feel at ease in a pub after—' her voice was smothered by the crowd bellowing, clapping and whistling at the act on stage.

I leaned in so she could hear me and took in her scent. 'I think you'll be safe enough tonight.'

She had to stand on tiptoes to reply. Her lips were

millimetres from my earlobe, and knowing that was disproportionately arousing.

'But will they be safe with me?' she said, looking around
the crowd. 'Fen told me the guys at the pub were likely to
have been sent by a Collective. Have you heard anything
more from Richard? Did they—' she swallowed and didn't
finish her sentence.

'Don't worry, they got out fine.' I was aware even as I lied
that it was a red flag. This overwhelming desire to protect
her, even from the truth about herself, could be my
undoing.

'I thought I had problems when only your lot were after
me,' she said, lifting her eyes to the ceiling and shaking
her head.

'Come on, let me get you a drink.'

I led her towards the bar, going around to the side where
there were fewer people, and signalled to the bartender. He
immediately stopped serving his current client and came
over to me to clasp my arm, slap my shoulder and take
my order.

'I'm impressed. Bit of favouritism in action there,'
she said.

'His dad works for me. Known the boy since he was
eight or nine and I helped him with his university fees, so
I'd expect some preference.'

She nodded. 'That's nice.'

'I really like this pub. It's one of the only buildings I've
never wanted to suggest improvements to.'

'Suppose that's an occupational hazard? I can't really
appreciate the space right now – it's too full, too dark, and
the noise overpowers everything for me. I like quiet.'

I laughed, genuinely amused. 'It's music, not noise.'

She smiled and tilted her head back and forth. 'Tomayto, tomahto.'

'A musician boyfriend is a perfect match for you, clearly.'

Her face froze. I put my hand out to touch her forearm.

'Hey, I'm just kidding.'

'I think I'm just tired. Savannah worked me over pretty hard again today as I was late for our session.'

'Let's find a table,' I said. Abigail picked up her gin and tonic and walked across the pub to a corner at the furthest point from the stage. Almost under the eaves, there was an unoccupied wooden table and two chairs. I pulled out a chair for her and she sat down, facing the stage whereas I had my back to it.

A tall man with dark tousled hair, wearing a black shirt took the stage, calling the audience's attention.

'That's Brandon,' I whispered. 'He looks like a rock star, doesn't he? I think Sav and him have a bit of a thing going on.'

'We are supposed to be having a thirty-minute break from the amazing Christina Crowl,' the crowd cheered and clapped, 'but we are fortunate enough to have been joined this evening by a fine musician who is visiting the area and whose music, I believe, many of you may know. I don't think I can allow the opportunity to pass us by, so will you please welcome David Hannon – the songwriter. He's going to play you a few numbers which I'm sure will surprise you.'

The crowd clapped, but not quite as supportively as they had for Christina, and Abigail watched David rise on to the stage with the kind of euphoria on his face that only music gave him.

'Hello, Glenkubright!' The crowd yelled back. 'You have no idea who I am, do you?' There was a collective laugh from the crowd. 'That's okay, I'm a behind-the-scenes kind of guy – I apologise if I'm nowhere near as good as the great performers who usually sing these songs, but they are my songs so you are getting them straight from the horse's mouth.'

He sat down at the piano and positioned the mike, taking a dramatic pause before he began to play the first chords of the song that had been number one across America and the UK for over seven weeks this year. The crowd went wild as his raspy, sultry voice rose and they began to sing the lyrics back to him.

'My God, he's amazing,' I said out loud.

Abigail nodded. 'He is, and apart from the punching-you part, just about the nicest guy you'll ever meet.'

I turned to look at her and took in every millimetre of her face. The music and the crowd were so loud that I had to whisper the question that was fighting to get out right into her ear.

'But do you love him?'

She pulled away, but then had to lean back in as I'd never have heard the reply otherwise.

'That's an unnecessary question.'

'You're very different.'

'Yin and yang create balance.'

'Perhaps.' I sipped my beer and studied her face.

'Don't look at me like that. He's 100% on my side.'

'You didn't answer my question.'

'Because I don't need to.'

She turned her head to the music. David was a wizard enchanting the crowd. We both watched Sav jumping up and down at the front of the stage, completely under his spell. Abigail's smile was one of regret.

'I do wish I loved music the way these people do.'

I took off my leather coat and laid it across my knee, putting my keys and phone on the table. Abigail picked up a little figurine on my keys. In the alcove's shadows, she looked so beautiful, her dark hair and eyelashes giving her face even greater contrast.

The small iron figurine of a saint was one I'd collected at a market some time ago. The figure was old and made cheaply in iron. She fingered its surface like a blind person reading Braille.

'What an unusual thing.'

I leaned even closer to her so she could hear me, and as I did, I felt the softness of her skin touch my lip. I fought the urge to kiss her, sitting in this alcove which seemed perfectly made for dark deeds. The angles we were at meant that if she only turned her head by ten degrees, our lips would meet. I took a swig of beer and glanced towards the stage to distract myself. David was singing a slower song now and the audience swayed.

'This wee laddie has been on my keys since my first year at university. I picked him up from a stall at Chapel Street Market in London when I was studying at uni. He's St Anthony, the patron saint of lost souls.'

She rolled the little iron figure over and over in her hands. Although she was facing the stage, her eyes seemed to be seeing something much further away than David.

'Guilt upon my conscience like rust upon my soul,' she said.

'What?' I looked at her and my heart picked up the pace of its beat.

'Guilt upon my conscience like rust upon my soul,' she repeated. 'Does that mean anything to you?'

I shook my head. 'Naw.' My mouth felt dry.

She continued rolling the figurine back and forward between the palms of her hands. 'Must be a saying I've heard at some time or other.' There was something in the way she studied me that made me feel she knew I was lying.

I took a long drink of my beer. 'How are the sessions with Fen going?'

She shrugged. 'I've managed to project successfully, but it all keeps cutting out, and I'm so desperate to get past this first stage.' She looked down, and I watched embarrassment enter her face.

'What?' I was intrigued.

She swallowed and turned the figurine in her fingers again. 'Projecting is a bit like sex. It's fun and gives you an enormous high temporarily, but I'm longing for the profundity of what comes after – the baby.'

This time it was my turn to blush, which was completely ridiculous given we were both adults, but all I could think about was the sex part with her and I felt like my thinking was exposed. I felt my mood slump a little. She'd made progress – already. I'd started to daydream that it might take many months – that we'd be together for many months.

'Cutting out is just your confidence dropping. Projecting at all is huge progress for a beginner. He must be a good teacher.'

'Why don't you teach me? That's why I came here, after all, because you promised to help me.'

I rubbed my forehead with my fingertips, trying to marshal an excuse. 'I'm busy,' I said. It sounded completely pathetic. 'Fen has been around a lot longer than me and has wider skills than I have; he will be able to teach you more.'

'I'd rather it was you.' She bit her lip. Perhaps she hadn't meant to say that thought out loud.

For a moment, something pulsed between us both. I moved my hand closer to hers on the table, just enough for our fingertips to touch. Her expression was so serious, her eyes hypnotising. I summoned some energy into my fingertips. It was the subtlest tingle. I didn't want to frighten her. As I let it go, it ran down my fingers and out to her own. A second later, I sent another one.

She stiffened.

'You feel that, don't you?'

She nodded once. I sent the ripple again, slightly stronger this time so that it might roam further, up to her wrist and along her forearm.

'Send it back to me,' I told her.

She shook her head. 'I don't know how to. How do I push a sensation?'

'Try using your mind rather than your body. Tell it to go home.' I sent another pulse.

'It's disobedient,' she said, a smile curving on her lips.

I moved my hand and placed it on top of hers. She didn't move. Her hand was soft and warm. I wanted to stroke the length of it, but I controlled that impulse.

'Look at me, Abigail,' and she lifted her eyes. A prickling like pins and needles started in my fingertips; I allowed the sensation to swell. 'It will be stronger this time. Send it back to me when it feels strongest.'

I let it go. She tensed as soon as she felt it. Being properly in contact with her, I could feel it when it reached her forearm and the sensation peaked. The unexpected intensity of it made her breath catch in her throat, then it was gone.

'Concentrate. You let it escape.'

I sent the impulse again. I felt it travel into her and shoot up her forearm.

'Damn!' She shook her head in frustration as it got away again.

The third time she was ready for it. I felt her block it just past her wrist and send it back in my direction. I returned the sensation, stronger this time, and she responded. I wondered if she could feel how hard it was for me to hold my power back. I was desperate to let it go. I wanted to share the power in me with her, allow it to wash over her.

'Abigail, Abigail!' David's voice made us both start. The place where I was in my own head made the interruption painful. Abigail pulled her hand away.

The venomous look on David's face made me jump up from my seat. There was no way I was going to let him hit me unawares for the second time.

Abigail stood up too and pushed David back. 'The music was awesome,' she said.

'What were you doing?'

'I was showing Abigail how to control the energy within her. That is why she's staying with me after all, to learn.' My voice was very controlled. Those who worked for me knew that was when they were in most danger.

'Not a very appropriate time.'

There was a vein standing out on David's forehead, and I couldn't help taking some pleasure in tormenting him further. 'It's hard to describe to someone how to exchange energy the first time. It's much easier to show them. It's an exercise, like throwing and catching a ball. It helps ignition and control.'

'Knowing Abigail a lot better than you do, I'm sure she is more than capable of igniting herself.'

'It just seemed like a good opportunity,' Abigail put in, but her expression said she regretted it instantly.

'I'm sure it was a perfect opportunity – together in the dark,' David barked.

I folded my arms. David turned away and walked towards the bar. Abigail threw an apologetic glance my way and set off after him.

**18**

———

**ABIGAIL**

I was expecting David to be prickly with me the next morning. The pub wasn't the place to have a row and he'd been aloof with me the rest of the night, so when Terry offered to take me home early, I'd gone. We'd missed each other in the morning, too, as I had a session with Fen, and David had been sleeping off his late night. Then he'd texted me to say he'd gone to have a late breakfast in town with Brandon, who was going to show him around.

I'd been hoping we'd manage a walk between my sessions to iron things out, but I couldn't have been more grateful to avoid it. I would have to lie to his face to reassure him there was nothing between me and Robert. The attraction kindling between us had the potential to be a roaring inferno, though we were both suppressing it. When he'd sent those pulses through my fingers last night, I'd felt all manner of sensations that I certainly shouldn't feel for any other man than David. He'd stirred me up so completely and with only the most minor contact.

Fen and I were in the kitchen around 5pm, after my usual

afternoon session with Savannah. He was showing me some images of a new artist he was interested in. David swept into the kitchen, dropped his keys on the stone island and collapsed on to a stool. He'd had his hair cut super-short, leaving only a little hair along his jawline. It suited him, making his look all about his grey-green eyes. He smiled at us both. I couldn't even respond with my own smile because I was so surprised to see him looking this happy and energised. In my head, I'd been building up his hurt about last night. The need for us to talk had become inflated as every hour passed. Looking at him, I realised it was distinctly possible that there wouldn't be any necessity for a fight.

'I've had a great day! Glenkubright is the coolest place. Brandon knows everyone and even their dogs' names.' He shook his head. 'You need to see what he's done there to believe it. He's sewn art into every crevice of the town. He's teamed up every street with an artist, encouraging them to use the streets as their gallery, so the town has tonnes of murals, even on the lampposts. They have the world's first keyhole artist who designs a unique keyhole for your door. He was an out-of-work blacksmith, but now makes one-of-a-kind door-knockers and keyholes. People are coming to the town just to see the weird and wonderful streets. If you walk down any road, it's like a visit to Tate Modern.

'Of course, the more people who visit for gigs or to see the art, the more coffee shops, restaurants and gift shops they need – now Glenkubright's high street is full of successful businesses, and artist/craftsmen from all over Scotland are moving to the area. Oh, by the way, he's got some guy coming into town tonight he thinks I should meet. Do you mind if I go?' he asked, looking at me.

My heart swelled. I would have agreed to just about

anything to be forgiven. The guilt I'd been holding on to evaporated.

'Not at all! That sounds great.' I sent up grateful thoughts to Brandon for getting me off the hook.

'Do you wanna come?' he asked, picking up the keys to fiddle with them.

My mind whirred while I thought how I should answer this diplomatically. It was about the last thing I wanted to do.

'I'm pretty tired, but if you want the company, then—'

I saw something pass across his face – relief or disappointment? Why were people so much harder to read than metals? I knew exactly where I was with metal.

Savannah appeared as silently as a phantom from the hallway. She put her fingers up to her mouth and then sprang forward, giving David a sudden push off his seat which made him almost fall over in shock. The stool clattered to the ground. She laughed at his reaction.

'Looks like you need to work on your awareness, David.'

'I knew you were there the whole time,' he said, picking up the stool.

'Oo, like the hair – very tough guy.'

She raised one hand up and stroked David's hair just above his ear. My jaw dropped open, but it was Fen who coughed for me, reminding Savannah that we were there. She pulled out her phone and leaned into David, showing him the screen.

'Brandon just texted me to invite me to dinner with Nathan Martin and you tonight. Do you wanna ride with me on the Ducati?' She hopped up on to the island so that she was facing David and completely blocking my view of him with her back.

'Nice,' said David.

I felt a lick of jealousy roll across my stomach. 'I'm sure Terry won't mind if you take the car. Motorbikes scare me, especially in the dark. People drive too fast on country lanes,' I said.

'Huh?' said Savannah, turning around to look at me. 'Something else you're scared of.'

I gave her a stare which I hoped was eloquent. Bitch!

She turned back to David. 'You need to impress this guy, Nathan Martin. He's a music director, got a dozen bands – definitely someone you should know. If there's an opportunity, you should play him that song you played for me yesterday.'

David shook his head. 'I hate being pushy about my music. It's not really my way.'

'There's nothing pushy about it if the situation presents itself. Just be on the lookout for it, is all. Don't worry – I'll be there to help and maybe even to open the door to the opportunity,' she said, putting a hand on his shoulder and using it for support as she hopped down. 'Any-hoo, I'm going to get ready, so I'll meet you down here at 6.30pm?' She patted David's shoulder as she turned towards the door.

I didn't know what needled me the most: her sage advice or the constant touching of David. To add insult to injury, an hour later, I had to watch her descend from her room looking even more sexy and happy than she had the previous night. She'd parked her Ducati outside and I was forced to wave them off as they sailed down the drive together, him on the back of her bike as passenger, nestled up behind her long leather-clad body. I wore a fixed smile, but my overriding inclination was to rip Savannah's head off. Mind you, that wouldn't have been so easy. I could hardly lift my arms, they ached so fiercely after the session I'd had with her that day.

As the two disappeared, I had a fleeting thought – maybe I could project myself to Glenkubright and watch them. I dismissed it immediately. First, it was seriously unlikely that I could manage to do that. Second, why would I do that to myself? Did I really want to see Savannah fawning all over David? No, but the desire to do it remained strong.

Fen was leaning against the back door as I turned in.

'You are quite a talented actress. That was definitely a passable impression of someone being happy that their boyfriend is being driven off by a motorbiking siren.'

I walked over to Fen and slumped against him, burying my head in his chest, and he put his arm around me and leaned his head down on top of mine.

'Oh dear,' he whispered, sympathetically. 'You two are such a tangle.'

'He's good for me in so many ways.'

Fen nodded, looking thoughtful. 'That's true, but could you ever love anyone else?'

Robert's face flashed into my mind, and at the same instant, I felt Fen's intrusion in my head. Some natural reflex took over in me. I felt a kind of kick, and the next instant he was gone.

'Fen! Don't do that!'

He looked at me with a penitent grin. 'Sorry. It's just so nice to know you're right sometimes. It's not enough to guess. Nice reflexes, by the way – that was sharp work.'

'How can people not feel you? It's like having an elephant tread on your brain.'

'Now, now. I'm not sure an elephant is fair. You're a more sensitive case than most. I'll have to tread more carefully in the future.'

'You will not tread at all, thank you very much! What happened to gaining my trust?'

He shrugged and pursed his lips. 'What can I say? I am a flawed character.'

I couldn't afford to relax around him. It was just too easy to forget what was natural for him to do.

My eyes felt itchy with fatigue and my body sluggish. I needed rest.

'I'm off to bed,' I said, not bothering to mute the grumpiness I felt.

As I trudged upstairs, pressing my left-hand side hard against the wall so as not to be drawn across to the handrail which was cooing for me, Fen's unsubtle intrusion bothered me. Savannah's rigorous workouts were nothing compared to how exhausting it was to have to keep my guard up all the time, even around my so-called friends. Everyone had their own agenda here, and they would press their advantage if they had the slightest opportunity.

Putting all thoughts of David and Savannah out of my head, I fell asleep almost immediately.

WHEN I WOKE JUST before 1am and turned over, I realised that David was still not back. That's when my mind fired up, and its path was a fruitless one. Scenes of David making love to Savannah in every possible way made sleep a place I could sense, but not draw near.

I began by projecting myself out and simply exploring the house to see if they were here somewhere, but they weren't. I decided to try making it to the other side of the lake, just to see if I could, though I'd only managed it once so far in my sessions with Fen. That wasn't too hard, so then I moved on towards the gate.

Without warning, my projection failed, and I found myself back in bed. My head gave a throb, but I was undeterred. Within seconds, I was back at the lake, and this time I made it through to the gate, moving over the ground faster than I ever could have done on foot. We'd turned right to Glenkubright last night within a few yards of being outside the gate.

Again, without warning, I found myself back in bed. How frustrating was this? The only good thing was that I seemed to be able to get back to the point I'd previously been at more quickly than I had the first time.

The journey limped along in this disjointed way – road, bed, road, bed – all the way until I hit the small town and paused outside the pub on the dark street. Rangy trees were spread around the churchyard and lights were festooned between their branches, giving the space a welcoming glow. I looked up at the church spire, lit by the garlands of lights, in wonder. This way of moving was incredible. If I wanted to, I could walk through the church walls and move up to the top of the steeple. Then my power failed, and I was back in bed.

I was back at the church again in a few minutes. There were still a few people around the streets and sitting on the benches in the churchyard. It was like watching a silent film. I could see their mouths move, chatter spilling from their lips, spirits fuelled perhaps by what they'd been listening to in the pub and their energy effervescing, but the silence was complete.

With a little pit-stop back to my bed in between, I made it inside the pub, passing Savannah's bike on the pavement. Inside, the pub was bright and the staff were busy cleaning down tables and shifting glasses over to the bar. With the lights on full, the pub had a completely different vibe to last night.

Brandon, Savannah, David and another man stood at the bar, and Brandon had a line of shot glasses laid out. I watched him spin the bottle of tequila he held in his hand expertly like a juggler and fill the glasses, one after the other, in a continuous run. Then my mind glitched out and I was back in bed.

This time I actually yelled in frustration and slammed my feet up and down on the mattress, but I started the journey over again and was there in time to see their sour expressions from licking the salt and biting down on limes. Savannah caught hold of David's arm, laughter cascading from her mouth, and she staggered against him. David held her up. Brandon leaned into David and made some comment in his ear which made David laugh, too. I moved positions, and as I did, Savanah flicked her long golden hair which disappeared all the way through my lights. The sensation was odd, like static, and it propelled me back to my bed.

Returning, I could see Savannah's eyes were crossing slightly. She was supposed to be driving them home! I hoped there was a taxi firm in the area. It would be ironic if they called me to ask for a lift home and I was with them as they did. Brandon and the man with him were certainly a few drinks south of sober, too, and I wondered how many shots they'd had. I wasn't sure about David. He held his drink well, but his eyes were glittering. I looked into his handsome, open face and my heart felt heavy. Fen was right: David and I were such a tangle.

Brandon was looking a little dishevelled, but otherwise every bit the rock and roll man. Wearing a black T-shirt, jeans and blue trilby, he was talking and walking towards the piano with the bottle of tequila in his right hand. He hopped up the stairs and sat down at the old wooden upright which was at the side of the stage. He put his hands together and pressed down on the keys. The chords he played must have been recognisable because Savannah responded immediately and followed him, singing to his tune, seeming entirely uninhibited.

It felt like I'd swallowed a stone. She could sing too? She looked so relaxed, and though that could have been the alcohol, I'd seen David come alive like that before, just from people's attention. Completely unlike me.

Brandon continued to play and began to sing, too. Savannah's confidence was sexy beyond measure, and I could imagine the type of raspy, soulful voice that she probably had, based on her natural tone. A couple of the staff lifted their heads from their tasks to watch her.

I looked at David and his face made my heart tear. For an instant, he was spellbound. The other guy, Nathan, picked up their shot glasses and walked across the floor and up on to the stage, too. He lined the glasses up on the top of the piano, took Brandon's bottle and poured them each another shot. Brandon swept his hand down the length of the piano in conclusion to the song, then stood. They all grasped their glasses and knocked back another shot.

Savannah touched Nathan's arm and inclined her head towards David. The three of them by the piano looked at David, and then there was an exchange of calling, with David shaking his head and waving them down. Savannah beckoned him, and Brandon nodded and welcomed David into the piano seat.

David moved round to the piano, tapping the fingertips of one hand against his side as he walked. Savannah had given him the perfect opportunity to play his new song. I hoped he wasn't too drunk to do it justice. Sax was his favourite instrument, but piano had been luckier for him.

When he began to play, Brandon, Savannah and Nathan all went still. They just listened as David sang too, and although I couldn't hear it, I knew why. People always did this when David played. They stilled and went on a journey in the landscape of their minds, and I always felt separate from it, as though I was on the outside of the experience instead of within it. And it was then I realised with crystal clarity that Savannah's rampant flirting wasn't our real problem.

For him it was music, for me it was metals. We were born out of diverse cultures, and I would never get his world; never be able to participate in it and share his love for it; and he would spend his life struggling with why I had my strange relationship with metal. He could no more enter my world than I could his, and all the Savannahs and Roberts didn't mean a thing.

When David finished, there was a pause before they all clapped him. He stood up and Nathan leaned over the piano and slapped him on the shoulder, then Nathan walked round to the other side and leaned against the instrument as they began to chat. Savannah winked at Brandon and they moved away, giving the others some space by sitting on the edge of the stage together. They chatted and laughed until Savannah looked at the time on her phone, stretched her hands upwards and shook her head. Brandon clearly didn't like what he was hearing and was making gestures that firmly said no. Savannah shrugged as she hopped off the stage. Her ankle gave way and she staggered, laughing uncontrollably and grabbing on to Brandon for support.

Brandon interrupted Nathan and David, pointing at

Savannah. Then Brandon shouted something to his remaining staff and made a farewell gesture. David, Savannah and Nathan followed him as he went for the pub's side door. I hoped David wasn't stupid enough to let Brandon drive them home: he looked more drunk than Savannah.

Brandon turned left on to the street and walked to the next house on the block. The houses were stone Victorian terraces with solid bay windows in front and a couple of steps up to the doorway. Brandon walked to the front door, fumbled in his pocket for keys and finally pulled them out, needing to concentrate closely to identify the key he needed.

He opened the door and led them into a hallway. Then an idea, with all the appeal of a rotting fish, made its presence known to me – maybe he was offering them a room for the night. I felt queasy, even though technically my stomach was miles away. I couldn't follow them – even the idea made me sweat. David managed to close the door on me as I stood on the threshold, which took me back to my bed instantaneously.

I stared aggressively at the ceiling, then closed my eyes, ready to set forth, but a tiny thought needled its way in just before I took flight.

What more do you want to see?

The part of my heart that held David fluttered in protest at my pause, but I forced my eyes open and glared at the ceiling again. My head gave an almighty throb. Paracetamol. I needed to see paracetamol.

**19**

---

## ROBERT

Every so often, I thought I could hear someone moving across the floor in the room above me. I looked at the time – it was close to 2am. I sat up to be sure. I wasn't completely certain because the wind was shrieking around the outside of the house. Even if thoughts of Abigail didn't keep me awake, that would.

The room above mine was the Gallery – Savannah had the code, but she preferred Netflix to art. No-one else should have the lift code to take them to that room.

Silence. I rolled on to my side and tried to empty my head, but even though I managed to ban her face, I could feel Abigail's presence in the shadows of my mind. Loneliness was piling in. Usually when it joined me, I made short work of it – went to an event and took home someone I had no intention of seeing again. It was a sticking plaster on a gushing wound, but better than nothing. Tonight, the idea of someone other than Abigail being in my bed made me feel more desperate.

Philip had rung again today, 'Just for a little update'. I resented the intrusion so much that I was barely able to be civil with him. I knew my truculent behaviour couldn't be reassuring him, but the bastard seemed to have a sixth sense for knowing when I was feeling most conflicted.

The footsteps started again. I got up and put my dressing gown on. I'd created an open plan penthouse space on the top floor of the house, where from the outside, the clear glass turned into the decorative stained glass, and I'd located the lift specifically so that it connected to my room. An innocent looking door on the far side of my room hid the entrance to the lift. I tapped in the pin code.

As I neared the top floor, I started feeling annoyed. It must be Fen. I'd shown him the paintings the other day with Terry, but he'd been so desperate to photograph everything, and I wouldn't let him. Was there nowhere safe from that man invading my privacy?

As the doors parted, my brain wouldn't compute. Abigail faced me, and embarrassment flooded her expression. She was wearing only a short slip, bed-socks and a loose jumper. Her eyes widened in surprise and she tugged her slip down slightly, though there was nothing more of it to lengthen. My brain kept searching for Fen, even though he was nowhere to be seen.

We stood and gawped at each other.

'I'm sorry, Robert, did I disturb you? I couldn't sleep. Terry told me the code on the drive home from the pub the other night. He said you wouldn't mind if I looked. I realise I should have asked.' She bit her bottom lip.

I felt a flood of relief; a rush of elation. Abigail was here. Not in bed with David. I recognised the ridiculousness of this reaction – that circumstance was only temporary.

'D'ya like my paintings?'

'I like all of them, but I'm most intrigued with this.' She signalled over to a display desk in the centre of the room and stepped towards it. Freezing dread ran along my spine. I sucked in a shallow breath. There was a chance I could side-step this if I just kept my cool. 'Whatever can require such a high-tech case?' She pressed her finger to the digital display in one corner with its humidity readings. 'Why can't I see inside?' Her voice wavered; she wasn't just interested, she sensed there was something telling inside.

'It has light filters on it which keep the glass dark.'

'Is it a manuscript – is the ink fading?'

I swallowed. 'Would you like something to drink?'

She looked at me with suspicious eyes. 'Robert, don't be coy – what's inside the case?'

'Just a map – bought at auction – from HMS *Endeavour*, Captain Cook's ship. I could do with a hot chocolate,' I said, turning away.

She caught my arm. 'I'd like to see it.'

'Every time I look at it, it risks the object. It's incredibly fragile, almost more jelly than paper.'

'Robert?' Her body was very still, except that she continually clenched and unclenched one hand, pushing her nails into the flesh of her palms. 'Show me.'

My eyes were pleading and hers were unyielding. I pressed a code into the digital panel and the glass cleared. Revealed beneath was a gold seal cast with a snake eating its own tail. The words Et *Illuminati Auream* circled the image. Next to the seal was an ear, preserved but black with decay.

She gasped as she realised what it was and stepped back, putting her hand across her mouth. There was tears in her eyes a moment later.

I pressed the code in again and the glass filter obscured it.

'It's part of our initiation gift. We are all given a relic.'

'From an alchemist.' There was no question in her voice.

'I wonder if I'll be lucky enough to have parts of me sitting alongside such great contemporary art in the years to come,' she said with a laugh that was chilling.

I could taste salt in my mouth as I forced myself to shake my head. Her ivory skin had lost its usually warm shade. She turned away, rubbing her hand across her forehead. I caught a glance of the brutally damaged skin on her hands.

'I should go,' she said. 'I need to go.'

I blocked her way. 'Abigail, this shouldn't change anything. It's just an object. I've been honest from the start – you know I'm one of them. This was part of a ceremony and I'm obliged to house it.'

'Hard to be level-headed when you're faced with such a stark reality.' Her expression was taut.

'Please, let me get you a drink. You won't sleep anyway.'

'Why did you lie?'

'Why do you think?'

Her shoulders slumped a little and she nodded. I continued to stare into her eyes as she did mine. I felt a rigid band tightening itself across my chest. Why did it have to be her? The band tightened again as I became very aware that I only had to move my body forward six inches to touch her lips.

I swallowed the thought down. 'Some hot chocolate? I can add brandy if that helps.'

A sort of pained but amused expression spread over her face. 'Well, you better not be considering waking Savannah up to go get us some because I can tell you for certain that she's not home.'

That was why she was up here. David couldn't be home either. I wasn't sure whether to berate Sav tomorrow or give her a bonus.

'I can assure you that I am more than capable of conjuring up hot chocolate without Sav's services.' I inclined my arm and she took a step, then stopped a moment, glancing at me before taking another. 'How's the projecting coming on?' I asked, going for conversation which I hoped would stop her thinking about the ear. Her expression was a little set, but she continued to follow me over to the far side of the room.

'I think I can say I've cracked the distance issue I was having, though not the cutting out.'

I could have kicked myself for asking her about her progress. I didn't want to know. Her answer only gave me pain with the reminder that we were moving closer to a day that I was beginning to dread.

At the far side of the room, there was a bank of panelled units. I pressed one of the panels, felt the spring release. It revealed a half-dozen tall, slender white porcelain cups. As I was about to lift one out, she put a hand out and clenched my arm.

'Wait – what are they?'

Leaning into me and standing up on the balls of her feet, she pushed the porcelain cups aside and reached for two heavy-bottomed and inelegantly crafted earthenware cups which had been hidden – carthorses among the thoroughbreds. She lifted them both down and stared at them.

'They were my first attempt at throwing cups.'

'You made these? They're terrible!'

I gave a slight laugh. 'Yes, they really are, but they remind me where I started from. I'm a little better with fifteen years under my belt.'

'What I mean is, I like them. They have heart.'

'Does the rest of the house not have heart?' I felt choked at her comment.

'No, I love the house! But, it's faultless. I'm partial to flaws.'

'If you like the cups so much, take a look at this.' I bent down and met her bare legs, which were barring my way. The desire to strum the length of her leg and push the hem of her slip aside to reveal more was so strong that my groin ached. With more control than I've ever had to exert, I stood and placed a hand on her soft waist to move her across slightly. I opened another hidden cupboard and retrieved a teapot which I'd never shown anyone. It only had a vague resemblance to other items of that name. It had a girth with a bulge and a spout that narrowed at some points to such a slender diameter that liquid would struggle to get through.

When she saw it, something lit up in her eyes. I wished I could have known her at a time when fear and worry didn't taint all of her expressions.

'You should put this on display alongside—' the pause was unpleasant as we both thought of the ear in the case, '— alongside the paintings,' she finished.

'I doubt I'll ever master the art, but it gives me ideas for my designs. I have a nice workshop; I'll show you it sometime.'

She nodded and took a deep breath while the coffee machine finished filling the second cup.

'Glad to see that Terry's art is prominently featured, but I was wondering why you've called it The Tamashadzov Gallery?' Then she took a sharp breath. 'That's not something to do with them, too, is it?' She shook her head and her hair swished about her jawline. She tilted her head up to examine my eyes and I felt an urge, as strong as the tug of the tide, pulling me towards her lips. If the machine hadn't beeped at that instant, I'd have definitely crossed a hard line.

Collecting the carthorse cups, I led her over to a bench in the centre of the Gallery, facing one of Terry's paintings: a portrait of Thérèse leaning out of a window, gazing at Venice's lagoon. The benches weren't long, forcing us to sit close.

'It was my grandfather's name: the jeweller I told you about. His family were Russian immigrants. My da' said that he loved puzzles, which is sort of ironic seeing as his life turned out to be one.' I paused. 'Am I allowed to go on?'

She gave a slight drop of her chin.

There was a part of me that knew telling her this story was an unnecessary risk. When I handed her over to The Golden Illuminati, she could tell them everything, but by the time she did, I'd have my jewellery collection back. And if she did, I would have to rely on blagging my way out of any accusations. There was very little chance they would ever connect me to my grandfather because of a twist of fate that had severed our names.

The other part of me wanted her to know the full story so that at some time in the future, she might, at least, understand why I'd betrayed her.

'My grandfather's disappearance decimated his family. My grandmother couldn't sell the family home because no-one knew whether he was dead or not. He was just missing. She had no other income and the staff and creditors in my grandfather's business took his stock in lieu of payment. My grandmother was forced to beg for help from her own family, not far from here, in Scotland. She took secretarial work in Edinburgh, leaving the children with her family.

'After her mother died, she married again, but her new husband wouldn't take the children. She found a home for children whose parents couldn't afford to keep them to take my da' and his sister. It had strict Presbyterian roots, was the type of loveless place which no child should ever have to grow up in. My da's childhood was one of abuse, starvation and poverty, until by a stroke of luck, he and his sister were adopted. He was fourteen, while she was only eleven, and they took on a new family name.

'The adoption was arranged from within the church. It happened a lot in those days – a route around the government system. It's unlikely that it was legally registered, or at least my da' was never able to obtain proof of his adoption, so Edward Tamashadzov, my father, stopped existing in 1963 and became Teddy Kirkpatrick.

'His new family changed his name by deed poll, and the children's home burned down in the 1970s. My da' always said that it must have been payback from one of its residents. There wasn't more than ash left of the place, so if any records were ever kept of the children there, they were lost in the fire. It's unlikely anyone would be able to place him as ever having been there.

'Once he became an adult, his every spare moment was devoted to finding out what had happened to his father and what should have been our inheritance: the jewellery collection. He fixated on the loss to such an extent that he became an alcoholic, and it wasn't long after that he developed pancreatic cancer. Ironically, three months after he was gone, I received my invitation to join The Golden Illuminati, and so the gateway opened to confirm his theories.'

'How did you make it to here with that kind of background?'

'Might have been because of it. I had a good brain and was artistic, so I did well at school and made it to an excellent selective secondary. I spent as much time at school and studying as I could because home wasn't such a great place.

There's no doubt that luck has played a significant part, too – several times.

'Once I helped a man who was in terrible distress because his dog had been run over by some moron who hadn't stopped to help. I took the pair of them to a local vet, stayed with him all day until the dog came through his operation, and got them both home. I checked in with him once or twice after that just to be sure all was well. Six months later, I turned up to my architecture interview at the Bartlett Building at University College, London, and guess who my principal examiner was?'

Abigail's eyes were wide, but the howling uncertainty that had been there not long before was beginning to lessen.

'Or think of the odds of this: I'm invited to a party in Milan and go along because I can't really get out of it. Miriam, my host, insists I go. The house is amazing, really something special. I don't know anyone, so I find a quiet little room, which is a study just off the main hall. There's a large leather ink blotter with paper in it. I sit at the desk and begin to draw. In my head rises the most incredible building, like a series of windsurfers' sails at various heights, as if lifted by an invisible sea. I'd never thought of it before. I'm there for a few hours, adding every tiny detail, then I finish the drawing, find Miriam, and we go home.

'Less than a week later, I get a phone call from Miriam. She asks me the strangest question – did I draw a building on a desk when we went to that party? I confirm I did. Turns out it was Domenico Milliardo's private desk, and he turns out to be the Supreme Head of The Golden Illuminati, and he's looking for an architect to design a tower for his empire in the business district. He wants my building – the one I drew that night.

'I sometimes think that maybe I've been born with my

father's and grandfather's share of luck. Maybe it's just the universe paying its debts.'

'Are you very like your grandfather?'

'From what my da' used to tell me, our abilities are a match. Da' didn't talk about abilities precisely, but instead eccentricities. From Da's description, my grandfather's eccentricities were a lot like my own, plus he was a designer, though his was jewellery, of course.'

She rubbed her eyes and turned to me. 'I need to go back to bed. Let me wash your cup.' Her hand touched my own as she moved to take my cup and, not hesitating, I clasped hers. And though she pulled back slightly, I was unable to let it go. Instead, I held on and pulled her towards me, kissing her with all that I felt in that moment spilling from my heart.

As our lips touched, I felt the band snap in my chest and the elixir of happiness poured out across my torso. It was made more perfect by how unfamiliar it was. Never had I kissed a woman and lost who I was and where I was so utterly. Every ounce of our situation was blasted away by the connection between us. She responded so completely that I was able to slow each caress down, knowing that I had no need to hurry. I was hitting every note like a virtuoso.

A thought of taking her to my room dashed across my brain, but as it did, it was as if she saw the thought too, because I felt the struggle within her. It took a few moments before she was able to pull back.

'I can't, Robert,' she said, breathing deeply.

I couldn't have hidden the look of desolation that I felt very well because she dropped her eyes to the floor and shook her head slightly. She put her hands to my chest and pushed me away as she stood up. I tried to clasp at her hand, but she slipped it.

'Do you know what an alloy is?' she said, and her voice sounded choked.

'What? An alloy?' I fought to grasp what she was talking about.

'It's a mixture of metals.'

I looked at her, confused.

'When I'm with you, I feel like that's what you are – there's two parts to you that are blended, and yet entirely different.' The words pierced me even though it wasn't fair that they should. I wanted her to trust me – to love me. 'Even if I didn't feel this way, it isn't the way I'd want us to start. It might be the way other people do things, but not me.'

I stood up, but she backed away, keeping her hands up. I wanted to pull her into my arms, but her eyes forbade me.

'Abigail, please.'

She kept moving backwards, keeping eye contact, but making her escape. At the door, she glanced over at the display case before slipping out.

I turned on the case, all my desire turning to anger, and had it open even before her footsteps had died away. I grabbed out the golden seal and scooped up the hideously brittle ear. Marching over to one of the windows on the far side of the Gallery, I grappled clumsily with the catch, my hand in a clawed grip as I struggled to keep hold of the seal at the same time. As the window came open, the seal dropped to the floor.

The cool night air made my hot skin sting. I put all my frustration and need into hurling the monstrous relic into the darkness, then I knelt and picked up the golden seal. I was about to send it shooting into the night when either the rowdy highland winds or the ghosts of my ancestors hit me with such force that I staggered back three paces. The fight went out of me and I let my hand, grasping the seal, drop to my side.

I moved back towards the window and lifted my hand, pulling it shut. Turning away, I slipped the seal into my pocket.

**20**

---

## ABIGAIL

David returned to our bed just before 7am. My own late night meant that I had got less sleep than usual, but once David climbed in, I couldn't stay there. My flesh crawled at the thought that his skin might be tainted by the touch of Savannah, and at the same time I was filled with guilt as the feel of Robert's lips on my own was still so fresh in my mind.

Fen swapped his session with Savannah's that morning, so after breakfast, I warmed up with a skipping rope in front of the long mirrors in the gym room. I hadn't been particularly unfit when we'd started our sessions, but I'd never done formal training of this kind before. To my surprise, the rhythmic beat of the skipping rope was just what I needed to steady my mind, which was pitching back and forth between anger and guilt.

Kissing Robert hadn't been some tit-for-tat reaction to David staying out with Savannah, and yet it would probably sound like that if I told David. When I told David. I didn't want to think of him kissing Savannah the way I'd kissed

Robert, but I'd be an idiot not to consider that scenario was both possible and likely.

Besides the kiss, there was a lot more I had to think over that had come out of my night stroll in Robert's gallery. That desiccated ear had very nearly sent me sprinting into the night, angry Collectives out there waiting for me or not. There was also the ramifications of what The Golden Illuminati had done to his family to consider. He presented it to me as him gaining control of his tattered family history, but I could see the pattern of the abused becoming the abuser. He seemed so intense with me, and yet he didn't seem involved in any specific strategy to strike against them. I didn't like Terry's plan of using me to get evidence against them, but at least there was intent there.

The way the house door slammed shut and Savannah's gait as she marched across the courtyard told me she was in a prickly mood. She picked up a rope and started skipping at double my speed. I felt no inclination to try to keep pace with her and the way she twisted her mouth told me that this annoyed her. I finished skipping before her.

'Why are you stopping?' she said with a chime of annoyance.

'You were late. I started before you.'

She turned back to the mirror, her face tight, and continued. Evidently, she saw her own sour expression reflected back at her and quickly relaxed it. I was unsure why she was in a bad mood with me. I, on the other hand, had the perfect excuse to be less than charming with her.

She threw down her rope after our warm-up time was done and went over to the shelves to take a drink from her water bottle, but even her drinking was fierce. Had David turned her advances down last night, or was she just hungover and annoyed that she had to do a session with me at all?

The door opened. Usually this was the time Terry appeared, but to my surprise, it was Robert with Remi at his heels. Momentarily, I felt elation, and then embarrassment. Savannah raised her hand to him, a gesture that was a little lacklustre.

He looked good this morning. His hair was swept back from his face; he wore a round-neck jumper, blue with strands of silver-grey – the shades all found in his eyes, and jeans. He looked much less the woodsman and more the successful international architect.

It hadn't been easy to break that kiss. Maybe it was just that I didn't trust him. There was definitely something there that I felt, but couldn't define. It was like the first time I worked with spelter. I could always feel the lead within it beneath the other familiar blended metals, like a bum note in a perfect chord.

'I'm here to see how Abigail's progressing,' he said to Savannah, turning his eyes on me. This wasn't good. My progress in this arena was nothing to boast about.

The coach house door opened again and Terry arrived.

'Are you staying? You can hold my supplies,' Terry said, handing Robert a box.

'Bed and board not enough for ye? Do I need to be your skivvy too?' said Robert, taking the box from Terry.

When Terry had given me a lift back from the pub, he'd broached the subject of his plan with me again, but I'd shut him down immediately so that there was no confusion about my position. I'd advised him to turn to Robert for the help he needed gathering evidence – perhaps with Robert out of his office for once, Terry would take the opportunity to do that today.

He'd been silent for the rest of the journey, but as I was getting out of the car, he'd said, 'Don't hold it against me, Abigail. I had to ask. You understand, don't you?'

I did understand. I wouldn't agree, but more than anyone else in the world, I did understand the pain, the injustice of losing Thérèse. And so for me at least, the topic was put to bed.

'Before we start, I might just go get myself a coffee. Would you like one, Robert? I got up at 4am and painted so my body clock is all out of whack. Sav can get Abi ready to show us some ninja tricks then.'

What did Terry have to say that for? He knew as well as Savannah and I that I was about as useless as the day I'd started. Now Robert would have expectations.

'I tell you what, I'll go and make you both a coffee. You get yourself set up, Terry,' said Savannah. 'Abigail knows the drill. She can get started without me – show them what you can do.'

Although her smile was controlled, her eyes danced with mockery. Bitch! I suspected her late night meant that she needed the caffeine more than Terry. She slipped out of the coach house door at lightning speed and I watched her ponytail swing in high arcs as she made her way into the house.

I needed to stall for as long as possible, so I approached Terry and asked him if I could glance over his sketchbook. He looked surprised, but complied. As I looked at the pages, my own form that he'd drawn disappeared before my eyes, and all I could see was Savannah's superiority: her elegance; her poise like a dancer; her sharp reactions to my blunt blows; the power that bounded from her body. Was David as familiar as I was with all these traits now?

'Abigail, you'd better get started. Sav will be back in a

moment and you don't want her miffed,' Terry said, taking back his pad and turning over to a new sheet.

I walked over to my nemesis, the post, and looked at it. The aim was simple: to strike a solid kick from a side angle at a point which would have been a man's knee. Why was the reality so damned hard? Though I could technically hit the post, my power seemed to be sucked out of me the minute I actually made contact with the wood.

Trying to ignore Robert's gaze, I studied the post, and something occurred to me for the first time. Maybe wood was my nemesis. Wood and Savannah. Every time I anticipated moving through wood when I projected, I got the feeling of being in a vat of maggots and having them wriggle all over my skin. The reality was different when I was outside my body; it didn't feel anywhere near as bad as I'd imagined it to be.

I stood back and looked at the post with fresh eyes. This was probably not the time to try out a new idea, but I had an inkling that there was something to it. I closed my eyes for a moment or two. Though I was now well practised in how to find the glimmer of light that was the sweet spot in my head, I just checked in to ensure it was where it always was. It flashed at me like a lighthouse. Then I opened my eyes, took up the position Savannah had shown me and swung my leg with all the force I could muster. At the moment before my leg connected with the post, I slipped into my sweet spot of light.

As my leg hit the target, I felt no pain for once, but heard an almighty bang like the firing of a gun in my head. The post, which had been fixed to the floor, flew across the room, straight at the coach house door at the instant it was opened by Savannah holding two cups of coffee. Her expression of surprise in the second before the post hit her was something I will always treasure.

It hit her square in the forehead. The coffee flew through the air as she reeled back on to the paving stones behind her.

Robert's jaw was slack. Terry couldn't have looked more surprised if the post had flown over and hit him. For a moment, we all stayed rooted to our spots, none of us running to help Savannah. Then we all scrambled at once. It was the first time outside of a slapstick comedy episode that I'd ever seen three people try to jostle their way out of a door at the same time. Caught in a momentary bottleneck, we finally popped out.

Savannah was conscious, but panting. I'd done that panting before – she was trying to contain the pain.

'What the hell happened?' she said, looking up into Robert's face.

He shook his head. 'You're miraculous, Sav. I constantly underestimate your talents. Clearly, there's still work to be done on her aim, but that was amazing. You have a gift for teaching!'

Robert helped her to sit up, slowly. Before our eyes, a purple lump was growing and filling the crevice between her eyebrows and the bridge of her nose. To make it worse, dividing the lump in half was a perfectly straight indent: a line where the corner of the post must have hit her.

When I leaned down to help her, she snapped at me, making me rear back. I had to swallow my smile. It was funny that she could possibly think I had planned to send that missile at her with such perfect split-second timing. In the back of my mind, a note trilled: unless it had been a matter for my unconscious mind. There'd been nothing to suggest so far in my training that I had any such competence. But if she was mad with me now, she was going to be hopping when she looked in the mirror.

All three of us were staring at the emerging lump which was morphing outwards before our very eyes.

'Let's get some ice on that head, shall we?' Robert's voice was jaunty, but I knew him well enough by now to realise that this man's default was dour. If he'd been jaunty with me, I would have been worried. I stared after them as Savannah leaned on Robert's arm and walked slowly across the courtyard.

I turned to Terry. 'Now, if you don't paint that, I'll never forgive you. For once, I would like to star in one of your masterpieces as someone other than the punch bag.'

Terry shook his head, giving me a rueful grin. 'I couldn't paint that even if I tried. It was all in the speed.'

He walked over to the post, which was now lying innocently on the paving in the little area outside the coach house, and picked it up. 'Do you see these fixings?' He spun a bolt head which was being kept in place by a steel plate welded to the base of the post. 'You hit that so hard, you sheared four bolts.' He shook his head and touched the other bolt heads which were wobbling on the plate. 'I can't figure out how you did it.'

The opportunity to have a conversation which should have taken place many months ago was finally here. I put my hand up to his own, forcing him to look at me.

'You don't really believe me about the alchemy, do you? I can see it in the way you and David look at one another when I mention it.'

Terry cleared his throat. 'Well, you have to see it from our point of view. You'd been under an unbelievable amount of pressure, being a captive of those lunatics and witnessing what they did to my Thérèse. Then there was the whole cutting your hands business. It was classic self-harming, borderline suicidal behaviour, Abigail. They'd been pouring this insane drivel into your head about alchemy, brainwashing you, and we thought that you had imagined certain things. I ... we thought that you had created explanations so that you could cope with what had happened.'

I looked at him fiercely. 'But you're prepared to subject me to all that again and possibly worse so that this time you can film it?'

'Don't make it sound like I want to film it for kicks! It's the only way I can think of to flush them out. We need a case opening. Once the police start digging, they might find Pandora's Box.'

'Robert is on the inside. It makes sense that he finds the evidence.'

'Evidence of what? You're the first potential alchemist they've had in a generation. The trail is cold on all the others, plus they are very tidy about their projects, which is how they've been at this so long without detection. Robert says there is nothing you could describe as physical evidence of anything worse than a historical interest in alchemy.'

'The trail can't be cold on Thérèse.'

Terry shrugged. 'It seems to be.'

'Why did you encourage me to come here if that was your plan?'

'It wasn't doing you any good being back at the foundry—'

'And you thought if you got me away, you might be able to persuade me to hand myself over to them?'

Terry walked back into the coach house and leaned the post against the equipment shelving. He crossed the room and sat down heavily on the old sofa under the stairs, and I tried to calm down. I joined him, sitting shoulder to shoulder with him.

'Tell me again why I would consider doing this. All the risk is on me.'

'Because you'll never be able to live a normal life with them threatening to take you again.'

Fen's offer flitted across my mind. Initially, I'd felt quite excited by the idea – the potential safety was more than appealing, but the more I thought about it, the more ridiculous it seemed. My world was about metals: I was a patineur and alchemist. I couldn't live trying to do anything else. At best, I'd be a puppet within a Collective and, frankly, if I ever mastered the alchemy, I could hire my own security. Selfish it might be, but I didn't want to be involved in pseudo-politics.

Terry continued, 'I presume Robert has told you about what happened to his family by now?'

I gave a slight nod.

'I thought that might make you more open to my idea. You must see how many others there've been like you, maybe thousands of families who have had their lives needlessly ruined by these people.' He paused and swallowed down what must have been pain. 'But, if you agree, I want you to go in as prepared as you can be. I thought this place was a good option. Here you can forge a relationship with people who could help you from the outside and learn more skills. It provides temporary safety and, just as important, a change.'

I had no faith that we could deal The Golden Illuminati a blow significant enough to do lasting damage. They were big; they were rich; their members were powerful cogs in society – judges, politicians, businessmen, mafia, even police. They would fight hard for survival.

'Terry, I need you to really listen to me. My life will never be normal because I can do something that defies all explanation. I realise it's hard for you to accept – I can hardly believe it myself. But I did transform that tiny piece of metal last year, and every so often, I do something startling like I did today.' I nodded at the post. 'But, I can't control it yet. I've spent the past year trying to replicate what I did, and I didn't progress at all until I came here.' I turned towards him and patted his hand. 'I'm not going to do it, Terry. I'm sorry, but there's nothing that will persuade me. I was lucky last time, but they won't underestimate me again.'

**21**

---

## ROBERT

The kettle boiled. I was making Sav a cup of sweet tea for the want of something to do and was considering whether it might be better to take her into Perth to be seen at the hospital when a message came through on my watch. Laura, my secretary at my practice in London, had marked it urgent. I scanned the headline. It was an email from my lawyer confirming that the transfer of the deeds for this house had gone through to be held by an independent solicitor in London Bridge for the next five years.

I ran my hands through my hair and then slammed them down on the work surface. 'Fock!'

It suddenly felt very hot in the kitchen, and then I got a stabbing pain in my gut which forced me to double over. There was a lot of saliva in my mouth and I jerked towards the sink.

It felt like my intestines were being twisted by invisible hands and pulled in two opposing directions. I braced myself against the pain and lowered my head so that I was staring at the floor and sucked in some air in through my teeth. Why had I signed that damn penalty clause? Like some kind of blinkered zealot, I'd been certain that nothing could turn me from my path. My stomach twisted a notch further and I felt sweat break out on my forehead.

I must be a masochist allowing Abigail to get close to me. A sensible man wouldn't allow situations like last night to occur. With all I had to lose, I should be more guarded, but when I was close to her, all that went out of my head.

The back door banged, and Remi trotted in and licked my hand. I looked down at his straightforward face. If there was anyone I wished I could talk this over with, it was him. He would have given me some crumb of comfort. Abigail followed him in, and I must have looked as bad as I felt because she was next to me in an instant, her brow furrowing. She put her hand to my arm.

'Robert, what's wrong?'

I felt the faint fizzle of her energy run from my arm down to my wrist and seep into my pulse. Suddenly my whole body was beating with need for her, and again my guts twisted.

I turned the tap and forced my face down into the stream of cold water.

'Robert, you look like you're having a panic attack,' she said, stroking the hair back off my face as it was falling forward and getting wet. 'You should sit down.'

Her stroke was gentle, loving. I reared back and bashed into one of the stools at the island counter, making it clatter on the floor and then into the one next to it while my legs scrabbled to create distance between us.

'I don't believe in panic attacks,' I managed to gasp.

Her eyes were concerned, but also wary. She was alarmed by my behaviour. Hell, I was alarmed by my behaviour.

'Where's that tea?' Fen's voice echoed down the corridor.

I couldn't deal with the damned tea right now.

Abigail looked at the empty cup. 'Shall I?' she asked.

I nodded – why was my throat so dry? It felt like it was narrowing.

She opened the utensil drawer and I caught a glimpse of her hands. They looked almost skinless, they were so raw. She lifted the kettle to fill the cup

'Pretty, aren't they?' she said as she caught my eyes on her hands.

I didn't have words.

'You go in. You look like you need to sit down.'

When I was almost at the door, she said my name. I paused, looking back at her.

'I didn't hit you with the post, too, did I?' A slight smile formed on her lips and suddenly the evil invisible hands in my guts stopped their twisting and let go. The relief was incredible.

'Go on.' She picked up the tea and nodded towards the door.

Sav lay in my study. The lump was the size of a plum tomato and a shade not dissimilar to that of an aubergine. Pulling my car keys from my pocket, I hovered near the wood burner. I was no longer in pain, but my body felt all wrong. I should get Sav to the hospital for a check-up, and maybe while I was there, I should get a once over myself. The pain had gone, but now my chest felt tight. I tried to rub the uncomfortable feeling away.

David was kneeling next to Sav, pressing ice to her forehead. Fen was sitting forward on the couch, rubbing his hand over the bristles on his jaw. As Abigail handed Sav the tea, she looked awkward.

'Robert made it,' she blurted out.

'Thanks, boss,' said Sav. 'I must look bad because that's about ... the second cuppa you've ever made me.' She gave me a wink.

David stood to avoid the tea, but his jaw tightened. 'What the hell did you do, Abi? Savannah's head is a mess.'

Abigail drew in a sharp breath as if he'd slapped her. 'Err, have you not seen the state of me over the last two weeks?'

'There's no question it was an accident, David,' Sav said, putting out a hand and touching his wrist.

The injustice of his assumption sent a surge of adrenaline through me. This man made me want to rip his head off, but I only got as far as thinking it because my phone buzzed. I pulled it out of my pocket and stared at the name: Philip. God, he picked his moments. I punched at the screen to send him to answer phone. Remi came and stood by my side, poking me with his nose, which was his way of lending moral support.

David was still staring at Abigail and folded his arms in front of him, as if that was likely to give him a better answer.

'Of course it was an accident, but need I point out that Savannah has been encouraging me to commit during every single lesson? Don't beat me with a stick just because I did it for once.'

'And you expect me to believe that?'

Abigail nodded her head slightly. 'What else could it have been?'

'Oh, I don't know – jealousy?'

Sav and Fen must have made an almost identical noise of surprise in unison because the resulting sound was loud.

'Do I have a reason to be jealous?' Abigail's voice was innocent, but her eyes were knowing. 'Exactly how could I have sent a post flying across the room to hit Savannah, directly at the split second she opened that door, with jealousy?'

'I don't know, but I do know that you've admitted this precise concern to me before. Idiot that I am, I dismissed it, but maybe I shouldn't have done. We are all cooped up here to cultivate your gift, but I, for one, will not help the cultivation of an ability to hurt people. None of us are ignorant of what you did to that man last year, and by your account, it was a necessary evil. I've never questioned that, but it's becoming a common theme, isn't it? I won't stand by and support you harming people I care about out of spite. It puts an entirely new spin on things.'

My phone buzzed again. I looked down. Damn it, the man was ringing again! My head began to swim. I looked at the phone, then at Abigail. I was very aware of my breathing. I fiddled with the little iron figurine of St Anthony on my keys and ignored the vibrating phone. What was it that Abigail had said that night in the pub after she'd touched this keyring? My mind groped for the words which had come so close to the truth that they'd scared me.

Anger was making Abigail's body quiver. 'I've only ever hurt someone when I've been threatened myself.'

'Threatened has a wide definition,' David shot back.

Finally, my thoughts came together. 'Guilt upon my conscience like rust upon my soul,' I said, aloud.

Everyone looked at me. Fen raised his eyebrows. David's expression said he'd noticed better things than me on the sole of his shoe.

'What?' he said with a slight shake of his head and an irritated expression on his face. 'Is that supposed to be some observation about your own role in this affair?'

I could see in his expression that despite how cool he was playing it, I'd needled him without intending to do so, and it felt fantastic. My head cleared a little and my heart slowed from its gallop. This was the end of the line for them. Didn't relationships always end over an issue that wasn't the issue? The depths of my stomach twinged again.

'David, might I make an observation?' said Fen, standing up. 'No-one who knows you could fear that the modern knight-in-shining-armour is dead. The other morning, you were very quick to fell Robert just for the possibility of harming Abigail, and now you are taking on Abigail to defend Savannah, but really you are seeing dragons where they don't exist. It's not uncommon for there to be a few mishaps when Underworlders are feeling for their abilities. There's no need to place blame.' Fen's voice was silvery and charming. 'I tell you what, let's go and take a coffee, you and I.' He stood up. 'We haven't had the opportunity to really get acquainted yet. Give everyone a chance to cool off.'

For the first time since he'd joined our troop, I felt sincerely grateful to Fenrear.

Abigail walked over to Sav. David ignored Fen and stood his ground as if she might lunge at Sav if he weren't there to guard her. Abigail knelt so that she was at Sav's eye line.

'I'm really sorry, Savannah. I can tell you that it was more a dislike for that bloody post than it was anything personal between us.'

Sav nodded. She usually had a smart retort in any situation, but she stayed mute this one time. Possibly due to her lump, or possibly due to the fireworks all of us could feel shooting through the room.

Abigail stood up, and without a look at any one of us, she withdrew. She was just into the corridor when David followed her. At the door, he said, 'I'm going to go and stay with Brandon in Glenkubright for a few days.'

We didn't hear Abigail's reply. Fen looked at me and

raised his eyebrows. Sav pressed the ice pack over the swelling again, but I detected a smile hidden below her hand.

'Sav, do you feel up to getting into the car? I want a doctor to look at you. Remi, you'd enjoy a drive, boy, wouldn't you?'

But Remi was nowhere to be seen. He'd left my side and gone with Abigail.

## 22

## ABIGAIL

I retreated to the book room near the kitchen and Remi padded in behind me. Throwing myself down on the sofa, I let go of the tears which had been backing up, waiting rowdily inside while I defended myself in Robert's study. The well-upholstered cushions cocooned me as I curled up, cat-like. The tears tossed a match as a parting gesture and my chest lit up with pain.

My thoughts were running fast. I'd never known David to be angry like that before. This morning, as I'd skipped during my warm up, I'd assumed it would be my own fury with him and Savannah that would end us – not that it really mattered how the end arrived. Perhaps I didn't have any right to mourn my relationship with David after what had happened with Robert last night. But, I couldn't help it. When I thought about Savannah and David sleeping together, which I was sure they had, it made me want to howl.

Then there was Robert and his bizarre behaviour. It only supported my instinct that there was something to be careful of there. David had called Robert clam-hearted, but that wasn't it. The Robert I knew kissed me like the world was ending, his heart wide open, making my body hum, and yet where was he now? And where had he been when David had been attacking me?

The door opened, and I felt expectation hop in my chest. Was it Robert? When Fen came into view, I gave a low moan.

He tilted his head and pursed his lips. 'Shall I make you a cup of tea?'

I smiled, shaking my head. 'I don't think that will fix things.'

He took hold of the nearest armchair and dragged it over to the sofa. Once seated, he let out a deep and tragic sigh. I looked at his face. He was about as mournful as I felt.

'What's wrong with you?'

'Well, I missed it all. You must consider how upsetting that is for me.'

I snorted. 'Yes, I can see how your day must have been ruined.'

'Did he cheat?'

I swallowed down the tears threatening to rise and roll again, and sat up, bending my knees so that I could rest my head on them. 'Probably. It doesn't really matter. He's picked a side.'

'How dramatic and overly simplistic.' His voice softened. 'It was bound to happen, you know. In one way or another.'

'Because of Savannah?'

'Because Robert's your match. You have powers in common. That's so rare.'

'So do you and I.'

'Not really. I don't project in the same way that you two do, and in general, I do prefer blondes.' He smiled and gave me a gentle push.

'Oh, don't joke. It's too awful.'

'On the contrary, I think things have worked out perfectly. David would be happier with someone like Sav, maybe even Sav.'

The thought turned my stomach.

Fen held up his hands. 'I'm not saying it has to be Sav, but our world isn't his. Look at what you did today, Abigail. It's a huge step forward. Underworlders have their own folklore about coming into their powers. There's a term, "avowal of power", meaning you must honestly acknowledge the power you have and be all in. That's the only way to make the miraculous things we can do possible. That honesty and belief is not something you can apply to some parts of your life and not others. You need to be honest with yourself about David, good man though he is, and the same about your gift. It is your gift and you have to commit to all that it brings.'

'You sound like Savannah. That's all she's been saying in my lessons for days: commit, commit, commit. I'm sick of hearing it.'

'I know she's not your favourite person, but she's hit upon exactly what's holding you back – in more than your fighting. You aren't certain about anything. You aren't certain about your power, even though you know you have it; you aren't certain if you want David, or if you love Robert, or whether you should be hiding away or living your life. Fear has a leash on you. Think back over last year – when you decided to get out of that cell, were you uncertain or were you sure, despite the consequences?'

'And what did that certainty turn me into in the process? What did I become, Fen? A murderer; a psychopath. A week ago, I set people on fire; today, I nearly broke Savannah's head. I've no control over this gift, but I know that it keeps leading me into darker and darker places. I'm scared of who

I might be if I commit. I'm holding on tighter to myself than ever because there might not be any controlling me if I let go. I don't want to embrace my ability, my world, or Robert who's hiding something. With David, I was safe.'

'Well, no wonder he slept with Savannah.' Fen put his arm out and took hold of my hand. 'Oh dear, duck, our lives are never easy.'

FEN LEFT me to myself after that. My mind whirred for a while longer, but ended up not solving anything, only tiring itself out. I found my eyes closing and didn't fight it.

My hands were on fire in my dream. I was back in the pub facing the man with the earring. This time I didn't throw any alcohol – I just touched him with my hands and he burst into flames.

I awoke, startled. My skin was wet with sweat and my hands felt so hot, it was no wonder I was having dreams about fire. The skin was having a complete tantrum.

The house was quiet. Remi was still at the foot of my chair. I needed comfort. I'd denied myself metal long enough, and though I had walls between me and the hallway, I could hear the dulcet tones of the handrail whispering, 'Choose me.'

I stood up and hoped that David had already gone. I wasn't in the mood for round two. The last thing I wanted to do was bump into him on the stairs.

My kit was in the old stables. I'd had it sent up by courier, imagining that I'd need it in the line of furthering my alchemical skills, though so far it had remained redundant. I leaned against the whitewashed wall of the stable and looked at the sleek wooden box. It wasn't my old kit, which had been another casualty at the hands of The Golden Illuminati, but this one was nice enough. My old kit had been so much a part of me that I still mourned it, and its contents had saved my life.

Laying both my irritated hands on the cool bronze was exquisite. The screaming itch of the psoriasis quietened, leaving a quivering excitement beneath my skin. It was a thoroughbred of a casting and I could do no less than stroke its surface while it continued to get at me.

'Choose me! Choose me!'

It had plenty of decent quality copper within it and was lost-wax cast, so the surface was perfection. Someone had taken a lot of trouble over the metal finishing, so the joins were almost invisible, and the surface was brushed to a satiny pink, which had begun to tarnish with handling to a soft penny. I closed my eyes and waited for the right colour combination to come to me. The request crept up shyly to my hands and gave me a nudge, like a cat asking for a stroke: the shades in Robert's eyes: a blend of browns with a blue thread weaving throughout.

I moved to my kit and laid out the brushes and chemicals I'd need for the work. My aim was to use methods that wouldn't result in a lot of strong fumes circulating in the house, which I doubted the residents would thank me for, but this did restrict my range of techniques. I cut myself some copper wool and drew out a pot of pumice powder that I'd premixed into a paste. Beginning at the top, I scoured the metal, rubbing the paste into every crevice. The texture of the bronze made this hard to do by hand and I returned to my kit for a small copper brush, like a toothbrush. I worked over a section and cleaned off the resulting dirty residue with some rag and a soap solution before continuing.

Over an hour later, when I was about three-quarters of the way down the rail, the back door slammed and I heard voices. I felt an urge to hide in case it was David, but Robert and Savannah appeared. Savannah was sporting a red bandanna covering her forehead. They both stopped as they took in what I was doing.

I looked at Robert, who glanced away and up the handrail.

'What did the hospital say?' I asked.

Savannah shrugged. 'We didn't need to go. I got Robert to take me to see Dr McLean, the GP who covers the village. He looked and said it should be fine. He kept me a while under observation, but doesn't think there's a concussion. Just says to use some Arnica on it.'

'Let's get you to your room to rest,' said Robert, who gave me a wide birth as he escorted Savannah upstairs. This felt like a slap. Maybe he saw things the same way David did. I turned my attention back to the handrail as they passed by. At least it was non-judgmental.

When I'd finished the prep work, I took up a pot containing a thick orangey-coloured liquid, a slender paintbrush and a round-ended brush with a handle. Dipping the paintbrush into the paste lightly, I then ran it up the length of the rail, careful to move the chemical in and out of the plait in such a way that the colour that would form would look continuous. While the chemical reacted with the metal, I removed it with my round-ended brush at the moment when the perfect shade formed. This was not a system that could be timed. It was a feeling I got from the metal: a certainty that the reaction had gone far enough. I pressed the brush into the metal and pulled away the chemical, revealing a ripe, rich brown-bronze shade. I burnished it when it displayed itself, making the colour shine even more, proud of its own accomplishment.

At some point, I heard Robert leave Savannah's room and continue up the staircase towards his own, without coming down to talk to me. If I hadn't been feeling so settled by the work, I might have tackled him, but Robert's cool behaviour couldn't pierce my calm right now. I wasn't even tempted to follow him.

Next, I took up a thinner liquid marked liver of sulphur. I added a couple of chunks of yellowy-brown crystal to the mixture, and with another clean paintbrush, I drew the chemical over the bronze. This one also turned brown, but as I continued to work it into the metal, the colour deepened and darkened, and with patience became almost ebony in shade. The warm bronze looked stark against the cold black, but I took a little copper wool and gently feathered the line where the two colours met. Reaching the top of the stair-case, I looked down. Old penny to ebony shades blended together, crisscrossing through the texture of the plait.

I was beginning to feel nourished by the work. As I glanced down, it looked magnificent already, but something was missing. It needed a contrast, something to make it stand out: blue.

Blue was a tricky colour to form. It needed heat, and had been one of the steps in the process which I'd used last year to create my first and only piece of gold. Since last year, I'd thought over the steps I'd taken in the transformation so many times. Was it essential to move the metal through several different shades, as the texts I'd found suggested, or was that just a warm-up exercise for the alchemist? What other purpose could the colouring work be for?

I mixed myself some potassium ferrocyanide and got out my little plumber's torch. By heating the metal to precisely the right temperature and introducing the chemical at exactly the right moment, I caused a thread of sapphire blue to appear through the bronze. Each time the colour was revealed, I felt excitement drum up my pulse and a deep urge for going further grow inside me. When I reached the bottom of the rail, I didn't even pause to admire my work, so frantic did I feel.

I moved to my kit again, picked up the Stanley knife, flooded its blade in methylated spirits and took a firm grip of it. My blood was up and my heartbeat echoed in my ears. Standing over the rail, I gave myself a moment of delicious anticipation, but as I was about to press the blade into my left hand, there was an intake of breath above me.

I glanced up. Remi had his head stuck between the banisters, looking down at me. Above him was Robert, staring down at me, too. The tug of what I was so desperate to do was too strong to be distracted. I ignored my audience and pressed the blade into my left hand, not too deeply, but the blood began to flow immediately. I clasped the bronze, and within a couple of seconds, I'd found the sweet spot of light in my mind that seemed to be the keyhole to all my power.

I was on the fringe of my body. Not fully projected, but somewhere in between places. The lights grew around me and the connection to the metal took on a greater strength, as though it was drinking from me. Now I couldn't have let go, even if I'd wanted to, and I lost my sense of boundaries: where I began and the metal ended. The intensity of the light was dialling up around me in a steady incremental way. My sight was beginning to fade out, but just as the light pressed in upon me, a thought slipped into my mind.

David and Savannah going into the house in Glenkubright together and the door closing behind them.

In that second, I lost it. Instead of the lights and me in union, they began to fight me. They swirled around, swarming faster and more furiously than anything I'd ever experienced before.

I tried to let go of the metal, but it wouldn't let go of me, and the lights were so piercing that I couldn't see any way back into my own head. Where my head was in relation to my consciousness, I wasn't even sure. I began to shake, and the frenzied lights divided more and more, to the point where I was utterly blinded by them.

The new pace of the lights was punishing. I felt consumed by their power, like I was caught in the sea being turned and tumbled by huge waves breaking over my head. This was nothing like my previous alchemical experience. The wildness and intensity were impossible to control, and I was beginning to lose all sense of myself.

'Abigail! Abigail!' A voice penetrated the swirling haze. The combination of terror and disorientation was impeding my ability to think.

'I'm scared,' I tried to say, but wasn't sure if the words formed in my mouth, wherever that was.

'I'm here,' the voice was calm.

I still couldn't orient myself.

Then more lights joined my own, but they were differ-ent. These were solid and a different shade. They surrounded my own scattered ones and compressed them, forming a boundary line. Things stilled, and I was able to sense their source: Robert. I felt him taking control of the chaos and my fear began to be extinguished by his calm. Things felt more solid. I had the sense he was holding me, though where he began and I ended, I wasn't sure. Our bodies hummed together, their lights enfolding and exploring inside and out of one another. The sensation shifted, becoming warm, intimate, delicious and definitely not platonic.

I was not inclined to move out of this blissful state ever, until I felt a stronger sensation in the place where my hand still touched the metal.

'Send your energy here.' The words were his, but inside my own head. I felt his energy flowing in the direction of my left hand, and mine followed. My contact with the metal strengthened and my energy poured into it. The metal responded to me. This time my lights didn't scatter; this time the connection grew stronger. He was a part of it, like a funnel, but I was the water flowing through it.

'You're doing it, Abi, you are in control of this.'

My heart swelled in gratitude to him before an almighty sensation tore through my body. It was so sudden: white light, noiseless. A pulse that ripped us both apart, and then silence.

**23**

ROBERT

I hit the wall with such force that my ears rang. My position as I met the stairs was inelegant: my legs up and my head pointing downward. I didn't black out, but I couldn't get up immediately. My lungs felt like they'd curled up, and all I could do was open my mouth and hope some air would drift inside.

I could see Abigail from this position. Remi was at the bottom of the stairs, licking her face. She had fallen the opposite way to me, landing on the hall floor, flat out. Her hand moved over Remi's shoulder – she was okay.

After a moment or two, my chest began to relax, and I was able to roll on to my side and right myself. All that I'd been feeling for her, seconds before the blast, came flooding back. Though my lungs protested, I found my legs were more cooperative. They got me down the steps in about the same amount of time as I'd been thrown up them. Putting my hand to her head, I leaned over her, gazing at her chestnut eyes which were lit by a ring of lights around the irises.

I touched her hair and whispered, 'Are you okay?'

'I can't see.'

I froze and took a grip on her arm.

'It should be temporary – at least it was last time it happened,' she said.

I relaxed.

She sat up, stopping just in front of my face. I slipped my hand along the side of her cheek and she leaned into it. I lifted her face slightly and met her lips with my own. She kissed me back with the same sizzle that had burned between us when our psychic bodies had joined, but in this form, I felt hyper-sensitised: just indulging in the fullness of her lips made me nearly tip over the edge; the warmth of her mouth was an almost unbearably sensuous pleasure.

From slightly above us came the sound of a slow-clap. We pulled apart and I turned to see David, up on the mezzanine level, outside Savannah's door, leaning over the banisters.

'That didn't take you long,' David's voice dropped down on us.

Abigail stiffened.

'Depends how you look at it. I've wanted to kiss her like that since the first day we met,' I said, standing up.

'I thought you'd gone,' said Abigail.

'Sorry to disappoint you,' he replied.

Abigail stood too, and I noticed the lights in her eyes were racing in circles. She was so mild so often that it was easy to think of her as someone who needed protecting, but as I saw those eyes, I felt a flicker of concern for David, disloyal though that was.

'You spent the night with Savannah and defended her over me. You don't get to be upset about this,' she said, anger putting steel into her voice.

David walked down the stairs. He stopped just before reaching the bottom.

'I know we're over, Abigail. It was probably never going to work out. We should never have been more than a perfect holiday romance, but please listen to one thing I have to say. I don't like this man. Don't put your trust in him. I may not have special abilities like you, but I can feel the secrets slithering inside him. He may be like you in some ways, but I know you – and he's not like you, fundamentally.'

'I thought it was my fundamentals you objected to.'

'He'll hurt you, maybe even betray you.'

I stepped in front of her so that David and I were inches apart. 'I will not,' I said and knew that this time the final decision had been made. I could never hurt her, whatever the price. The futility of what I'd been trying to do for the last several days had dawned on me when our lights merged: light could not hurt light, it could only mingle.

He moved down the last step and a glass jar filled with a chemical which Abigail must have been using hit his foot. Whether by accident or spite, David's foot met it with enough energy to send the container shooting across the hall floor and smashing into the wall. The chemical splattered all over the floor as David strode through the hallway door, slamming it so that it echoed up the hallway.

Within seconds, a shout came from above. 'All okay?' It was Terry's voice, but Fen's head was next to his, looking down on us.

'Nothing to worry about. Abigail is having a little trouble with her eyes. Something got knocked over is all.'

'Coming down,' yelled Fen.

I took Abigail's hand and gave it a little squeeze. She didn't respond, still staring through the door after David.

'You need to clean up that chemical fast. It will damage your wood,' she said.

'Whoa, Abi!' Terry's voice was all amazement. 'What's going on with your eyes?'

'I'm okay, really. It won't last long.'

'Err, Terry?' Fen's voice was high and warbling.

'I'll help you get that glass up,' said Terry to me as he crouched down to the floor to lift the larger pieces.

Fen cleared his throat. 'Err, Terry, Robert, will you please take a look at this?'

Terry made an irritated clicking sound. 'There's bloody glass all over the place here. Give us a minute.'

'No, I can't, really,' Fen insisted.

'What is it, Fen?' Abigail's voice was concerned.

'Well, let me tell you what I see,' said Fen. 'Several delicate shades of bronze and blue weaving through the threads of the handrail, and one distinct golden handprint.'

Silence fell upon our group as we huddled around the rail. I leaned forward, sliding my hand along the surface to touch the startling gold mark. She'd done it. The three of us couldn't tear our eyes away from it.

Abigail walked over to the steps and sat down on the lowest. 'But I lost control,' she said, her face looking up in my direction. That had been horrible to witness: her body slamming back and forth, as limp as a rag doll yet snared by the metal. I'd just held her at first to stop her neck being snapped from one of the violent tugs, but as soon as we'd touched, I'd known the problem wasn't physical.

Projecting out of myself and going into her cloud had been like being hit by a wave breaking. My own essence was pummelled before it mingled with hers. I became as much a part of her body as her mind and I could feel her fear and panic, and something else with us – an underlying presence;

a quiet, steadying influence. At first, I couldn't register what it was, but then it occurred to me that it was the metal clinging on to her hand. Like me, it was trying to stop her being hurt.

I bent down to her. 'But you regained it,' I said, taking her hand. She shook her head and looked down at the floor, her expression distressed. 'I felt the metal beg you. Its request was in our blended minds: please. You wanted to pull away, but to me, going towards it felt like the right thing to do, and so I directed your energy there.'

'It's incredible,' said Terry.

'It will change everything,' said Fen.

Still holding her hand, I stood up and pulled her to her feet.

'I'm going to take Abigail up,' I told Terry and Fen.

'I'll clear this away. Fen, get a broom,' said Terry.

I clasped her fingertips and led her up to my room.

MY ARMS TIGHTENED around Abigail the moment the door closed. She leaned back into me and put one hand to my head as I dropped my lips to her neck. My desire for her wasn't a gentle candle-like burn. It was a mighty fire licked up by wind, devouring everything in its path. Holding myself back from her for so long meant that something as slight as my lips running the slide of her soft skin was disproportionately arousing, and I was gripped by the need to take her quickly.

She turned to face me, her body pressing against my own, and I found myself needing to take shallow breaths to hold myself together. I tried to focus on small steps: releasing her dark hair from its tie, letting it spill around her neck. She slid the vest top up and away from her body. My hands fell into step behind the path of her own, passing up and along every curve until I made it to her shoulders, toned from hard work rather than gym lifts. We kissed again, and I let my thumb stroke from the nape of her neck down her long, slender back, checked from going further only by the top of her jeans.

I tried not to open my eyes. Even a glance of her semi-naked body pushed me closer to an edge that was perilously crumbling away. I hoped she'd take it as a compliment that this first time might be over before it had really started. I'd walled up my feelings, but now they could see the light, they were fighting to be free.

I saw my own lights begin to escape my body and crowd around us as if calling to hers to come out and play. They ran down her hair, flowed inside her mouth, cascaded down her breasts. She pressed me away momentarily and undid her jeans, shaking them to the floor. Her hand felt for my buttons, releasing them without delay, though to my desperate mind it seemed an unbearably slow pace.

My skin glowed with light and she ran her hands over it and my shoulders as she discarded my shirt on the floor. We stopped and stared at one another, knowing that this was the moment. As I lifted her up and carried her to the bed, laying her beneath me, the tightness of my trousers was matched only by the ache in my heart.

As I leaned over her, I cursed The Golden Illuminati. They'd ruined the lives of three generations of my family now. I knew that the physical release I would gain from being allowed to love Abigail in this moment would be paid for royally, but I was far past sense or self-preservation. As I slipped off my trousers, I felt fire licking up the sides of my throat. If I told her the truth, she'd run. If she discovered it through Sav, the Society, or Fen, she'd never be able to trust me, and I'd lose her and everything else anyway.

Our lights were having their own game now, spreading out and into the room, twisting around one another like shoots of plants growing and entwining. At the moment that we joined completely, the world drifted away, and pleasure extinguished every dark corner of my mind. Just as I knew I couldn't hold on for any longer, her voice materialised in my mind.

'Robert, why are you crying?'

## 24

## ROBERT

We didn't leave our room for the rest of the day. Despite the tearful climax to our first time, I didn't tell her the truth. There was nothing I could see to be gained by it.

I woke before she did. It was just after 5.15am and my stomach growled. I decided to make us coffee. The Gallery was nearer than the kitchen and I knew she'd enjoy the wonky cups again. To avoid waking her, I didn't use the lift; instead, I walked the stairs and, passing one of the only guest rooms not in use, I took advantage of its bathroom to take a quick shower.

Wonky cups in hand, and in less than half an hour, I came back to find my bed empty. Sipping from my cup, I made my way downstairs to find her. She was sitting at the foot of the stairs, looking at the gold handprint on the rail.

'Look at my hands,' she turned them over. When I'd seen them before, they had been too painful even to look at. Now, the skin looked calm. The scars were still there, and the incision remained that she'd made in her palm yesterday, but overall the psoriasis seemed to have melted away.

'I'm not sure what's more amazing: that I made that mark,' she nodded at the handrail, 'or the improvement in condition of my skin.'

I sat down next to her on the step and passed her the cup. 'Congratulations – you've found your gift.'

'I couldn't have done it without you there.'

'Ridiculous woman! It was all you.'

She rested her head against my shoulder and I felt the heat of happiness spread through my body.

Everything had changed last night. My head was clear today, and I felt settled – such an unfamiliar feeling. There would be no more angst over what to do about The Golden Illuminati, but one thing was certain: I would never hand her over to them. I was letting the jewels go, letting my family history go. We would figure out a way around that.

'I want to show you something. Let's go for a walk,' I said.

She stiffened very slightly. 'I've hardly been outside since we arrived. I don't feel safe out there – it's so open.'

'Aren't I a strapping enough bodyguard for you?' I said, banging her knee playfully with my own. 'Come on.' I stood and offered her my hand.

'Well, seeing as I definitely won't be working out with Savannah today,' she said, 'I suppose I do have space in my schedule.' She took my hand and I pulled her on to her feet so that her lips met my own for a moment. Remi shoved his nose between us and leaned forward, forcing us apart.

'I might leave you here, Rem,' I said, giving his head a pat. 'His rheumatism seems to have flared up and he's been a bit lame the last couple of days.'

We moved through the courtyard and towards the back of the house. It was a perfect morning – pale, shimmery shades of light flooding the land like something out of a

Turner painting. The only thing to be heard was our feet crunching the gravel along the path, along with the warm gusts of wind as they blew against the grass every few seconds.

Abigail leaned into me and I put my arm around her, feeling euphoric. The jingle of happiness turned into a chorus of bells, and I had to resist the urge to scoop her up and swing her round like a couple in some cheesy musical. This felt so right. I wanted to declare it to the hills that rolled all the way around us, shout it to the sky. How could I have deceived myself so completely? I didn't want to think about the details now; I just had a sense that everything was settled. I wanted to enjoy the present moment.

It had been the same during the night. I'd meant to tell her how I felt, but when it came to it, it seemed unnecessary. Words were redundant. Anyway, we had plenty of time for that.

We wandered downhill through the field for about five minutes.

'Where are we going, Robert?'

'I feel a wee bit mean telling you this, but I haven't shown you the best part of this house yet.'

Even though I'd owned this place above seven years, it never ceased to enchant me. Big sculptural trees were at different points on the hill, making me think that they must have walked there from the nearest wood. It was the perfect landscape for lovers, and it suddenly struck me how long I'd lived here without ever having someone's hand to hold as I walked this path. I longed to pull her down into the long grass and show her again how I felt about her, but it wasn't warm enough for that.

The path veered off to the left, and as we rounded the bend, I heard her make a noise of surprise. I'd placed the huge structure at this precise point so that it would achieve this very reaction. We both stared down at the two colossal shavings of iron silhouetted against the sky.

'Richard Serra,' she breathed, hardly above a whisper.

I couldn't pull my eyes from her. The colour in her ivory skin was up, tinting her cheeks and contrasting with her dark hair; she'd never looked more beautiful. She got why I'd spent untold money buying this monumental sculpture and toiled to have it installed in this perfect epic landscape: one of the few backdrops that could really do the shape justice. I watched her face quiver and tense, then she took a huge leap from a standing start and sprinted down the hill towards the sculpture. I watched her run like a child, pelting faster than her legs could carry her. She rammed into the great face of the sculpture and, panting, laid herself against the surface, lifting both hands and laying them either side of her face.

Approaching at a much more sedate pace, I noticed her eyes were closed, as if she'd come across a much-loved family member unexpectedly. When she opened her eyes, I took the opportunity to push her up against the sculpture and kiss her, but her body wasn't compliant as it had been last night. She was stiff, her mind ticking.

I pulled away. 'Tell me.'

She turned her head to the side as if listening to something and leaned her back against the surface, touching her fingertips to it. Her expression became a little self-conscious.

'Sometimes, metals tell me things. When I think back, it was the first glimmer I had of something unexplainable that I could do.'

I patted the mighty rusty elevation. 'Is it telling you that I'm a bad-boy millionaire bachelor? If so, tell it not to worry – last night closed that chapter.'

I smiled at her. She eyed me with an expression that I didn't understand.

'Actually, it gave me a warning for you.'

I continued to watch her, but raised my eyebrows.

'It said, "Take care".'

I looked around at the open land. 'Not much I can get harmed by here, other than that rogue sheep over there, and how do you know the message is for me?'

She took a deep breath and her forehead furrowed. 'Maybe you aren't seeing the whole picture.'

'I think I'll stick with taking security advice from Savannah rather than my sculptures.'

She shrugged, and colour rose in her cheeks. I'd been trying to be funny, but had made her feel foolish.

'Are all metals the same? Could an alchemist turn anything?' I said, scrabbling to make up for the last comment.

'No, they're not the same at all. This fellow is quite sweet, though he looks like a fearsome beast. Anything iron-based, like this steel, I've found to be generally kind.'

'Kind, how?'

She ran her hands over the roughened surface of the steel. 'Last year I escaped because I listened to a message from some iron bars in my cell. That makes me sound unhinged, I know, but I'm alive because I listened.'

'You're alive because you are clever and brave.'

'And murderous, don't forget that,' she said, her chest rising slowly as she said it and a bleak look coming into her eyes.

I offered her my hand. 'Let's walk this bit together.'

She stayed adjacent to the surface of the sculpture, running one hand along its face as she moved. I guided her towards a corridor-like segment where another mighty sheet of steel ran in parallel to the first. We had to go single file here because of the narrowness. I directed her to look up as we moved through this section. I knew every step of this walkway, and the profiles of the two surfaces, wavering in and out against the skyline, were a joy to see.

At the end of the walk, we arrived in the centre of the sculpture and I began to feel excited. I had a little surprise to show her. The middle of the sculpture formed a circular space like a curl, and here the ground was paved in triangles meeting at a point in the centre. Her hand was still touching the metal surface, reluctant to let go, or perhaps to cease the conversation she was having with it.

I pulled a key fob from my pocket and clicked it without her paying too much attention. Instantly, the ground we were both standing on began to sink and move, and Abigail gave a yelp, grabbing on to me. I steadied her, and she looked into my eyes for an explanation which I wasn't about to give.

Each triangle sank a few inches lower than the previous one, resulting in the start of a stone staircase, which then met a conventional spiral stair and disappeared deep into the earth. Abigail couldn't have looked more surprised if the sculpture had risen up and flown away.

'Come on,' I said, behaving as nonchalantly as I could which made me laugh inside. She stood stock still on the upper steps and I had to give her hand a little tug to get her going. 'It's okay.'

Her eyes settled on me and something in the exchange tipped the balance and she began to move down the steps. As soon as we'd both made it below ground level, I clicked the fob again and the triangular segments closed. Abigail looked up at the disappearing sky and tensed.

As the roof closed, the space became very dark, with

only the occasional small spotlight embedded in the wall at each turn of the staircase.

'Are you trying to keep your electric bills down?' she said with a nerviness to her voice. 'What's with the gothic darkness?'

'Ay, it's black as the Earl of Hell's waistcoat,' I said, giving her my broadest Scottish accent.

She laughed as she walked the last few stairs to the bottom. I waited for her and kissed the uncertain expression from her lips. The freedom to do that was still so novel that it made me giddy. My mind started racing off towards what else we could do down here.

'I think darkness is a bit like silence: it heightens your other senses.'

'I don't care for it myself. Once I walked through a tunnel of utter darkness. There was nothing profound about it.'

'In that case—' I leaned over to a panel on the wall and pressed a button. Light built, revealing the entire cavernous space. The walls, which were shaped similarly to the sculpture above – free-flowing like a river, had light cascading down them. Around the perimeter were endless shelves, curving too. The concern on Abigail's face fell away and she darted towards the shelves when she saw their contents. Thousands of ceramic items were set on every shelf: clocks and bowls, platters, cups and sculptures.

'What is this place, Robert?'

'It's my ceramic curiosity shop, a folly and a man-cave. All rolled into one. The architecture I build is all about unexpected spaces and I couldn't resist treating myself to one when it came to my own house.' I felt a twinge in my stomach as I said, 'My own house'; it wouldn't be mine much longer. This sculpture and the gallery would be the bits I would miss the most. I'd never be able to replicate this. It would be unlikely that I'd have the money, or the heart to.

'You've collected all these?' she said, peering more closely at the groups of exquisite items on the shelves.

'Most yes, but I told you that pottery was my hobby. Some of them are mine. I throw pots and make things, and break things, and I do it for no other reason than the love of creating.'

A phone rang, echoing through the space. I walked to my desk at the back of the Gallery and picked it up.

'Robert, you left your mobile phone here on the kitchen table. There's been about fifty calls from Geraint in Berlin. You'd better call him. Something must be up.'

I thanked Sav and quickly dialled Geraint, who began with a torrent of Welsh obscenities directed at me. There'd been a huge delivery of glass for the project, and none of it fitted. I'd sent out the order, and if the mistake was ours, it would cost us a vast amount of money, not to mention the impact on the other trades of the delay. Even the frantic stress that was pouring down the phone couldn't derail my upbeat mood, though.

'I'll get up to my laptop right away and call you when the documents are in front of me. I'm sorry, Geraint. I'll make some arrangements, fly out to you and take some of the strain off.'

Geraint grumbled some words back at me.

I found Abigail in my pottery workshop, examining my workbench and tools. It was a fully lit space with a wheel and large slabs of clay.

'I've got to go back up to the house. Problems in Berlin need my attention.'

'You know, this place is where you want to be in case of a nuclear strike, or alien invasion. You should get cases of tinned goods, a few weapons, and then if it comes, you'll be sorted.'

'We'll be sorted,' I said, offering her my hand. 'I need to go. I'm sorry to cut the visit short.'

She nodded. 'But we can come back? Throw some pots together?'

'Well, I always work alone in here, but I guess I could make an exception,' I said, leading her towards the stairs.

'Can I open the ceiling?' I passed her the fob, taking the opportunity to stroke her wrists with my fingertips as I did. Halfway up the stairs, she clicked it, making the ceiling slide back. A shower of daylight and fresh air streamed over us.

Outside, we walked back through the rusty steel corridor, single file. She was ahead of me and couldn't help herself from touching the walls continually. I wondered whether I could take her to Berlin with me. I couldn't avoid going: Geraint had sounded like he was cracking under the strain, and in truth, even I had never run a project of this scale with as little backup as I'd given him, so he'd outperformed expectations to hold the fort this long.

I put my hand out to touch her waist as we approached the point where we exited into the landscape. She stopped stock still in an oddly stiff position. I slipped past her and moved into the field.

As I did, she yelled, 'No!'

I turned to see her distressed expression, which I didn't understand, and was vaguely aware of another sound like ice cracking. And then a bullet barrelled into me.

## 25

# ABIGAIL

The steel told me there was danger, but my shout of warning was too late to stop Robert. The bullet hit. I'd been deep in a daydream about the kind of life Robert and I could have here together. It was like watching a rerun of an accident I'd already seen and I didn't have the presence of mind to intervene.

He made no sound when it hit, but looked down at his leg, surprised, and then crumpled to the ground. I stared at him, disbelieving my own eyes, before looking around. There was a man on the hill. He had been leaning his gun on a sculptural tree between parted branches that I had so admired. He stood up and we locked eyes.

The man moved out from behind the tree and, slinging his sniper gun over his shoulder, took a step down the hill towards us.

I looked down at Robert. Possibilities of how to get help were chasing around my brain. Could I ring someone? The man wasn't running, but his stride was long and his intent clear. This guy didn't need to hurry – he had us right where he wanted us. We were going to die here in the lap of this sculpture.

Robert was conscious and lay blinking, perfectly calm. His eyes were on the clouds as though he was just making out their shapes. I glanced at the man again, halfway down the hill now, and I threw myself to the floor.

'Give me your hands,' I yelled at Robert.

He gave a groan and twisted slightly, jolting at the pain this caused.

'Give me your hands!'

He obeyed this time, providing me with one hand entirely smothered in his blood.

I'm a small thing, but I'm wiry, and years of foundry work have made me stronger than most men of my size. I took hold of both his hands and pulled for all I was worth until he was standing up and draped over me.

'I need to get us back into your workshop – now,' I said as we staggered forward like two drunkards. There was no strength in him; I was holding him up. Glancing down at his leg, I could see a lot of blood, but knowing our attacker must be almost upon us, I threw my shoulders into it and pushed us forward.

'Come on, Robert, or we are going to be dead in two minutes. I can't drag you all the way.'

The terror in my voice must have registered. His noises of pain were primal. This was a wounded animal's response and was agony to my ears: real suffering.

I moved as quickly as I could with a huge man hanging over my shoulders. I willed him to help me, though I was fairly sure he had passed out. This horrific dragging dance had us crashing into one wall of the sculpture's corridor and then another. I kept glancing over my shoulder, sure that I'd see the gun pointed at my back.

We were almost at the centre. I scrabbled in Robert's pocket for the fob, and grasping it in my hand, watched and prayed as the stone slabs began to slide open. But I knew it was too late.

I felt his presence like some ghoulish spectre, and horror clutched my heart. The man, who I now saw was dressed exactly the same way as the guys who'd attacked us in the pub – black combats and cut-off T-shirt, with cropped military hair – walked into the space.

I shoved Robert off my shoulders towards the stairs, but he didn't manage a single step. He fell like a tree, hitting the ground with bone-crunching effect. His neck whipped back the moment before his head hit the top step of the stairs, and for a moment, I panicked that he may die from this blow rather than the gunshot.

The man moved towards me. I stepped away, mirroring him, and glanced at Robert. I couldn't tell if he was breathing or not, but it probably didn't matter – we were both going to be dead in seconds. I looked back at the assassin.

The man smiled a smug sort of smile. He knew he had me and I was trapped by the sculpture's curling walls in this small space. He stepped again, and this time I stayed put, allowing him to come closer. And then I did the only thing I could think of. I threw myself forward and to his left, before he had time to lift his gun fully. I couldn't have found that sweet spot in my head if it had had an arrow pointing at it, I was too terrified. Instead, I threw out my side-downward kick to the knee with 100% commitment.

I hit it with bullseye precision, but the impact made the fob I'd been clutching fly out of my hand. He groaned and fell towards me, letting off a gunshot, which went high and ricocheted off the statue.

Even with my best attempt, I knew I had done no significant damage – only toppled him, and we fell together. His hand shot out and grabbed my ankle, then my wrist, and I knew I was in trouble. Though he met the ground before me, his arms were long, and he managed to throw a punch quickly, making contact with my stomach. It sent every molecule of air careering out of my lungs. I keeled over, hit the floor, and lay staring at the warm shade of rust on the surface of the sculpture.

Curled into a ball, I knew I was done. My brain was functioning, but my lungs wouldn't when I most needed them to breathe. I could hear him getting to his feet. I tried to sniff some air through my nose, but even that hurt.

His shadow fell upon me, and I closed my eyes. Would he shoot me in the head while I was lying in this foetal position, unable even to take another breath?

'Up,' he shouted. His voice had a heavy accent, and when I didn't respond, he kicked me hard in the lower back. The pain in my side blew up and the pain of my squeezed lungs seemed to unite with it. Now my whole body was ablaze.

'Up,' he shouted again, hitting me this time in the side of the head with the butt of his rifle.

As I started to move, inch by inch, I saw the fob on the ground. Raising myself a little, I picked it up and slid the ring on to my finger. He grabbed my hair, yanking me on to my knees. I was dizzy, unable to breathe more than the tiniest bit and the pain was making me sweat. He let go of my head and stepped back. Now released, I fell against the metal, and put out my hands.

It was in my ears, my mind, my hands, in every cell of my body. 'Strike me,' it directed. Without questioning the instruction for an instant, I reared back, lifting my hands above my head, and hit the metal with every ounce of commitment in my being. As my hands came down, I saw the golden glow of my projection swell and move ahead of them. As the glow met the metal, we connected and, as if the sculpture was wired to the mains, my body quivered with power. The metal sang.

It was a billion nails scratching down the steel's surface and a million gongs being struck simultaneously. The sculpture roared in proportion to its magnificence, and the noise was like being inside a thunderclap.

My light grew more intense around me, but in my head, the sound softened and was dialled down almost to silence. My body was pulsing with energy. I turned to see the effect on my assailant and was amazed.

He was down on one knee, like he had been the recipient of a blunt uppercut. His face was completely contorted, and he looked at me, putting out his hand – actually begging me for help. Tears were pouring down his cheeks and he was encasing one ear with his hand. The gun was discarded on the ground.

I was on my feet in an instant. Keen to keep the metal singing, I held my hand against the surface and leaned down to pick up the gun. The man didn't even seem to be aware of it. He was incapable of moving. I staggered and bent over, for to stand upright seemed impossible.

As quickly as I could, I moved around the small circumference of the statue's centre towards Robert. He was still motionless on the floor and rivulets of blood were filling up the spaces between the cobbles. With the gun in my hand, I had no chance of moving him, so I had no choice but to drop it. As I took my hand off the metal, the noise ceased and my glow disappeared. I grabbed Robert's forearms and hauled him.

It wasn't pretty; it wasn't elegant; it wasn't a hero's rescue – it was dirty desperation that pulled him down five stairs, bashing his head brutally on every step, but as we made it in, I clicked the fob on my finger. The entrance closed over us.

## 26

# ABIGAIL

He was in the most ridiculous position, head down, legs up the stairs, but I wasn't capable in that moment of righting him. I could only collapse down next to him and clutch at his body.

I pulled and squeezed the fabric in my hands and buried my face in his back, gasping in breaths and mumbling, 'I'm sorry.' Though I was stationary, I felt dizzy and my body was shaking. I pressed harder against him and he groaned.

'You saved us.' His voice was muffled due to his position, but his hand flapped somewhere close to me, groping for mine.

I turned my head. 'You wouldn't be bleeding to death if it wasn't for me.' The word "death" brought me up short. I may have slipped away from danger, but Robert was still grappling with it. He couldn't afford to lose time.

'We can use a belt as a tourniquet. Are you wearing a belt?' I pushed myself up on to my feet and clambered over his body to get to the lower stairs. The light was too dim to see his face, but his shallow breathing made my stomach churn.

Don't die, don't die.

I needed to slow the bleeding and get an ambulance here at light speed. When Savannah had been hurt, Robert had said the hospital was in Perth: a significant distance.

'We need to keep the leg elevated,' I said, swatting around his waist, looking for the belt.

'Do you have first aid training?' he said, his voice hardly above a whisper.

I shook my head. 'One of the apprentices at our foundry sliced through his leg muscle with an angle grinder. The head foundryman tied his leg to slow the bleeding.' Bile rose unexpectedly into my throat and I swallowed it down. What if someone else I loved died because of me? I had to get help, fast.

'I know this will hurt, but I need to turn you over. You'll have to help me.'

The pain must have been awesome. Although he never made a sound, his body tremored, and as he made it on to his back, his face had a sheen of sweat across it. The wound was oozing blood. The fabric all around it was saturated. Slipping the belt around his bleeding leg, I hesitated.

He put a hand out and grabbed my wrist. 'Abigail, there's things I need tae tell ye.'

Knowing I was about to hurt him very much, I brushed his words aside, fearing I might lose courage. 'I'm sorry,' I said, tears in my eyes. I wrenched my hand from his and pulled the belt tight around the leg.

He cried out this time, and I saw his eyes widen and then lose focus.

I bent and kissed his damp skin, my hands shaking violently as I knew I had to hurt him more. I pulled the belt tighter again.

'I'm sorry, I'm sorry.'

'Woman, you're no Florence Nightingale!' His eyes closed, and he lay panting.

My face was wet with tears as I fumbled around, trying to find a way to secure the belt. I wedged it in on itself, and his blood was all over my hands: a warm, sticky layer.

'I need to call Savannah. She'll know what to do. I don't know the number for the house.'

'It's speed dial 1,' he mumbled, 'and turn up the lights. I don't want to die in this darkness.' His voice was raspy.

I stood on legs that didn't feel safe. 'You said it heightened your other senses.'

He coughed. 'I'm an architect. I say all sorts of crap.'

I could hear the drone of the sniper's voice directly above us, muffled by the ceiling. He must be speaking to someone on his phone.

'He better not be calling for backup,' I said, taking two steps down the staircase. Suddenly, I felt as though someone had swiped my knees out from under me. My legs buckled, and I stumbled down the remaining stairs, biting my tongue in the process. I met the floor on all fours, tasting my own blood.

An image filled my mind: a dark room; a collection of jewellery. There was an old man with red hair standing alongside a display case. I wasn't looking in at the scene, I had a role in it. Three emotions were blended as one as I stared at the jewels; a chord played to perfection: a high note of excitement, a softer mid-tone of resolve and a yearning bass so melancholic it was hard to bear. I could feel the control being exerted over the hands of whomever I inhabited. It was all they could do to stop themselves from smashing the glass and taking the jewellery up then and there.

The redheaded man said, 'Abigail is the only deal we are interested in making, Robert.'

Robert coughed and the images were gone. I pulled myself up from the floor. My head felt foggy. What had I just seen? I moved towards the back of the room in search of his desk, licking the blood from my split lip. My thoughts raced back and forth over all that was forming in my mind. The image had been so sharp, not like a dream where things blur and details are unaccounted for. He'd betrayed me. The fears I'd had about his loyalty, which had flitted about me during my stay here in Scotland, had vanished last night. Now, their ghoulish forms returned. How could that be? The Robert I'd been with last night couldn't have sold me out, and yet I'd seen it.

It might have all been down to the stress of fighting for our lives. My steps slowed – I wanted to race back to him, lying on the stairs, and demand the truth, but this was not the time for that.

My hands were feeling unusually hot and the skin was beginning to prickle. It wasn't my usual psoriasis itch. The sensation in my hands was becoming more uncomfortable by the second. I needed to rinse them of Robert's blood, which must be irritating them, so I darted into his workshop.

As I thought about Robert's blood on my hands, under-standing pulled me up short. Messages had materialised in my head before, but never quite like this. It must have been another metal friend of mine: iron, in his blood, showing me his secrets.

I gulped back the tears crowding my throat and felt doused in cold stupidity. If there was one thing I was completely sure of, it was that iron wouldn't lie to me. But Robert would. I'd sensed it, but now I knew I'd been played.

The relationship between Robert and me was fabricated. He'd been doing whatever it took to secure those jewels and make good on the promises to his father. I wished I hadn't realised his secret when his life was in my hands.

Pushing back all the heartbreak I was feeling, I stood up straight. I needed to be practical now and get him help; I wasn't too far gone to deny him that.

Almost at the sink, I was hit again with more images. The smack of these ones had me falling hard against the worktop. I was inside his head again: it was the day he'd come to the foundry and we'd met. Just as he reached the top of the ladder, I felt his heart change stride as he laid eyes on me for the first time. Desire scorched through him as he took me in.

Another flash and we were in the upstairs room in The Coach House pub. I could feel what he'd been experiencing when he'd touched me in his out-of-body state. It was water flowing into water and coalescing.

Another flash and we were on the step together this very morning, looking over the view, and he was happy – joyously, giddily, childishly happy. His sense of peace was entire because he was filled up with love for me. We stood up to walk, hand in hand, our energies mingling over the bridge they provided.

The images fell back and I pulled myself up and thrust my hands into the sink, turning on the tap. My head felt like it had glue running through it, but as I watched the blood mix with the water and trickle away, I felt relief replace some of the hurt. He did love me. It wasn't a pretence. He hadn't expected it and he couldn't help himself.

'Abigail!' Robert's voice reached me.

I grabbed a cloth, dried my hands and fled to his desk where I phoned Savannah. She picked up immediately.

'What's going on down there?' she yelled at me before I could even get words out of my mouth. 'We heard this really weird noise, and of course, no-one has their mobile with them, so Terry's gone down to see that you are alright.'

My heart froze. 'Terry ... you need to call him, Savannah. Robert's been shot. The guy who did it is still here. Call the police and get an ambulance here fast, otherwise Robert's going to bleed to death.'

I put the phone down. Running over to the stairs, I lay my hand on the rail and felt something wet on its surface. I looked at my hand – more blood. Robert was leaking through the staircase struts. The lights flickered in my head again, and it felt like someone was squeezing the base of my neck very intensely.

This time it was different. I heard a voice. I recognised the redheaded man's distinctive tone.

'If by any chance you misinformed us, we would have to invoke a penalty clause...I believe you have a very fine residence in Scotland.'

I felt love and loss spin together, turning over and over like a coin flipped into the air: my face; the house; my face; the jewels; my face. With each turn, his feelings for the jewels, the house, me washed over me, and then it clicked: the jewels and his beautiful home were the cost of his loving me.

I slipped back to reality and looked up at Robert, who was quiet. Oh, what had he done? Everything made sense now, and yet we were so far from sense it wasn't true. I moved up the stairs, my feet feeling weighed down by the muddiness of our situation.

At the top, I knelt, putting my hand to his head, and just that simple connection triggered my heart to run over with love for him. I truly loved this mixed-up good-bad genius-idiot man. This was a feeling so deep, it felt like my soul had been rewritten. It was the most unsuitable moment to feel such a powerful thing, but I had no control over it. My tears dropped one after the other on to his shirt.

His eyes were closed, but they fluttered open.

'I need to go,' I said, biting down on my bottom lip to control the crying. His body tensed. He reached out and closed his hand over mine.

'Don't go – please. If I'm going to die, I want you beside me.' His accent was heavier than usual, the pain wiping away the fine education that silvered his speech. 'A've got things ay need to tell ya—' He swallowed. 'You should take the opportunity while ya' can – a Scotsman has to be near death to be vulnerable.' He half-smiled. 'Ay should have said this last night.'

I shook my head, trying to stop the tears again. I needed to be strong if I was going to help Terry – a blubbering ally wouldn't be much use to him. I swiped the tears that wouldn't stay back with my other hand.

'Nothing needs to be said now, but I do need to go. Terry's coming down to us—' but he gripped my wrist tighter.

'What I feel for you, I've never felt for anyone else. If I was an honest man, I'd have told you the day we met. Fenrear knew it – he said you were my match, and you are. Don't leave me here, Abigail.' He lifted his hand to my cheek and I gripped on to it.

There was a muffled shout from above, making me raise my eyes to the ceiling.

'It's Terry. I can't leave him to die. He doesn't even have a weapon. You'll be safe here – I'll come back.'

'Don't go, dammit, woman! He wanted to hand you to them. Is it worth dying for a man like that?'

Fear and tension quivered in every cell of my body, but for the first time in a long time, I wanted to laugh. I didn't let myself; it wasn't the time. I leaned towards him and kissed his temple and then his lips, pouring into them as gently as I could all the love I felt for him.

'If I held that against everyone I love, I wouldn't have anyone left.'

He gripped my hand even more tightly and searched my eyes, but I pulled my hand away from him and stood, pulling out the fob from my pocket, pressing it, and watched the ceiling of the stairs open up.

## 27

## ABIGAIL

Terry was facing the gunman, who had the rifle pointed at his chest. Under any other circumstances, I would have laughed at Terry's expression of surprise as I emerged from the ground. The sniper's head whipped round to me and there was hesitation in his eyes. He glanced at my hands, but then all three of us were distracted at the same moment by the deafening sound of an aircraft flying low and fast. It went directly over the top of the sculpture.

There was no hesitation this time. The man sprinted forward and barged past Terry, knocking him sideways.

Terry jumped up. He was looking with concern at me.

'You okay?'

He gave me a quick, urgent hug. I looked down and realised that I was covered in Robert's blood.

'I am, but Robert's been shot. Savannah has called the police.'

'I'm going after him,' Terry said and turned to run after the man. I tried to grab hold of him, but his strength pulled me along as well. I ended up letting go and following him.

'He has a gun!' I shouted at Terry's back.

'Can't shoot that type of weapon when he's running away.'

'He's not one of them, Terry.'

'Of course, he is. Who else could it be?'

This wasn't really the time to explain the other possibility, so I settled for, 'Someone else.'

We arrived at the mouth of the sculpture. The guy was a quarter of the way up the hill and was waving his arms at a compact orange jet which had gone way past by now. Did he think the jet was going to land in this field and pick him up? Terry broke cover and had made it a little way up the hill when the roar of the jet grew louder again. It was returning in our direction.

Terry slowed, and I knew why. Although it was impossible, the plane was going to fly right at us. There was something terrifying about seeing it moving at high speed towards us. Suddenly I felt a distinct and tangible charge in the air. Every hair on my body rose to attention and began to hum a warning. I shouted for Terry to stop. This time there must have been something in my voice which resonated with him because he obeyed. My brain was bypassed as my instincts took over.

I ran to him, pulled him to the left and yelled, 'Get down!'

Throwing us both to the ground, I rolled as tightly as I could next to him and moved through the sweet spot of light in my head. In that instant, I felt rather than heard the explosion. I was in that silent place where noise is absent, but I felt the ground flinch and shake in fear at this monstrosity falling out of the sky.

I sensed the presence of metal in the air immediately – metal in motion. Terry and I clung to each other as my lights wrapped us in their tendrils. Great hunks of metal jetted through the air at high speed and cannoned into the ground centimetres from us. Razor-sharp fragments rained down in a mighty deluge. We lay together in my light, pressed to the ground as the bomb storm raged around us.

I closed my eyes to block out the scene and concentrated on dialling up my projection the way I'd practised in my lessons with Fen. I lost sense of time as I waited for the inevitable blow that would finish us off. It was when I felt Terry relax that I opened my eyes.

Smoke was rising from the grass and there was a smell of burning. I could see almost nothing, at first. I leaned up on to my elbows and squinted around the landscape. The jet was gone, but every inch of the field around the sculpture was covered in jagged lumps of steaming metal. Everywhere, almost without exception, apart from where I and Terry lay.

I looked up the hill to where our assassin had been running. He was dead. A lump of metal had gone directly into his chest. There were a few sheep that were smeared with blood and not moving either. One of the trees smouldered. Hardly an inch of the statue's surface had escaped. It was gouged, dented and scored all the way along its length. At one end, there was a gaping hole, edges of jagged steel curling back on themselves where an explosive had run right through it.

The wind blew my hair away from my face. I could hear the dull sound of sirens far away. Terry was staring at the field.

'What the hell just happened?' he asked.

I shook my head. 'Some kind of bomb?'

Terry rolled on to his back and stared at the sky, then he began to laugh, but it was more hysteria than humour.

Two police Range Rovers came around the bend at the top of the hill. They drove along the path, then emergency stopped as they saw the state of the field. A medical helicopter arrived, too. The complications of getting Robert out from the centre of a bombsite dawned on me.

I stood up and surveyed the scene again. There was hardly a section of grass that didn't have shrapnel covering it. I looked down at Terry, offering my hand to help him stand.

'I don't know what the odds of us surviving that were, but we must have somebody watching over us, is all I can say – or possibly it was just dumb luck?' said Terry.

I pulled him to his feet. 'That wasn't luck. It was an example of brilliant stupidity. You're never going to kill an alchemist with metal.'

Terry ran a hand over his face. 'They won't be allowed to negotiate this field until a team has assessed it. I doubt they even have munitions teams around here.'

My shock at having survived the blast began to wane as I thought about Robert. He was going to die alone, if he wasn't dead already. He'd begged me not to let that happen.

'We have to get him out and fast.'

Terry looked at me. 'What exactly are you proposing we do? It's not wheatsheaves we're surrounded by, it's bomb casings – if we're lucky.'

I looked towards the sculpture. 'We go in and bring him out ourselves. I'll need you because I can't carry him.'

'We will get blown to smithereens. I've already skirted death today. Don't feel like chancing it twice.'

'So, you'll just let him die in there? Would you be saying the same thing if it were Thérèse?'

He ran his hand over his lips. 'That's not fair. At the very least, we should hear from the police about what ideas they have. Emergency services deal with emergencies. Maybe they can drop down into the sculpture if the helicopter hovers over the top and pulls him up.'

'They won't. How can you even consider leaving him?' I was shouting at Terry now.

'Because it's a suicide mission. Look, Abi, I'm sorry for Robert. I really am. He and I have been friends for many years, but since Thérèse died, my only goal has been to bring down The Golden Illuminati, and this risks that. There are professionals up there on the hill.' He pointed. 'Let them handle it.'

'So, you want to just sit tight here and wait for rescue? All the while, he's dying in there.'

'Precisely.' Terry nodded, threw his hands up in the air and turned away to look up the hill, pulling his phone from his pocket. Savannah answered him immediately. She was at the top of the hill with the police. Terry made his enquiries and floated the idea of the helicopter rescue. Then he shook his head and covered the phone.

'They say it's a cluster bomb and they definitely have to wait for a bomb squad. They say that they'll need multiple teams to deal with this. Apparently, there are very likely bomblets which failed to explode on impact.' He raised his eyebrows. 'If there's one in the sculpture, and they try to bring the helicopter over it to lift Robert out, it could jeopardise the helicopter. They need the all-clear before they do something like that.'

I pulled the phone from Terry's hand. 'Savannah, he needs help now. You have to impress upon them how necessary speed is.' Savannah made a whimpering sound. 'I've got an idea, but you need to make sure the ambulance is ready for us, okay?'

'Abigail, I'm sorry about—'

I closed the phone down and turned my attention to Terry. I thought of Robert on the steps, blood dripping through the stairs. It was the thought of his blood that delivered me the perfect solution.

'You know that thing you wanted me to do?'

Terry's eyes narrowed, and he nodded. 'Turn yourself in to them?'

'I'll do it if you help me get him out.'

Terry looked at me. 'If we die doing this, it defeats the purpose.'

'You said it was the only way. If I don't go in, you don't have a case.'

He thought about this for a moment, his eyes skirting from one hunk of metal to another in the field. 'Okay. I suppose walking through a minefield with an alchemist is safer than doing it without one.'

He wasn't to know that this bait cost me nothing. I couldn't let Robert die or lose his beautiful house or the jewels for me – not when I knew he'd decided to give them up for me. I could forgive him the deal. I knew the circumstances, and who was I to judge a person for straying into dark places for their own ends?

Staring at the shell-infested field, I felt my confidence wobble. I wasn't sure that my relationship with metals would be any help at all to guide us through these shells. At first glance, the sub-shells looked to be made from aluminium: the only metal I'd always had an aversion to.

I turned to Terry. 'Before we risk our lives, I'll go and make sure he's alive.' He looked concerned. 'Don't worry – it's a trick Fen taught me. I'll be back very soon.'

I lay down on the grass and projected out of my body to the centre of the sculpture. The stairs were still open, and I steeled myself at the top of them: there was a very real chance that I was too late.

Robert was in the same position I'd left him. I held my breath as I pressed my projected body to his. His chest moved shallowly up and down, and relief flooded through me. Laying my head down on his chest, I closed my eyes. He took in a sharp breath and I lifted myself up to see his eyelids open.

His lips moved slowly enough for me to read them. 'I'm still here,' he said. He knew it was me. I leaned forward and put my lips to his, blending my essence with his and encountering only the slightest ripple. Before we had gushed together and now his pool was almost still.

Hold on, please, just a little bit longer, I willed.

Hard as it was to leave him again, I rushed back to Terry as fast as I could. Terry had his phone to his ear and gave me a look of relief when I opened my eyes.

'He's alive, but we can't wait.'

Terry nodded, and I looked out over the route we would have to take. I'd never looked at metal and felt it to be menacing before, but this was. It wasn't the stuff of the sculpture, where an artist had weaved creative magic into its surface. Destruction had been the intent of this metal and I felt it without even touching it.

I bent down to one of the fragmented casings and put my hand to it, closing my eyes. My touch was a shock to it. It wasn't sure it liked me. I felt the haughtiness of the aluminium; it wouldn't stoop to engage with me. I turned the casing over gingerly, trying not to bang the one next to it, which from this angle looked entire. As I flipped it over, my heart rang like a bell in my chest, not with fear, but hope.

Copper – my friend, copper. The main component of

bronze. It was angular like a misshapen arrow. As my fingers ran its length, I sent out an enquiry in my mind.

'Talk to me.'

It began quietly. It wasn't a single voice like when I'd touched the walls of the mighty, wise Serra sculpture. What I could hear couldn't be described as coherent. I sensed many voices rather than one. These shells weren't individuals; they spoke together, and the language was infantile. Whatever sophisticated purpose the copper had in the bomb, the heat and energy of the explosion had melted it. The propulsion had formed it into a lethal piece of shrapnel, stripping it down to its crudest form. I concentrated, but it was more like the whir of dozens of fans than a voice: a wordless, babbling chatter. But I didn't need a conversation, only its help.

I looked at Terry and nodded. 'Right, ready? I'll go first.'

He nodded. We picked our way past the clearer sections where there was a glimpse of grass and just enough space to step between the cast-off pieces. We couldn't take a direct path because the way the bombs had dropped was far too dense. We twisted and turned, but there were points where the path stopped entirely.

I dropped down to the closest empty casing. My heart couldn't have beat any faster as I touched it. If ever in my life there was a time to believe in my power as an alchemist, this was it.

'Guide me,' I asked of the metal. An excited drone rose through my fingers and in my head. I saw the path stretching out from me to the mouth of the sculpture. It wasn't a sweeping curve, but a jagged, awkward line.

I stood up and without hesitation took a step into the sea of metal so that I was ankle deep. I held my breath, as though that might stop a bomb exploding, but all was quiet.

'Terry, it's very important you only tread where I do, okay?' He nodded, pursing his lips. This must be much worse for him.

I turned back to the path and saw the next step in my mind. Pace by pace, we stepped forward, the metal jangling against our ankles, making fear shoot up and into our chests. I had to keep stopping and bending to touch and re-visualise the correct path.

We were about fifteen feet from the sculpture and I was concentrating hard on swinging sharply right or left when the medical helicopter hovered over our heads. With a booming microphone, someone shouted down at us. We could feel the wind rocking us, and now the pieces of metal jangled against each other too.

'Go back! Go back! It's not safe,' the voice boomed at us.

I gave Terry a glance, my fear brimming over. Even his short hair seemed to be wafted by the helicopter. His expression cracked and he grinned at me.

'No shit, Sherlock,' he said, looking at the man in the helicopter. 'Keep going, Abi, we're nearly there.'

The helicopter kept swooping around us with more dread warnings. It made it harder to concentrate on the metal's messages because there was more noise and the shells were quaking.

Putting our heads down and pushing forward, we made it to the entrance of the sculpture's corridor. Very few metal pieces had entered there, and a clear path opened up. Both of us fell against the statue's walls, our chests heaving like we'd run instead of slow-walked the section.

Terry leaned forward and put his arms around me, kissing me on the top of my head. 'Well, if I didn't get it before, Abigail, I sure do now. I can see why everyone's after you.'

Hopping over a few stray shells, we ran down to where the staircase was open at the mouth of the sculpture. Terry took the lead. He climbed over Robert and put his hand to his throat to check his pulse.

'Alive.' He looked up at me. 'Come on, boy. Let's go.' He leaned down and scooped up Robert, who didn't respond. The awkwardness of the narrow staircase and the length of Robert's limbs made their exit a jolting, ungainly series of steps, but once outside, Terry adjusted his position.

'Terry, you can't carry him like that. You need to be able to see your feet. It will be worse for him, but if we get blown up then it will all be a bit pointless. Throw him over your shoulder.'

As if I was the captain, he obeyed. I was beginning to feel panic getting a grip of me. My chest was getting tighter. Could I really pull this off?

I took hold of Robert's hand as it dangled down and gave it a squeeze. There was no response which made my chest tighten further. I pushed ahead of Terry to look out at our easiest path to safety. The helicopter had set down about the length of two football pitches away. Three-quarters of a pitch had the treacherous metal, and then the remainder was a safety zone. The paramedics were now standing watching us, which was better at least than zooming around our heads, frightening us.

I looked back at Terry for reassurance. His shirt was smeared with Robert's blood. Bending down, I touched one of the casings. The babble rose up again and the path appeared in my mind. It was fairly straight this time and I stepped forward into it, but felt my nerves breaking through any calm I could form. This kept fracturing the image I had of the path we needed to take.

As we crept towards them, so the paramedics crept

closer to us. When we finally stepped out and passed Robert's body over to them, I felt my head swim – I hadn't been breathing for at least the last fifty yards. I sat, dazed, looking back at the deadly route we'd just walked.

The paramedics swarmed us and began working on Robert's barely alive body.

'I'm sorry, but we can only take one of you with us,' a paramedic said.

'It's got to be you, Terry. I have some things I need to do here.'

The paramedics were preparing Robert to go. I dropped to my knees.

'Wait!' I took his hand, but just when I needed to say something meaningful, my words jammed in my throat. I stared at him dumbly, and then I felt the tiniest pulse of energy run down my fingers and into my hand. It was barely a flicker, but I caught it like a pro and sent it back to him just as the paramedics lifted the stretcher and raced towards the helicopter.

Terry looked horrified. 'Don't tell me you're going back through that!' He pointed up the hill.

I shook my head. 'Alchemist or not, I think I'll take the scenic route.' I smiled at him. 'Go!' I pushed his back with both my hands towards the helicopter.

28

## ABIGAIL

It took me a while to walk back. I skirted around the perimeter of the metal-contaminated field and into the wide openness, but I could hardly draw my eyes away from the bombsite. To have survived was incredible and I felt a shift take place within me.

I'd accepted it. Some things are harder to do than they should be, or maybe some personalities make things harder than they need to be. I'd transformed base metal into gold, heard messages from metals, and made a huge steel sculpture scream, but I hadn't believed in any of it. I'd kept looking for an explanation that fitted in with the scientific education I'd had, as if that would make what I could do valid.

Ironically, it was the science that had been holding me back. I'd been clinging on to it so hard that I hadn't realised it was drowning me. There was no explanation, but it didn't make any of what I'd done less true.

When I finally made it back to the house and opened the door, I was met by a half-dozen officials and police who seemed to have taken over the kitchen as their office. After being questioned and someone had made me a coffee, I went to get changed out of my blood-soaked clothes. On the way past Robert's study, I slipped in. I found Savannah sitting on the couch, staring into space. She looked glassy-eyed as she turned her head to me. The swelling on her forehead was still purple, but it had gone down a little. It was only yesterday that had happened, and yet it seemed like a lifetime ago. Tear tracks ran through her make-up. She was clutching an empty coffee cup.

'I should put a bag together for Robert and take it to the hospital,' she said. Her voice choked on the last word and I witnessed the toughest woman I'd ever met being overcome with emotion. She screwed up her eyes, trying to block the tears, but they dodged her attempts and slipped by. 'He's my best friend. I don't know if I—,' she looked down, '—have it in me to go.'

I took a deep breath. Even seeing her this vulnerable, I felt a small inclination to be a bitch.

'You should have tried walking through a bomb-covered field, not knowing if he'd died alone on that staircase.'

But, I didn't say that. For all Savannah's dynamic fighting strength, I'd finally found her weakness: Robert. I could understand that.

I walked across to her and sat down, giving her hand a squeeze.

'He made it this far without the medics. That's got to be a good sign.'

She looked up at me and her expression wasn't that of the old Savannah: cold or derisive.

'I didn't get you before. Didn't understand your way. Then I watched you walk through that field and I saw the strength in you.'

'I know about the deal he made, Savannah.'

Her eyes lost their distant look. 'Did he tell you?'

I shook my head. 'But I know – everything. What he'd have to sacrifice: the jewels and this house, and I'm not going to let him do that.'

She shook her head. 'You can't stop it now. After what you did for him, he's going to stand by you – I know him.'

I took a few slugs of my coffee and stood up. 'If you don't want Robert to lose everything, you're going to have to do exactly what I say. You'll have to delay going to the hospital for now. Where's Fen?'

Her eyes showed uncertainty. 'He's missed the whole thing. Went out to see clients in North Yorkshire and I haven't even been in touch with him yet.'

'Perfect. Leave him in the dark as long as possible.'

She was about to argue and I had to barge on to stop her.

'I want you to contact The Golden Illuminati and arrange an exchange for me. It can only be you acting on Robert's behalf. You've probably seen the handrail. The Golden Illuminati will be very interested in it. You'll email them video evidence of that golden handprint. Then you're going to take me to wherever their HQ is and you'll receive his payment for me.'

She looked at me with eyes that grew wider as the words sank in and shook her head. 'Did he tell you to do that?'

'No.'

'Then why would you do it?'

'Isn't it obvious? Because I love him, Savannah, and because I won't let him forfeit this house or that part of his history that he cares so much about for me. Such a loss would destroy us in the end anyway. No-one can give up such a huge part of themselves without feeling bitterness eventually. Terry has a plan. Robert can help him, and you too, I hope. You'll get me out.'

She swallowed and stood up, shaking her head a little. 'I'd have to talk to Robert. Oh, I can't talk to Robert. I don't know what to do.'

'Yes, you do. Did he ever give you instructions?'

'Yes, but it was different then.'

'You knew what the deal was all along. You're just carrying out the plan because he's unable to. Are you really going to let him lose this place?'

She rubbed her temples with shaking hands, hiding her face, and I knew now was the time to press her a little more.

'You owe me, Savannah—,' she pulled her hands from her eyes, '—for David.'

A pinch of colour came to her cheeks and she looked down at the ground. 'He's gone to London. In case you were wondering.'

I took a deep breath and said what I knew was true, but hurt to admit to her. 'He's gone because, there wasn't anything we could have said to each other to put things right, but he'll come back for you. David's not the one-night-stand kind of guy.'

'I don't need reassurance from you, of all people,' she snapped, some of the old crackle back in her voice.

'That's good because that's my last comment on the situation.'

I set off into the hall and she followed me in. She gazed at the golden handprint on the handrail.

'Have you got your phone?' I put out my hand to her.

She keyed in the pin and passed it over. I took a video which started at the rounded end of the handrail and moved along its curvy length, showing the beautiful blend of colours that I'd created, until it revealed my golden hand-print in stark contrast to the rest. I zoomed in on it just in case there was any doubt.

I handed the phone back to Savannah. 'Right, I'm going to get some things together. You need to make the arrangements, and for goodness sake, if Fen comes back, just focus your mind on Robert's injury. If by any chance he goes poking inside your head, you need to be worrying about Robert. That will be all he sees. Just emphasise that Terry needs his help at the hospital as soon as possible. Otherwise, he'll try to stop us.'

She nodded, her face almost porcelain in its pallor. The dynamic between the two of us had reversed completely. As I trudged up the steps to my room, I felt weariness descending on me. So, this was what certainty felt like. The next time I saw Fenrear, I'd have to tell him I was unimpressed by it. A drop of sadness made my throat ache: I'd miss Fen.

Terry had better have a good plan in place.

## 29

## ROBERT

I opened my eyes to see a nurse with dark hair, a heart-shaped face and blue eyes twinkling at me. I tried to moisten my lips which felt dry and she helped me to take a tiny sip of water from a beaker. I was hooked up to monitors and had various liquids coming in through a cannula in my arm.

'You're in recovery. On the mend now,' she said and patted my arm. 'I'm just here to check your vitals.' She popped a thermometer in my mouth and a little monitor on to my finger. Terry was in a chair a few feet away; he nodded at me with a slight smile. I could feel sleep tugging at me again.

I suddenly felt a spike of panic when I thought about my leg, which didn't hurt. I tried to move it, but it didn't respond. The thermometer prevented an outburst, but the nurse read my distress.

'It's okay. Just the anaesthetic – it's going to feel numb for a little while. Then you'll wish it still was.'

I relaxed and closed my eyes again. There was noise and bustle in my vicinity and it kept me from sleeping deeply, but I must have got a further hour's rest before the medics came in to move me back to my room. The pretty nurse escorted me while the porters pushed the bed along corridors. Terry followed, and our procession made it to the lift.

As the doors of the lift were about to close, I could hear someone shouting.

'Robert! Robert!'

Terry put his shoulder across the lift door to hold it open as Fen jogged up, slightly out of breath. He nodded his thanks to Terry and joined our group. He was wearing his fantastic red hat and the porter seemed unable to look anywhere else.

Terry was about to greet him when Fen raised his hand to him in a stop gesture and gave him the filthiest look.

'Don't!' Fen said, turning towards me. 'I leave you for a few hours and you end up here. What the hell happened?'

I shrugged and stole a glance at the nurse, who seemed to be looking at the notes she was clutching in her hand. The lift stopped. As I was being transferred, Fen stepped up to the side of the nurse.

'How serious is it?' he asked her in a quiet voice. 'There's something very urgent he might need to do.'

The nurse looked at him with amazed eyes. 'He's just out of theatre. I think doing things might have to wait,' she said, shaking her head. She settled me into my room before turning on Terry and Fen. 'He needs rest. Visitors shouldn't be here until 2.30pm,' she said, addressing Fen in particular.

'Give me quarter of an hour, nursey, and you won't see me after that.'

He nodded at her with his twinkling eyes. Her face twitched, but not with irritation. As she left the room, he swung round to me.

'We've got to get you out of here.'

Terry bounded forward to the bed. 'No, that's ridiculous!'

Fen turned on him. 'Don't you dare say that! It's entirely your fault he's got to get out of his sick bed.'

'My fault?' Terry looked bewildered.

'She's gone, Robert. She's on her way to them right now. We've got to stop her.'

'What? How do you know?' I asked, pushing myself up onto my elbows.

Fen sat down on the edge of the bed. 'I'm a whisperer, I hear things. I was in Thirsk, seeing someone about buying a beautiful little Stubbs print, and I heard it, clear as day: a conversation between Abigail and Savannah.' He glanced at Terry, and back at me. 'She was talking to Savannah, telling her she knew what you'd have to sacrifice, and she wanted Sav to email them a video of the handprint and take her to their HQ.'

I shook my head. 'Sav wouldn't do that without my say-so.'

Fen looked at me. 'Not exactly Abigail's biggest fan, is she?'

'You don't know her. She wouldn't do that.'

Fen took a deep breath. 'Would she if she thought that was what you wanted? Have you ever implied that?'

I'd more than implied it – damn! I'd downright told her to make sure she followed through if I couldn't.

'How reliable is this gift of yours, Fen? Have you tried phoning her?' I asked.

'I tell you, I'm right!' Fen snapped. 'I'm at least three times your age, Robert, and my gifts are sharper than they've ever been. But, by all means, try ringing – either of them, or the house. I would love to be wrong.'

Terry stayed very quiet and circled away from the bed, looking out of the window.

The grogginess of the anaesthetic was fighting with adrenaline. I wanted to slump into a deep coma, and at the same time leap out of bed and race down the corridor on a magically uninjured leg.

Terry cleared his throat. 'I think she's done the right thing.'

'What?' Fen's shout was so loud it brought the dark-haired nurse into the room.

'You'll have to go,' she said, pointing to the door. 'Arguing is absolutely not what he needs at this moment. Out!'

Fen glared at her. He slipped his hand into his pocket and pulled out a fat wad of £50 notes. He unsheathed six and offered them.

'I need ten more minutes. We won't shout again.'

She looked down at the money and up at his face, and down at the money again. I was certain she was about to scream for security, when instead her hand darted out and she pocketed the money like lightning. She spun around and left the room without another word.

'Oh my God,' said Terry. 'You just bribed a nurse!'

'Well, you just talked Abigail into a life sentence!'

Terry crossed his arms. 'I'm not going to defend myself. I can bring The Golden Illuminati down, but I need her inside, not out, to do it.'

Fen shook his head, rage making him quake. 'You've no idea what you've done! She is so important for bigger things than this stupid little society. How could she have listened to you?'

Terry glared back at Fen stubbornly. 'What does that mean, everything you'll have to sacrifice?' he asked me.

The fallout I'd have to face if Terry discovered the deal I'd made was the kind I wasn't up to coping with right now.

My brain felt like it was weighed down with lead; it took immense effort to expel even an unimaginative lie.

'She must mean what I'd have to sacrifice if The Golden Illuminati discovered I'd helped her.'

How could she have discovered what I'd have to sacrifice? Had Savannah told her? She was the only one who knew the details, and yet, I couldn't believe she would do that.

'It sounds to me like she's being idealistic, and if so, we really are in trouble. It's the idealistic souls in this world who become suicide bombers.'

'There's nothing I can do about any of this lying here!' I said, frustration making me feel wild.

'Well, you certainly can't leave the hospital,' said Terry. 'Dying isn't going to help the situation any.'

'I disagree,' said Fen.

'How can you disagree?' said Terry, whose face had almost turned puce at Fen's comment.

Fen gave Terry a scornful look and turned away from him. 'It has to be you, Robert. You love her, and unless I'm very wrong, she loves you too. You are the only one who will be able to talk her down. If they get her again, they'll never let her go. This time, they'll know she's bona fide and she won't be underestimated. She got very lucky the last time. I know you would be risking your life, but you have to do it. We need to get to wherever she's going before she does, to cut her off. It's our only chance.'

'What about David?' I said to Terry.

'It's over between them.'

'But he would never let her go to them, break up or not. I don't have his number. He might be in Glenkubright still. He could intervene, slow her down, even.'

We both turned to Terry. David was his nephew.

'I'm sorry, but I'm not going to give you his number. I think she's done the right thing, for her own reasons, and from this second on, all I'm going to do is try to help us both to terminate those Golden Illuminati bastards. I was always here to support Abigail, no other purpose.'

He picked up his leather jacket and was about to walk out of the room.

'Don't lie to yourself, Terry. You were here for your own ends, as we all were,' Fen said.

My eyes followed Terry out. I looked at Fen.

'Any other ideas?'

He nodded. 'Creativity is my strong point, and money always helps. I'm just going to find that little dark-haired nurse,' he said, slipping out of the room.

I waited in a state of helpless indecision as the minutes ticked by. Dressing wasn't possible with the drip still attached to me. I had tubes coming into my arms – should I just pull them out? There was a monitor too. If I disconnected that, it was sure to start beeping and bring someone in.

I was shaking with nervous tension – every minute slipping through my fingers seemed like a vital opportunity to stop her. I'd tried ringing Sav and Abigail; both had their phones shut off. Damn Sav – she'd never had her phone shut off to me, even when she'd gone on holiday.

Nearly forty minutes passed before Fen returned, pushing a hospital wheelchair. He was followed by the dark-haired nurse who moved around the bed and turned off the various liquids coming into my arm and disconnected them. She pressed some tape against the cannula to stop the tube flapping.

When she stood up, she met my eyes. 'Don't you dare judge me,' she said. 'I get off in five minutes anyway and it's my day off tomorrow. I have a son to put through university. It's not me deciding to play roulette with my friend's health,' she threw a look at Fen. 'I'm a good nurse. I'll do everything I can to help you.' She pursed her lips, but I could tell it was bravado. She didn't like what she'd agreed to, either. I could sympathise with that.

Fen was shaking his head. 'No-one is judging you, Gemma. Like you say, it's down to us and we appreciate your help – a lot. Gemma is going to be coming with us. To help as much as she can.'

'You do know how dangerous this is?' she said to me and her eyes were searching my own.

I smiled at her. 'He's not forcing me to go, if that's what you're asking.'

She gave a slight nod of her head and went to my bag and rifled through it for clothes, which she helped me put on. Fortunately, my legs were moving on command now, and we managed between us to haul on some baggy tracksuit bottoms.

'You're on your own for the next bit. You need to get him downstairs,' she said to Fen. 'I wouldn't be surprised if the police are somewhere around, waiting to talk to you, too. A gunshot wound won't be ignored. I'll meet you by A&E. I need to make a few phone calls and organise supplies to meet us at the airstrip and clock out of my shift.'

'Good girl, Gem. Get anything he might need. Money's not an issue.'

Gemma looked at Fen, then at me. She was wondering what all this was about. A gunshot and now racing somewhere to get away. She swallowed, then helped Fen lift me into the chair. I only put weight on one leg, but even that one felt like it might buckle under me.

Gemma went out first. She checked the corridor and gave a tiny nod.

Fen didn't hesitate. He had me out of that door and down the corridor to the entrance of the ward in a blink. He pressed a buzzer and the door opened.

Gemma stared after us. 'Go!' she mouthed.

## 30

## ROBERT

'Can you speed up any, son?' Fen pressed our taxi driver. His hands clenched in a way that suggested he might just strangle the man if his reply wasn't positive.

The driver glanced at Fen's hands. 'Man, are ye not lookin' at tha' road? We're doing over sixty now. These are windy roads. If something comes around that corner and I'm at seventy, we're all deid.'

Fen sighed. I was sweating. Each bend was throwing my weight on to my bad side, and the numbing effect of the anaesthetic was barely there at all now. There was no such thing as a comfortable position even though Gemma had done her best. I was lying along the seat with my back against the door and window. She had bolstered me up with blocks of foam that she'd secured from God only knows where. She was perched on the front of her seat with her nose almost pressed up to Fen's headrest. I closed my eyes and tried to breathe deeply. This drive was only the start of the journey to London. Surely, the next part wouldn't be this bad.

Fen glanced into the back at me. 'People had to travel long distances with gunshot wounds during the last war, and you've even had the damn bullet removed and the wound stitched up.'

I opened my eyes. 'I'm sorry. Is my pain annoying you?'

He turned his head back to the road and began to clench his hands again.

I smiled at Gemma. She was staring at the back of Fen's head with a poisonous expression on her face that didn't bode well for Fen when she got out.

'He's on edge. Don't mind him,' I said.

'Obviously, as you got yourself shot, you must be involved in something pretty heavy, but you seem like a nice guy. I would pick your friends better,' she said, holding up her hand. 'Just saying.' She took hold of my wrist and looked at her watch, checking my pulse. After a pause, she tutted. 'I'll be a lot happier when you are on the plane and hooked up to some blood and painkillers. I hope the supplies have arrived at the airfield.'

Her eyes were anxious. I suddenly felt sorry for her. Fen shouldn't have put her in this position, though from a selfish standpoint, I was glad he had.

'If I find out you're risking your life for drugs, or some other criminal activity, I'm going to be—'

The car jerked mercilessly, and I cried out.

'Nearly there now,' said Fen, his eyes on the satnav on his phone.

I swallowed down the nausea that had welled up inside me. 'It's not about money, it's about love,' I said as the pain worsened, forcing me to close my eyes and descend into my own world. Heartache was mixed with leg ache so that my whole body just ached. I'd tried to tell Abigail how I felt, but had I been clear that I loved her? My memory was patchy.

We'd never make it in time to stop her. She had too much of a head start. The chances were that she'd be in their custody hours before we even made it into London. Fen had organised a private aircraft for us and the flight wouldn't be long, but we'd still be hitting London in the evening traffic and then have to get across town.

## ABIGAIL

Even though we were on a train hurtling towards London, I had the feeling of creeping home drunk as a teenager and, despite all the precautions you take to be quiet, your parents catch you anyway. I wasn't quite sure how it would have come about, but I knew my weak link in the plan was Fenrear. He was too old and canny a dog not to suspect my disappearance was strange and investigate. My only hope was that I had enough of a head start in case Fen pursued me. I knew that if he caught up with me when I was still so far from my destination, my resolve might falter.

I let my mind slide to Robert. Savannah had rung the hospital when we'd been on the way to the station and was told he was stable and in recovery. It might have been naïvety on my part, but as he'd survived on that staircase without help for so long, I'd never contemplated that he wouldn't make it.

I couldn't let myself think about Robert too much, though. When I did, I started to doubt what I was doing. Robert being trapped in hospital was the best possible outcome to enable me to carry through my plan. If he'd have been well, he would have convinced me not to do it and I know I would have yielded.

Savannah hadn't come to sit with me since we'd boarded

the train. Instead, she stood in the hallway, making calls continuously. When I'd come out to enquire what was going on, she'd covered the microphone with her hand.

'We need some backup when we get to London. I'm not going into their HQ with you on my own. We need to ensure they uphold Robert's deal.'

I watched the train pull out of Doncaster station. I had at least a couple of hours still to go, and I could feel my resolve plummeting. I lay my head down on my arms and let my mind tumble over all that had happened in such a short space of time.

The adrenaline was waning. Back at the house, I'd felt drunk on engaging with my gift; invincible, even. Now, with every mile that the train travelled, I was feeling the sharp reality of what I'd decided to do and my nerve was beginning to go. What if The Golden Illuminati were going to punish me for my escape, or take some retribution for Pierro's murder? What if they didn't take me to where Terry had secured his job?

I looked down the corridor of the train towards the bar. Getting completely paralytic suddenly seemed appealing.

**Robert**

We landed near London and began the last part of our journey. Once we were in the car, a tight silence settled in between the three of us for most of the hour plus that we'd been in the car.

It took over an hour before we made it to Blackfriars Bridge where the light was beginning to retire and fade I was sulking. I'd asked Gemma at least three times already if there was anything else she could do to give my leg more strength in the short term, but her continued allegiance to the word "no" was getting on my nerves.

I tried a final time. Fen made a tsk noise and dived into his bag. From the front seat, he glanced at our driver.

'Eyes on the road, Luke,' he said as he passed me a jiffy bag filled with white powder, shaking it when I didn't immediately take it. He tapped his nose.

'Is it—?' I asked, staring at what was clearly around fifty grammes of cocaine.

'Don't look at me like that! I can't stand you bleating on to Gemma any more. She's done all she can. If you want something to give you some oomph, that will do it.'

I stared at Gemma whose eyes were fixed on the bag's contents.

'Will it help?' I asked her.

She rolled her eyes and sucked some air in between her teeth. 'Can make you more aggressive.' She gave a little shrug.

'Good enough,' I said, turning back to Fen. 'Got a straw?'

It isn't easy to snort cocaine without a flat surface to lay it on, but as we travelled along the Embankment and the traffic slowed, I managed to get a few large pinches into my hand and half snort, half knock it back. Either way, some must have made it to my brain, because as the Tower of London loomed in front of me, I was brimming with euphoria and confidence.

The car took a left turn, and it was then I wondered if I'd made a mistake and what I'd taken for cocaine was actually acid. I blinked, assuming it must be a hallucination, but the scene held: Abigail was in front of The Golden Illuminati Headquarters, almost halfway up the steps with two men in dark clothes shadowing her ascent.

Before our car had fully slowed, I'd flung open the door

and hurled myself out, hearing a squeal from Gemma as I did so.

'Abigail!'

She turned, and my heart lurched as I noticed the ashen shade of her skin and terrified expression. Her body stiffened.

I ignored the way my damaged leg protested. I was going to save her! I began to take the stairs, managing a half-dozen or so before my leg gave way. Suddenly, I couldn't gauge how far the next step was and I heard a popping in my head. To my surprise, I saw the steps rear up and meet me. I connected hard with their surface and my kneecap met with the nosing of the steps, sending a whole new dart of pain into the mix.

Feeling my head snap back and then bash into the granite, I saw stars burst across my vision. Then I rolled over several times down the steps, scraping my fragile leg mercilessly. I kept catching glimpses of Fen standing by the car, physically restraining Gemma.

Though my plan had been to arrive at the top of the steps as a proper hero rather than land at the bottom like some slap-stick clown, I found Abigail at my side, which had been the result I'd been aiming for anyway. I could feel my trousers soaking through with sticky, warm blood.

Abigail took my hand. 'You came.' It was half statement, half disbelief.

I was finding it hard to focus, but I knew what I wanted to say.

'Please don't do this, woman. You don't have to. I don't know what Sav's told you, but—'

Tears began to run down her cheeks, and she ran her fingers over my forehead and through my hair.

'Savannah didn't tell me anything. I saw it all when I

touched your blood on the staircase. I saw you with your dad as he lay dying in hospital; what the jewels mean to you; the deal you made with them.'

I grimaced. 'But, I didn't know you then.'

She put her fingers to my lips. 'You don't have to explain. I felt everything. I'm sure the jewels have a role to play. One that you don't even understand yet. They are very significant, and if I don't do this, you will lose so much.'

I turned her hand over and kissed the palm. 'I'll lose the most important thing of all if you do.'

She swept some tears away. 'You can't give them your beautiful house, your masterpieces, the Serra sculpture. I won't let you give them that sculpture, not when I can prevent it. Last time, no-one knew they had me. It'll be different this time.'

'I'll build another house.'

'Robert!' Savannah's voice made us both look to the doorway. She was outside, carrying a large black metallic box, accompanied by a bodyguard. My jewels were in that box. Abigail melted away as colours filled my vision: the lush green of the emerald, the pigeon blood red of the rubies in the bracelet. Cold spread through me and not because my blood was leaving my leg like it had better places to go, but because fear was taking possession of me. Losing either one of them would mean my soul would be torn right down the middle.

Sav's eyes darted to the man with her and I could tell she was struggling with whether to pass the precious box to him and come down to me or not.

One of the two men who'd been escorting Abigail bent and took hold of her elbow, forcing her to rise. 'It's time to go,' he said.

She'd followed my gaze and bent closer to whisper to

me, 'I want you to have them. It's too late to change anything – if you don't go, they'll suspect something, and you won't be able to help me.'

She stood and took a step away and I turned on my side and grabbed hold of her ankle. She staggered but pulled her foot out of my grip then moved quickly up the stairs. As she did, Fen, many years older than anyone here, moved like an arrow up the stairs and blocked her way. One of the men moved forward to brush him aside.

'Don't go, Abi. They'll never underestimate you again. This is a huge mistake.'

I was vaguely aware of Gemma beside me, applying pressure to my leg and with her phone pressed to her ear, calling an ambulance.

'Don't make this harder for me,' she said to Fen as the men forced him out of the way. Fen, the size of a terrier compared to these bulldogs, jostled his way back in front of them.

'Terry will get over Thérèse. Don't do this out of guilt. It won't bring Thérèse back,' he said.

'This isn't about Thérèse,' she shouted at him.

'It's about everything. You think giving yourself to them is the answer? You need to fight, not surrender.'

This time it was Abigail, not the guards, who pushed Fen away and she continued up the stairs. I watched in horror: it was like watching someone sleepwalk across a road into the path of an articulated lorry.

I rolled on to my front with a groan, pushing myself up on to my feet. It could have been the adrenaline, or Fen's cocaine, or the magnitude of all I felt for Abigail that blew away any awareness of my injury, but I launched myself forward and ran those stairs two at a time towards her, because I knew my life depended on it. I tackled her like a rugby pro, slamming both of us into the door so that she hit the solid oak with a thud and fell to the floor beneath me.

It was only moments later that I felt Fen join me in the tussle. We both grabbed hold of her. Fen tried to hoist her up, but she fought us like a wild cat.

'You can't do this! I won't let you do this! Not for me! Please ... don't do this!' I shouted as strong hands intervened. One minute I had hold of her, and the next Fen and I were being lifted off the ground and carried away. We both fought against the might of the men who previously had been escorting Abigail.

I stopped fighting. My energy and blood were ebbing away. She stood on the threshold, looking slightly dishevelled. She lifted her hand and banged on the door.

'Stop a moment,' I yelled at the man who held me. 'Stop!'

He paused. We were far enough away from her not to interfere now.

I shouted as loudly as I could, 'If you do this, Abigail, we're done. I swear, I won't come for you!'

I could hear the wail of an ambulance siren. Someone opened the huge door. There were tears in her eyes again, and a courageous smile on her lips. She lifted her chin.

'Yes you will,' she said, before walking inside.


# THE END


<<<<

>>>>

# ACKNOWLEDGMENTS

Thanks to my mother, and late father, who have encouraged me throughout my writing journey. Thanks to my husband, Iain, who supports and encourages me in so many thoughtful ways. Love and appreciation to Catherine Bower who has ridden the highs and lows of another novel with me. Love to Alison and Jim McLean who continue to support me in all that I do. Hugs to Paige Toon, superstar author and dear friend, who shares her passion for writing with me and is full of encouragement. Thanks to Dr Viva Judd for trying to school me about gunshot wounds – sorry Viva, some poetic licence has been used. Enormous gratitude to Mr Jim Smith, former member of the Intelligence Corps, for his information and guidance on cluster bombs. Finally, my sincere gratitude to my beta-readers, Catherine Bower, Helen Winstanley, Siân Fletcher, Rachel Phillipson who helped me to see my novel with new eyes.

# WANT TO KNOW MORE ABOUT …?

THE GOLDEN ILLUMINATI?
ALCHEMY
PATINATION
AND
THE ART THAT INSPIRES THE NOVELS?

JOIN MY READERS' GROUP AND RECEIVE EMAILS
FROM LUCY BRANCH WITH CONTENT THAT DELVES
DEEPER INTO THE THEMES OF THE SERIES

AT

www.lucybranch.com

## ABL PRESS

If you enjoyed this book, please review it. Reviews make a BIG difference to small presses like ours and if you haven't the time to review, please spread the word.

ABL PRESS
Lucy Branch loves hearing from her readers so if you would like to drop her a line – please do!
Email *lucy@antiquebronze.co.uk*

More Books by Lucy Branch

A Rarer Gift Than Gold (Book 1 in The Gold Gift Series)
Girl In A Golden Cage (Book 3 in The Gold Gift Series)

www.ingramcontent.com/pod-product-compliance
Lightning Source LLC
Chambersburg PA
CBHW071740190726
48292CB00003B/817